SHIELD HERO

Aneko Yusagi

Hidemasa Miyaji

Rishia

Chris

Glass

Itsuki put the medicinal herb to his mouth and started to play it, like a grass reed. The light of magic immediately sprang up in the vicinity.

Table of Contents

Prologue: The Coronation

"Make way for Queen Melty!"

After Melromarc's victory in the war against Faubrey, for all intents and purposes it had become the largest nation in the world. Siltvelt held the achievements of the previous queen in high regard, the one who had forged an excellent relationship with the Shield Hero and also fostered friendship with Siltvelt itself. The two nations now had an alliance that made their long years at each other's throats seem like a fleeting dream.

However, the two nations were also carrying on without bringing up the slave issue, placing a pin in that until a later date. For now they had simply formed an alliance in order to better prepare for the waves.

All of this was the result of defeating the whip seven star hero, Takt, and his band of hangers-on. Takt had apparently been a vanguard of the waves. Takt had been the one who interfered with our fight against the Phoenix and caused massive damage to the coalition army, not the least of which had been the loss of Atla.

We had proceeded to Faubrey, seeking to bring the seven star heroes to heel, who had shunned our summons and made no effort to participate in our battles. This had led to our first encounter with Takt, the one behind the whole messy plot. Falling right into his trap, I had been badly injured myself, and we lost the queen altogether.

I had been left to wander the border between life and death. During this freaky experience, and with the guidance of the shield spirit, I had even managed a reunion with Atla and Ost, now just spiritual energy. Trash, sinking into depression at the loss of the queen, was snapped back to himself by both the queen's final words and my own rage at him. But he was awakened as the staff seven star hero.

We then joined Trash in fighting the forces of Faubrey, as led by Takt. Due to Trash's strategy, the result was a victory. He had once been known across the land as the "Wisest King of Wisdom." For my part, I absolutely kicked the crap out of Takt, seizing my own personal victory.

We proceeded to torture the captive Takt and his retinue of women, trying to get them to reveal who was behind the waves. Just as it seemed we might get some answers, not only Takt's body but his very soul were shredded apart, ultimately leaving us with nothing.

In other news, there was also this nation called Shieldfreeden, which ostensibly espoused freedom but had sided with Takt. However, immediately after learning of his defeat, they had quickly changed their tune and replaced all the representatives from Takt's forces. They had then tried to sidle up to us, pointing the finger at those same disgraced representatives as the ones who orchestrated Shieldfreeden's involvement.

So much for a nation of liberty. As soon as they sensed things weren't going their way, they tried pulling all kinds of shifty stuff. At any other time, I might have just continued the war and rolled right over them, but Trash stated that it wasn't the time for such conflict, and we had to obey him.

Thanks to all that, Shieldfreeden stopped making ripples for the time being, but I didn't think we could really trust them going forward.

It was also decided that the defeated nations of Faubrey and Shieldfreeden would pay some serious reparations to Melromarc and Siltvelt. Almost all of that money was already earmarked to be used to fight the waves, for the sake of world peace and all that jazz. It wasn't hard to imagine the path that Shieldfreeden would be forced to walk in the future. Even after peace was achieved, Melromarc and Siltvelt would surely continue to demand money from them for all sorts of arbitrary reasons.

Just as I had started to think about exactly who we were facing—the enemy force that included Takt and Kyo and the one behind the waves—a seriously injured Ethnobalt had been found in my territory.

Ethnobalt had proceeded to inform us that some terrible stuff was going on over in Kizuna's world.

I wasn't sure whether to consider this good timing or bad, but after Raphtalia had been captured in aiding our escape from Takt's first trap, *she* had ended up escaping to Kizuna's world via a katana vassal weapon summons. This meant we needed to head to Kizuna's world to get Raphtalia back, and we were currently in the middle of those preparations.

Before that, though, I should finish explaining the situation in Faubrey. Putting together the pieces of everything that had happened so far, I realized Takt had executed everyone in the royal family who had stood against him. Any left alive had lost their authority due to having backed the losing side. Trash, of the Faubrey royal bloodline himself, had declared that as a hero he'd support the nation. The result of this had been Melty—Trash's daughter and next in line to be queen—getting the proverbial tap on the shoulder. Melromarc, now with Melty at the helm, had just become a major player on the world stage.

"Hooray for Queen Melty!"

The massive coronation for Melty was held in Melromarc. Not only the people but also the full coalition army was in attendance, celebrating the event. The envoy from the hostile nation Siltvelt was that old genmu guy. He was also among the well-wishers, heartily clapping his hands.

The coronation itself took place on the castle terrace, which could be seen from down in the square. As one of the heroes, I was also in attendance.

Trash, master of ceremonies for the coronation, was waiting for Melty to arrive in the throne room with crown in hand.

"The coronation of the queen of Melromarc will now begin," Trash proclaimed. Melty had changed into a gorgeous dress that looked incredibly hard to walk in and was shuffling her way toward Trash. She then stood in front of the throne and bowed her head to Trash.

"Well then, Melty Melromarc . . ." Trash said.

"I present myself," Melty offered.

"You have managed the territory ruled by the Shield Hero, aiding in maintaining the peace in his lands. I am told these deeds have turned a previously abandoned territory into a rich and successful one. This was no easy feat to achieve. All of the people of our nation of Melromarc expect even greater things from you in the future," Trash intoned. Shouts of support from those same people could be heard from outside. "As of this day, you shall lead our nation as the queen of Melromarc. You shall henceforth be known as Melty Q. Melromarc."

"I am humbled and overjoyed," Melty responded.

"Now, the crown." Trash proceeded to place the crown on Melty's head and then take a step back. "I hereby affirm the coronation of Melty Q. Melromarc."

More cheering and applause broke out. It was the moment in which Melromarc got a new queen, so some celebration was probably to be expected. Melty proceeded to the terrace and leaned out over the railing so the people could get a good look at her.

"Hooray for Queen Melty!"

"Hooray for the Queen!"

"Melromarc forever!"

These and other shouts rang up from the crowd. Although she was just one small girl, Melty smiled in the face of all of these expectations from her people.

"My most worthy subjects! I am Melty Q. Melromarc, the new queen of Melromarc. Will you please join me in continuing to fight, for the sake of this nation and for the sake of this world?" Melty's request was met with a roar of agreement. "This is the time for the world to come together and face the waves! I declare here and now that I will continue to support and continue to enact the wishes and requests of my mother, the previous queen!" More cheering and applause.

With that, the coronation came to an end. I saw it more as a presentation to the people than anything.

Melty sank down into the throne with an exhausted-sounding sigh. It was to be expected—the ceremony head featured the heroes, VIPs from across the nation, and representatives of the coalition army.

"Mel-chan, that was amazing! Everyone was cheering for you!" Filo offered from Melty's side, as just someone who was happy for the success of her close friend.

"Thank you, Filo," Melty replied.

"You've gotten pretty big for your boots, Melty," I also offered, mixing in some trademark sarcasm. "Queen of the largest nation in the world! You've risen a long way from when I first met you."

"What's with the attitude?" she retorted.

"Nothing in particular. I'm just wondering what Her Majesty Queen Melty, ruler of the vast nation of Melromarc, will get up to next?" I quipped.

"Seriously, why did this have to happen to me?" Melty muttered, definitely sounding displeased. Melty had never seemed like one who wished for personal advancement. She'd been born a princess, of course, so it hadn't really been something she had needed to go after actively herself. She was quite the contrast from her power-hungry sister, that was for sure.

"This is when the real work starts. For the sake of the people, and the sake of the world, you are going to have to do all sorts of difficult things," I reminded her.

"The same goes for you, Naofumi!" she bit back.

"Only until the waves end. You're stuck with this gig for the rest of your life. All I have to do is fight. You need to handle all the other stuff behind the front lines. Man, it's so easy being a hero!" I laid it on nice and thick.

"Bah! Just give it to me straight, why don't you? I'll show you!" she retorted. With a determined expression on her face,

Melty stood and raised both of her hands in order to attract everyone's attention. "Upon reflection of his great deeds during the uprising, I now bestow upon Shield Hero Naofumi Iwatani the title of archduke!" she proclaimed loudly.

What! The more important I got, the more annoying jobs it would force me to do!

"You little—" I started. Melty just laughed.

"Trying to force all the boring work onto me? Never!" she crowed.

"I'd rather die than take such a title! You take that back, right now!" I commanded.

"Who do you think you're talking to?! I am declaring this a royal edict!" Melty proceeded to put the boot in. Her further declaration was met with applause from the coalition army representatives. I could only wonder why they didn't bring Melty to task for her slovenly, childish behavior. But she wasn't finished yet. "I think Archduke Iwatani deserves all of the Faubrey territories that we obtained during this most recent conflict. Takt has left them badly scarred, to be sure, but they should still be able to provide some taxes." A nobleman spread out a map and outlined the territories to be given to me. As befitting the title of archduke, perhaps, it was a pretty big chunk of land.

"Stop pushing your own agenda!" I shouted. At that point, Trash stepped in, an uncharacteristic smile on his face as he gently raised his hands.

"Yet it is a fact that we won the war thanks to your actions, Hero Iwatani. Failure to reward you would reflect poorly on our nation," Trash pointed out.

"Trash! The exact same thing could be said about you!" I fired back. In fact, Trash had done the most out of anybody. Why does the title of "hero" attract this kind of trouble?

"I acted only as a representative of this nation, now as I have in the past," Trash replied. I mean, Trash was already second only to the queen. He was already in a top management position, basically. But I still couldn't accept my own sudden promotion.

"There are still many tasks that I need my new Archduke Naofumi to handle!" Melty stated.

"Shut it! Stop pushing everything onto me! I'm not going to be your archduke!" I replied.

"And I didn't want to become queen either! We don't have much choice, either of us!" Melty retorted.

"Fehhh! There's no need for either of you to reject your advancement so vehemently." Rishia cut into our conversation with a flat, relaxed voice.

This wasn't what I wanted. I had only sought territory to start with because I had wanted to provide a place where Raphtalia could live in peace until she died, once I left her behind. I certainly didn't want my next war to be waged on bundles of documents. Melty surely felt the same. She had already been fighting all the paperwork my territory produced. It wasn't hard to imagine the increase in volume she would see by becoming queen of such a massive nation.

"How did the king of Faubrey run his nation?" I asked. Takt had held the throne so briefly he didn't really count. He had probably just left everything to the more capable members of his gaggle of girls, anyway.

"It seems everything other than commands relating to basic policy was handled by his subordinates," Trash explained. He had lived in Faubrey in the past, of course, so he probably had quite a good handle on that stuff. "A capable ruler who truly thinks of their nation, and of their people, would likely take the lead in all things. Just like my wife did . . ." Trash drifted off, a distant look in his eyes. That shut Melty up, anyway. She had also seen everything the queen did.

"Is this going to be hard on you, Mel-chan?" Filo asked. *Boy, does the next queen of the filolials have it easy!*

"In all sorts of ways," I said. "Filo, we'll need you to support Melty too."

"Okay! I'm with you all the way!" Filo chirped brightly.

"Filo. Thank you," Melty replied. She had lost her mother and then executed most of those responsible. Melty might be putting a brave face on, but it had to be hard on her. Trash was back to his wise-king ways and so was likely supporting her. But having Filo around had to be helping ease her burden.

"Still, daughter, giving Hero Iwatani the title of archduke! I couldn't be prouder!" Trash continued.

"What? Why? Ah!" Melty turned to me with an "oh shit" look on her face. An archduke was a pretty high rank among nobles, I presumed. But I didn't know the exact pecking order in this world—or even at home.

"Hero Iwatani, you may not know this, so please allow me to explain. In our nation, archduke is second only to the queen. The rank you might usually call 'king,'" Trash stated. I took a moment to process this. I already knew that Melromarc was ruled by a queen. Trash had served as an interim king, which meant . . .

"Indeed. As interim king, I actually held the title of archduke." Trash filled in the blanks.

"Hold on," I said.

"You still don't see? With this, Queen Melty has finally approved you, Hero Iwatani, as her fiancé," Trash proclaimed. I made a noise in my throat. Melty was clutching her head too. The realization of what she had done now really hit her. "As you hold the position of Shield Hero, we will need the approval of those from Siltvelt for this, but . . . I presume that won't be a problem?" Trash turned and asked. The delegation from Siltvelt nodded in response.

"No problem at all, if you will also allow a number of our people to enter into marriage with the Shield Hero," came the reply. This was my chance! If I made things seem bad for Mel-romarc, I could get this whole silly idea thrown out completely.

"I refuse!" I stated flatly.

"Perhaps that is to be expected. How about allowing us to arrange marriages with your children, Shield Hero?" the delegate continued.

"I refuse!" I retorted again.

"We can always wait to decide this after the waves have been resolved," the delegate said, changing his approach. "You do seem open to marrying people from your own territory, I have heard."

Ah. Considering how depressed I had been after losing Atla, and the way I had been acting when recovering from that, I could see how I might have given that impression. I wasn't going to change my tune now. For the sake of the future, it might be best if those from the village did have . . . but just thinking the thought made my face red.

"I think that is enough on this topic—" Just as Melty also tried to steer the conversation onto other matters, Trash spoke up.

"If you don't desire to marry Hero Iwatani, I have someone else I might like to suggest to you, Queen Melty." The old man was looking at Fohl as he spoke.

Wait, Fohl? What?

"Huh?!" Fohl froze as though his spine had turned to ice

with Trash's eye upon him, and then he visibly recoiled. So he wasn't up for it. I could understand that.

The old genmu, also clearly having worked out who Trash was talking about, gave his own approving nod. "A forgotten remnant of the hakuko, the brother to Atla, and the Gauntlets Hero. He would also make a fine choice to serve as the bridge between our nations."

"Brother!" Fohl looked at me with pleading eyes. Seriously, he looked quite pathetic. As a white tiger demi-human, he looked a bit like a weepy kitten.

"Naofumi!" Melty joined him in looking at me—the eyes of the pair who would likely end up being forced together if I turned down this marriage. It wasn't like anyone would have to sleep with her, anyway. The marriage could just be for the sake of appearances.

It seemed as though Trash had a sister, and Fohl was the child of that sister. So he was just trying to give his nephew a helping hand.

"In which case, and in recognition of his deeds alongside Hero Iwatani, we must also give Master Fohl a suitable rank—something that lets everyone know he is worthy to run this nation. If anything was to happen to me—" Trash continued.

"Brother! Please, I'm begging you! Say something!" Fohl interjected. I shook my head, seemingly left with little choice.

"Okay, okay, just calm down. Taking Queen Melty's age

into account, she isn't in a position to bear children yet, I presume?" I asked.

"Hey!" Melty immediately glared at me again. Like I said, I didn't have any choice. If I didn't think up some kind of reason, I was going to be forced into this engagement.

"No need to worry about that," Trash responded. "Melty is quite capable of carrying a child." So she was quite an early bloomer . . . *Trash, hold on!*

"Why do you know that?!" I retorted.

"There was much about Melty written in my wife's diaries," he explained. He almost made it sound like a good thing, whimsical and sweet. The queen had known about Witch's virginity, after all, so I guess she would know about Melty too.

That was some serious surveillance, in any case. Also, it's not something she should really be leaving in her diary.

"What I mean is, I'd like to push such matters a little further into the future, in consideration of Melty's health. She is the queen of an entire nation now. Safety first. More than anything, to me she is still just a snotty little kid," I finally responded, as tactfully as I was able. What I really wanted to do was keep this whole thing as vague as possible and then get back to my own world, putting an end to it all.

"Snotty kid?!" Melty raged. "I'm quite the mature woman, thank you very much!"

"Dummy! Shut up!" I hissed back through my teeth. Trash was nodding though, a smile on his face.

"Then there is no problem," he said. "With the holding of this ceremony today, Queen Melty is now considered a woman. Therefore, Hero Iwatani, please take good care of her. I want to see the faces of my grandchildren sooner rather than later."

"Someone, please, take me away from here!" After she stepped on the landmine herself, Melty now begged for aid from some unknown quarter.

"Do you want to run away, Mel-chan?" Filo asked. The oblivious filolial was the only one her pleas for aid reached, however.

Chapter One: Talk of Love

Once Melty's coronation was completed, we returned to the village.

I still had quite a lot going on. Quite aside from anything else, we were preparing to set out on an expedition to another world. The familiar surroundings of the village really helped calm me down.

Then I saw Ren leading Eclair along. I thought it had been decided that Eclair would be transferred to the castle, where she would continue to guard Melty.

"How's it going with you?" I asked them.

"Not bad," Ren replied. "I hope this makes raising levels go a bit more smoothly."

Then I looked at Eclair.

"You said all that stuff about beating your knowledge into Ren, but you're the one getting schooled now. You should be grateful for this class-up over 100," I told her.

"Why are you acting all high and mighty, Hero Iwatani?" she retorted.

"I'm an archduke now. So I actually am high and mighty. That's what I wanted to tell you," I said.

"What! Archduke?!" Eclair exclaimed.

"You've gone up in the world? You don't seem very happy about it," Ren said.

"I'm not. It wasn't exactly my idea," I replied. Seriously, how did things end up like this? "Eclair, you just worry about protecting Melty."

"Of course I will. I will take my notes from Queen Melty's own capacity for rule and learn the ways of politics for myself!" Eclair stated enthusiastically. She could fight but wasn't all that skilled when it came to regional management. If she didn't get on top of her game, even village-newcomer Ruft would start to show her up.

"Eclair has such a positive attitude. I could learn a lot from her," Ren said, heaping more praise on her. Ren had respect for Eclair, that was for sure, and also paid careful attention to Wyndia. None of that was going to change.

Wyndia didn't seem very happy about it, however.

I signaled to Ren and moved close to his face.

"You ever going to confess your love for her?" I whispered in his ear.

"That's not what this is!" Ren protested.

"Oh? You prefer them young, do you?" I asked.

"Hey, that's more—" Ren started to say something and then stopped. He'd been about to say, "That's more your style." *Sorry, buddy. That's not the case.*

Or was it?

I was now basically engaged to Melty. That might look like a Lolita complex from the outside. There were lots of women around me with adult bodies but who were actually quite young too—Raphtalia, Filo, Shildina, Keel, even Atla. From that perspective, it did start to make me feel a bit strange.

"Of course, Naofumi, you're . . . Ah, it's nothing," Ren started, then stopped himself again.

"Sounds like you've got something to say. Go ahead, finish that sentence," I prompted him.

"I just mean . . . you know." Now Ren was looking over at where Fohl was lecturing the slaves training in the village. Why Fohl?

"What the hell kind of misunderstanding is this?" I inquired with an edge to my voice.

"What? I mean, Naofumi, don't you play for both—" Ren started.

"That's enough. Say no more!" I cut him off. I really needed to nip this in the bud. It was true I tried to sleep with Fohl—just once—but there were all sorts of context to that encounter. Still, he had an ugly mug, but his skin had felt pretty smooth. He had kinda smelled like Atla too.

"W-what do you want?!" As soon as I had that thought, Fohl turned and looked around, perhaps sensing something from my direction.

He was so sensitive to this kind of thing, seriously!

"Love is free, man. Don't you know that? I learned it recently," I said. It wasn't just what Atla had told me. I'd learned that love was required in order to keep you from having regrets.

I'd never dreamed that I'd come to regret doing nothing.

"Ren," I said.

"What?" he replied.

"Once the world is at peace, what do you want to do?" I asked.

"Yeah . . . good question," he replied. Perhaps reading what I was trying to say, he looked around the village. As it turned out, the spirits of the holy weapons would let us choose to either remain in this world or return home. I was planning on going back, but for Ren, remaining here might be a good choice.

"You're staying here?" I asked him.

"I don't know," Ren said. "Eclair, what do you want me to do?"

"Me? I'm not sure why you're asking for my opinion, but don't you have somewhere to go back to?" she replied.

"Yes. The world I originally came from. I haven't thought about it much since I came here, to what I thought was my ideal world," he explained.

"The choice is for you to make, so I'm not going to comment on that," I told him. "But if you have unfinished business, going back is definitely one choice. I can't say whether saving the world will allow for your sins to be forgiven, but—"

"Acting for the sake of others is one form of atonement, right? I get it," Ren interjected. The two of us had been through a lot together by now. We were comrades, even, with a solid understanding of one another.

From Eclair's reaction, though, it also looked like Ren's love life wasn't going anywhere soon.

"Ren. Might be time to give it some thought," I said.

"What?" he asked.

"Why don't you just settle for Wyndia?" I suggested. At my words, Gaelion made a surprised noise and glared in my direction. Yeah, he didn't like that. He wasn't willing to give his daughter away to Ren.

"About Wyndia . . . I am planning to take responsibility for that," he said. He wasn't making much progress on either front, then. Ren clearly had his own troubles to deal with.

"Little Naofumi!" Sadeena, in the distance, was waving eagerly in my direction.

"This is the difference between Naofumi and I, then . . ." Ren commented despondently. Hold on. He was including her too? For my part, I considered it impossible to tell if Sadeena really liked me or not.

"Look, Ren. You might not all be on the same page with everyone, but you do have quite a few people who like you, right?" I told him. Eclair and Wyndia were just bad picks, neither one of them having much interest in romance. But Ren was close to Keel, the weapon shop old guy, and that crowd.

"You're concerned with how people see you?" Eclair asked.

"No, that's not it. I'm talking about having your priorities in order, if and when the time comes," I replied.

"I see. The mental side of things is also important in battle. I've heard that fighting with someone you want to protect helps you bring out your full strength." Even Eclair seemed to have cottoned on to what we were talking about. Perhaps it was my role to cast the first stone.

"Eclair, if someone said they cared for you, what would you do?" I asked.

"I would be happy to have anyone feel that way about me. But unfortunately, I also don't have the time to think about love. I would politely turn them down," she explained.

"Even if, just for argument's sake, it was Ren who liked you?" I prodded.

"Even then," she confirmed. Oh boy. Ren immediately looked super depressed. He'd had his balls crushed before even getting to his confession. He might have sounded undecided, but it was pretty clear he liked her.

This didn't feel like an end to it either. I also didn't want his performance in battle to suffer due to a broken heart.

"Ren," I said.

"What?" he eventually replied.

"She's not the sharpest when it comes to matters of the heart. If such a situation actually came about, she might change her mind. If you get lucky, the one you confess to may then start to take notice of you. It's too soon to give up," I told him.

"Okay, okay. I get it," he said.

"But you also need to read the room a little. If you confess to her right now, I don't think she'll give you the nod. You need to get closer to her first and then let her know how you feel. Maybe even get the elation right after we save the world to give things a push," I advised.

"Yes. Yes, okay!" Ren gave an enthusiastic nod at my suggestion. That was easier than expected. My only experience with this kind of thing was dating simulators, of course, so I couldn't provide a detailed plan of action. This was perhaps something to ask Motoyasu about. In the past, at least, he might have provided some actionable intel, but as he was right now . . .

The reason I had kept my advice a little vague, using words like "maybe" and "I think," was so I wouldn't need to take any responsibility if he failed.

"Well then, Hero Iwatani. I will repay your kindness for everything I have been taught here. Now I take my leave." With that, Eclair used Ren's portal to return to the castle.

Chapter Two: Limit Break

As it turned out, Ethnobalt was with Sadeena and the others. Sadeena had not stopped trying to call me over.

"Little Naofumi, how are you doing?" she asked.

"Really not sure how to answer that one," I responded. The Melromarc wave had been taken care of, by the way. With the four holy heroes and the staff, claws, and projectile seven star heroes all suitably powered up, wave-level enemies were not such a problem anymore. It had been over within minutes of it starting. No enemy we could consider a threat had been included in the wave.

Maybe that was just how strong the heroes had become.

One piece of bad luck, however, was that we hadn't been matched with Kizuna's world during the wave. I had kind of been hoping that, if we had been matched with them, Raphtalia could have made it back to this world through one of the wave cracks. As more waves were going to continue to occur in nations across the world, the heroes were going to have to split up to handle them all. Needing to go and bail out Kizuna and her gang in another world was a pretty tall order, on top of all our troubles.

Ethnobalt had explained how the holy heroes, other than

Kizuna, had all been killed in her world. Control had been taken by a group who seemed to be a vanguard for the waves and also had access to the Takt-like power to steal people's weapons.

"Tell me, Ethnobalt. Just to confirm, when do you think it would be best to cross to Kizuna's world?" I asked. I had already returned the anchor accessory to him that he had previously given me. We could apparently use that trinket to cross over. However, there were some timing-based issues we needed to deal with first.

I had plenty of other stuff to be getting along with, of course. But I also wanted to go and save Raphtalia as quickly as possible.

"I think it will take three more days. Then I will be able to use the power of the accessory and take you across to our world," he replied.

"Okay. In which case, I'll use that time to make the required preparations," I said, then shouted, "Gaelion!" He replied with a rumbling squawk, flying in at my call. I'd noticed that he was operating independently from Wyndia a lot more recently.

After claiming the dragon cores from Takt's own Dragon Emperor, Gaelion had now ascended to the position of the greatest Dragon Emperor currently roaming the world. He had also acquired the knowledge about how to break the limit on the level cap.

In order to explain this limit-breaking knowledge, I need

to first explain about this world and the levels that exist here.

To put it simply, this world has an element very much like the "levels" seen in video games. Defeating monsters awards you with experience, and that experience can raise your level. However, everyone aside from heroes has a level cap in place, the first one at 40 and the second one at 100. In order to break the 40th-level cap, you can use—with permission from the state—a facility called a "dragon hourglass" to perform a class-up ritual. The method for breaking the 100th-level cap, however, had been lost to us until now. It was no longer lost though, because Gaelion now knew how to do it.

"Considering we're facing plenty more fighting in the future, think you could gather up everyone ready for the limit break and get it done?" I asked.

"Kwaa!" Gaelion responded affirmatively. He sounded pretty happy, perhaps pleased to be able to do something to help me out. That business with the class-ups for the monsters hadn't really gone his way.

"You certainly have some interesting techniques here in your world, Naofumi," Ethnobalt commented.

"What about in Kizuna's world?" I asked.

"There's a level cap, of course. If we could take this technique back with us, it might help us overcome our current troubles," Ethnobalt pondered.

"I bet the system isn't the same," I replied. Our world and

Kizuna's world were quite different from each other. Just as they handled the seven star weapons and vassal weapons differently, the methods for limit-breaking were probably different too.

After all, when I first visited that world, I had been dropped back to level 1.

"Let's head to the dragon hourglass in order to perform the limit-breaking class-ups. Anyone who meets the conditions, get ready to join us," I stated. The power-up method provided by the gauntlets seven star weapon now allowed us to distribute skill points. Increasing the skill level for my Portal Shield had boosted the number of locations I could register and the number of people I could take through the portal with me.

"We're here, we're here! Little Shildina, get ready!" Sadeena shouted eagerly.

"I was ready before you were," Shildina shot back. The killer whales were two of those who would be participating in the class-up experiment. Both of them were pretty strong, and both were already at the level 100 cap.

The reason for their high level was because, for whatever reason, the monsters in the sea awarded a substantial amount of experience.

"Raph!" said Raph-chan.

"Dafu!" said Raph-chan II. The pair of them looked pretty excited. *I guess it's about time these two got a class-up too.* There were still plenty of lingering questions about Raph-chan II, but she wasn't an enemy, and so it couldn't hurt . . . right?

"Hold on!" Ruft ran up, chasing the Raph-chans.

"Hey, Ruft. Working hard on raising your own level?" I asked.

"Yeah. I should be level 40 pretty soon," he replied.

"Good for you," I complimented him. He had definitely gotten taller recently. His face looked more mature too.

"Once I reach 40, I'm going to take the Raph-chan class-up. I really can't wait!" he exclaimed.

"Raph?" Raph-chan interjected. Oh boy. Had I gone wrong somewhere with raising this kid? Raphtalia hadn't been happy about it, but I had ostensibly agreed to the Raph-chan class-up that Ruft had mentioned.

"Shildina, you're going with the Shield Hero, aren't you?" Ruft asked.

"That's the plan," she replied.

"Once you get your class-up, let me join you in leveling up," he said. Shildina looked at me. If possible, I had wanted Ruft to remain young for a while longer and to grow up more gradually, but with everything that had happened recently, he likely had his own reasons for wanting this. He was also being trained in all sorts of fighting styles by all sorts of people. I couldn't waste his desire to work hard.

I gave a nod, and Shildina confirmed it too.

"Just within a range that isn't dangerous," she said.

"Okay. Thank you," he replied. The speed that Ruft was developing mentally really reminded me of Raphtalia. That was how swiftly he was making progress. No wonder he and Raphtalia were cousins.

"Dafu?" Then Ruft picked up Raph-chan II. I saw the perfect opportunity.

"Raph-chan II, you take good care of Ruft," I told her. Raph-chan II was actually the past Heavenly Emperor. If anything happened here while we were gone, she could turn into the form of the past Heavenly Emperor and fight to protect Ruft. She was strong too, although the transformation appeared to have a time limit.

". . . Dafu," came the eventual reply.

"Heh, being with this little one really relaxes me, even more so than when I'm with Raphtalia—so much that it makes me think having a mother might be like this," Ruft explained. I mean, she was basically his ancestor—like his however-many-greats grandma.

"Dafu . . ." Raph-chan II rubbed her cheeks a little, unsure of how to react to that, and so Ruft put her up on his shoulder and stroked her head. The words "Ruft exclusive Raph-chan" flashed through my mind.

Then I had another thought. If Raph-chan II was actually the past Heavenly Emperor, what about the original Raph-chan?

Did she also have the soul of someone we don't know about inside her?

"Raph," she said in that moment, striking a pose to prompt us to set out. Those among my allies who could talk to monsters hadn't mentioned any issues with her, so I guess it wasn't a problem.

"We'll deal with the class-ups first and then head out to level up right away," I said. Then I proceeded to send everyone who was going to get a class-up over to the dragon hourglass. The class-up rituals started at once.

"Here we go!" I said.

"Kwaa!" Gaelion squawked, starting to incant the magic as Sadeena touched the dragon hourglass.

"Here, in this moment, the Dragon Emperor commands you. Bestow a new role upon this warrior who fights alongside the hero in defense of this world. Oh world, oh dragon vein, oh truth itself! Unlock the true power of this individual!" He was incanting using telepathy, meaning I was the only one who could hear him. The actual Gaelion was basically squawking like a parrot. As he finished the words, a beam of light emitted from the dragon hourglass and extended to my shield, which glowed as though some form of verification had been completed. Then, just like normal, a list of options appeared, showing the paths that Sadeena could take.

Wondering if there was a chance in the modifier rate for

changing to a special class, I had a look at the options available to her. They were broadly divided between raising her abilities in her humanoid form and raising them when she was in her therianthrope form. It also looked like she could get some special abilities.

It felt a bit different from a normal class-up. With one of those, you could make detailed specifications about status. Of course, they did include special abilities too. This was closer to a monster class-up.

Shouldn't it normally be the other way around? Maybe this was due to Gaelion's protection. I went ahead and transferred the right to make the decisions over to Sadeena.

"Oh my. I'm really not sure what to pick. Which do you like, Little Naofumi?" Sadeena asked.

"You decide," I told her.

"Please. A girl wants someone they like to make these decisions for them," she replied.

"Is that so?" I responded. I didn't feel all that comfortable with deciding Sadeena's life for her.

"In that case, I'm going to choose to do fun things with you, Little Naofumi, and make lots of babies," she responded. I made a disturbed noise. Was that even a choice? I checked again, and there were plenty of items that came pretty close.

"Sadeena. Stop toying with sweet Naofumi," Shildina said.

"Oh please. I'm just having a little fun," Sadeena shot back.

"I'm the one who's going to make lots of children with him," Shildina continued.

"Oh my!" Sadeena responded.

"Sisters, enough!" I exclaimed. I couldn't tell if they were friendly or not, but their sexual harassment of me was identical! Seriously, at every turn they were there, making comments.

It looked like Sadeena had made her choice, anyway, as the hourglass glowed brightly and Sadeena absorbed the light.

When the light finally faded, Sadeena was smiling.

"That seems to be all of it. Little Naofumi, will you please take a look?" she asked.

"Sure thing," I responded and proceeded to check her status.

Wow. Her stats had increased so much I almost thought it was a joke. Almost double her previous stats! Once my own protection was overlaid on this, she might have attack power to rival that of a hero.

For the level 100 class-up, the modifier looked to be displayed as a percentage. I wasn't entirely sure what she had selected, but her previous, fairly evenly balanced stats now had a bit more of a slant to them. Of course, that might originate with the overall direction she had chosen.

"What did you choose?" I asked.

"Agility, strength, and then magic," she responded.

"Fair enough," I said. On top of all of this, she'd also

started to learn Hengen Muso Style! She was quite the monster!

With that, we proceeded with the limit-breaking class-ups for all of the high-level individuals from the village. Apparently, it would remove the level cap completely.

The two Raph-chans, chattering away as normal, also both got class-ups. Gaelion had a bit of a sour expression on his face. I could understand it—Raph-chan could probably learn to do this himself, if he wanted.

It was decided that Gaelion would continue to aid with the class-ups for everyone whom the heroes deemed worthy of their trust. We needed all the firepower we could get. Anyone we could trust needed to be made as powerful as possible in order to prepare for future waves.

"Right then. The killer whale sisters and I are now going to lead a party to level up in the ocean. This is about raising the standard all round, so if you want to join in, be ready for what that means," I said. Having finished the class-ups, we returned to the village at once and prepared to depart in three days' time.

It was true, of course, that once we got to Kizuna's world everyone who hadn't gone there last time would probably be kicked down to level 1. *Whatever.* They still had to be as powerful as possible when we returned. The killer whale sisters, in particular, were both really strong and yet had been stuck at level 100 for ages. That had really been a shame and a real waste. If we could boost the levels of Ruft and the others a little too, all the better.

I was even going to get Sadeena to train Ethnobalt. The effect of crossing between worlds had left Ethnobalt as weak as a monster called an usapil, which looked a bit like a rabbit. In his world, it was apparently called a "library rabbit."

A killer whale and a rabbit . . . for a moment that old story called "The Hare of Inaba" kinda hopped through my mind. But that was a shark, of course. Or was it a crocodile?

"Put this on, Ethnobalt, and go get really strong," I told him, passing him a pekkul costume that served as diving gear.

"What is this? Something Chris made?" he asked. I mean, I could see why the design would make him think that. It was just a coincidence though.

"It's based on a different model. A monster boss from a certain area dropped it," I said.

"So it's not order made? This design is quite something, I must say," he commented.

"I'm more interested in you than this suit," I responded. I had identified that Ethnobalt had the same kind of growth potential as Rishia. I'd gotten the old Hengen Muso lady involved and it had been just as I suspected. After checking Ethnobalt's body countless times, the old lady had shouted, "You see this maybe once every hundred years! It doesn't matter that he's a monster! This is quite the year we're having!" Pretty much what she had said with Rishia. Still, it meant I was right.

When I told her that there was basically a whole tribe of Ethnobalts in the other world, she had clutched her head as though she was really thinking hard about joining my little expedition. As it turned out, the old lady had been training those with potential in this world in order to help support Trash. Furthermore, after learning of the danger the old lady was in during the fight with Takt, her rather undependable son was also finally starting to take things seriously, and so she was hoping to train him too.

She was a mother, after all. Of course, her own son would be more important than some unknown but highly skilled group. However, I couldn't stop myself from wondering about the apparent age gap between mother and son.

Anyway, she'd said something about leaving the training of the library rabbits to Rishia. She'd also asked me to bring some back once my work there was done. So she wanted to raise some after all!

"I trained as hard as Rishia but still failed to achieve my true potential. I'll make the most of this opportunity, even if just for a short period!" Ethnobalt enthused.

"Holders of vassal weapons do have trouble learning life force," I sympathized. They could do it, but the requirement to use SP makes it hard to get a handle on, stopping them from achieving it easily. "Like you said, it's just a short period, but go and do your best. Then keep it up once we come back."

"That's what I'll do," he said. I did shake my head though. Having an intellectual-magician type like Ethnobalt learn the same martial arts as Rishia really seemed like a waste, coming from a former geek and gamer.

It being its own world, the rules in Kizuna's world were different. The only way to find out if application to magic was possible was to experiment with it. In either case, though, there was no harm in him being able to handle himself in close combat.

The killer whale sisters therefore led the way to leveling us up in the ocean.

"We came hunting before the war with Faubrey, didn't we, Little Naofumi? Let's push past even that point this time," Sadeena suggested.

"Sure. We can handle it," I replied. Once we arrived at the hunting ground, I started to cast All Liberation Aura. Just like when we finished off Takt, I used the X version. That meant we could *definitely* handle this. It was support magic so strong that the old Ren, Itsuki, and Motoyasu would have called it cheating for sure. Activating this turned most monsters into little more than wood to be chopped.

Living wood, though, so I still wasn't going to risk any messing around.

"All Liberation Aura X!" I placed support magic on everyone who had come with me.

"This is . . . quite incredible. I should be a low level, having crossed from another world. Having this level of power is quite astounding," Ethnobalt said, dressed in his costume, clearly quite impressed. "I should think using this power should allow us to easily aid Kizuna."

"I hope so too," I replied. I really just hoped we could hop over there, resolve their problems, and come back.

As we had this discussion, Sadeena and the others were speeding through the offing with us on their backs.

"Time to dive! Everyone hold on tight!" Sadeena said. Ethnobalt gasped as both of the sisters plunged down deeper and deeper toward the hunting grounds, with us still on their backs. They were going so fast! Multiple times faster than during our hunting trip prior to leaving for Faubrey, taking us down really deep in mere seconds. It was like being blasted into the deep by a rocket engine.

"Killer whale sisters! Stop!" I barely managed as Ethnobalt and Ruft started to writhe and moan. "Think about the water pressure—and whether we can all handle it!"

"Oh my! I'm quite surprised by this speed as well!" Sadeena replied.

"Wow . . . you guys are too light!" Shildina added. That sounded worth investigating. I deployed my Shooting Star Wall, just to be sure.

This was a skill housed in the Shield of Compassion that

Atla had bequeathed to me. The effect of this high-functioning skill was to deploy Shooting Star Shield on everyone I considered allies within a certain radius around me. It was even better if they were in some sort of formation, really giving a boost to the effects of each individual shield.

It was not without its issues, of course. If the resistance threshold was crossed, then all of the shields would break. It was ultimately just a Shooting Star Shield for everyone. While offering some resistance from attacks, it also caused issues with attack range when those with the shield active tried to engage in close combat. When used with a sword or other in-your-face weapon, the barrier would push the enemy back, making it harder to close in on them.

In any case, deploying Shooting Star Wall provided some respite from the water pressure.

"I thought . . . I was about to be crushed," Ethnobalt managed around gasps and heavy breathing.

"Me too," Ruft added. Both of them were spitting up blood. They couldn't hack it, as I had feared. I proceeded to cast some healing magic on them both. The rules in this world were different, and Raphtalia, S'yne, and I hadn't really been bothered by it, but high-speed diving into the ocean clearly caused some damage at low levels. Seriously, it could have even killed them.

"I'll keep Shooting Star Wall up, so let's continue deeper while raising our levels," I said.

"Oh my! All your demands, Little Naofumi, it's making my head spin!" Sadeena jibed.

"I could use wind magic to gather some air and alleviate the pressure . . . You could also put them behind you, sweet Naofumi." Shildina was being far more practical when compared to her sister, who was joking around.

"We also have to keep an eye on our remaining oxygen," I reminded them. "Take care as we dive." Something else I'd discovered on this hunt was that adding points to the underwater skill Bubble Shield not only increased the volume of oxygen it provided, but if I allocated at least three points, it created a kind of bubble membrane . . . basically creating an air bubble version of Shooting Star Shield.

As it turned out, it was a pretty convenient skill.

With that, we reached the ocean floor, and the killer whale sisters hunted down even more monsters than last time.

"Our limitations have been lifted! We are unleashed! Let's do this, little Shildina!" Sadeena was in full flow.

"You don't get to order me around. I can handle myself better than you!" her sister retorted.

"No fighting," I interjected. While watching the killer whale sisters swim along, I walked the ocean floor. Ruft and Ethnobalt were with me. Perhaps thanks to his increased level while we'd been down here, Ethnobalt had started illuminating his surroundings using his own magic.

"Those two seem very strong," Ethnobalt commented.

"They sure are. They joined me after I last saw Kizuna. They are definitely in the top five, not counting the heroes," I explained.

"I see. You have been bolstering your fighting forces considerably. I am relieved to hear it," Ethnobalt responded.

"I do what I can," I replied. Looking back now, I realized it had definitely been a long road since I said farewell to Kizuna and her allies. With days so packed with stuff going on, it was hard to believe it had just been four months.

"Raph," said Raph-chan, riding on Sadeena's shoulder and waving at Raph-chan II, who was being held by Ruft.

"Dafu," Raph-chan II replied.

"Two sisters, both water dragon miko priestesses, were swimming freely through the depths. It might not be long before they even surpass the water dragon himself. What do you think, Shield Hero?" Ruft asked me.

"Oh my! I think that might be going a little too far!" Shildina said. I personally wasn't so sure he was that far off the mark. Still, it wouldn't do for them to get too full of themselves.

We continued our hunting and continued to increase our levels.

Ethnobalt was racing up in levels even as he just continued to explore the seabed. As the main point of this was to raise Ruft's and Ethnobalt's levels, we hadn't taken on any higher-ranking monsters yet. There were apparently some incredibly powerful monsters down here, if you went looking for them.

"Ah, Shield Hero! I just reached level 40!" Ruft said.

"Sounds good. Want to go back?" I asked him.

"Might be a good idea. I can't increase any higher than this, and I don't want to hold everyone else back," he replied.

"Gotcha. I'll portal you back to the village," I told him.

"Okay. I'll take part in the training there," he said. Ruft really was a hard worker. So serious. "See you later!" I saw him waving, then used the portal and sent him back to the village.

"What next, then? You don't need a level 40 class-up, right, Ethnobalt?" I confirmed with him.

"That's right. Before I became a vassal weapon holder, I went through all sorts of training to become the library rabbit leader. The level 40 restriction seems to be an element unique to this world, and there's no sign of me stopping at level 40," he reported.

"Okay," I muttered, stroking Raph-chan II with both hands. Ruft had chosen to leave her behind with us. I had to admit, quite aside from my plans for Ruft, I had been hoping to have Ethnobalt undergo a Raph-chan-type class-up. I had really been wondering about what it would do to him.

"I'm not sure how to explain this, but I sense something from you right now very much like what I feel from Kizuna when she's planning some fresh mischief," Ethnobalt said.

"You do?" I said innocently. Was it so easy to tell when a hero was plotting something?

"Dafu," said Raph-chan II. As though reading my mind, she hopped up onto my head and started batting at my skull. It was cute. Okay then. I'd try to limit my evil notions, just like I did when Raphtalia was around.

"Right, Little Naofumi. You keep that little precious bundle safe. We're going to push things a bit harder!" Sadeena said.

"Go ahead," I told her. We followed the two sisters deeper into the ocean depths. Based on the experience we were receiving from the monsters, it looked like the recommended level for defeating them was 150, and Sadeena and Shildina were cutting through them one after the other. Ethnobalt looked pretty freaked out by the proceedings. They should have still been weaker than the Spirit Tortoise—or at least I hoped they were. I'd feel terrible for Ost if that wasn't the case. That said, we had defeated a fake hero who had claimed to be level 350.

Through these raging battles, Ethnobalt crossed level 60 in no time.

"Hey . . . can I have a moment? I'm actually pretty hungry," Ethnobalt said, clutching his stomach, which was definitely rumbling.

Ethnobalt was hiding in his human form, but just as Filo had been transformed by crossing to another world, Ethnobalt had been turned into a monster called a leshuant, a type of usapil, from his original form as a library rabbit. Considering his age, Ethnobalt apparently wouldn't have a rapid growth spurt, but his body still had to be growing a bit.

"Let's go back then. We've got most of the materials I was after too," I said. We needed to quickly carve up the huge—and strange—monsters found down on the ocean floor. I'd considered just putting them into my shield and then popping them out again at the dragon hourglass, but we'd defeated some monsters so big they would probably crush a few buildings if I did that. It might be best to just put up with the drop items. Some pretty good gear had dropped.

We finished the hunt and returned to the village.

As a result of our efforts, both Sadeena and Shildina had reached level 120. Twenty levels in one day was huge, and it made me do a double take to make sure we weren't back on the Cal Mira islands.

Once we were back in the village, I took Ruft to the dragon hourglass and performed a Raph-chan-style class-up on him. There was a puff of smoke just like with Raphtalia, but once it cleared, nothing much had changed.

"How do you feel, Ruft?" I asked him. Ruft inspected himself carefully but then tilted his head.

"I do feel stronger," he started. "But I don't really understand how."

"Fair enough," I responded.

"I was hoping to be able to transform like Shildina!" he said.

"If you keep working hard, you might be able to!" I encouraged him.

"You're right! I'll keep training!" he enthused.

"I wonder what kind of face little Raphtalia would pull if she saw this," Sadeena commented. An angry one, probably, but while the cat was away, the mice could class up however they liked. It made sense, anyway. When I thought about the future, we would need Ruft to also start pulling his weight.

"Right then, Shield Hero. Should I go to Melty now?" Ruft asked.

"Yeah . . . okay. Trash is at the castle too, so you'll learn a lot there. I'll want you to take part in leveling up when you can, but put your studies first," I instructed him. He nodded his agreement. I proceeded to send him to Melty, and then I returned to the village.

This was how we spent the three days prior to our departure: getting ready for the trip and mainly leveling up. The party went through a few variations, but Ethnobalt and I were a fixture. Sadeena also brought some of her own friends along.

When I looked at how Ethnobalt was coming along, his progress was a little slower than Rishia's, but around level 95, his stats suddenly started to really grow. However, before our departure, he hit the growth cap and stopped increasing. It looked like stopping at 100 was the same for him.

He was suffering restrictions from losing the vassal weapon and had also lost his SP. So I performed a limit break on him and enhanced him further. That said, I could only make my own exclamations in surprise at him raising close to 100 levels in just three days. I had to wonder what further potential lay in this seabed level-raising as suggested by the killer whale sisters. It seemed that taking a hero along further boosted the experience received. Ethnobalt had grown a lot since his arrival in the village and was now even a similar size to his library rabbit form. As for me, I had reached 150. It was good but still a far cry from a certain fake hero and his 350.

During that time, I also checked in with the weapon shop in Melromarc.

"Hey! Good to see you, kid. I saw the coronation of the princess!" The old guy greeted me with a smile, just like always, and I immediately felt at ease.

"I just came to say thank you," I told him. "All the gear you made us really helped during that last battle."

"Glad to hear it," he replied.

"Huh? Hey you, punk! You at least avenged Atla for me, right?" This question came from Motoyasu II, the old guy's master, as he appeared from the back of the store.

"That's right, although I didn't do it for you. Takt and his cronies have been punished, all across the world," I informed him.

"Surrounded by all those women, I don't understand why he felt the need to rule the world as well. I'd be happier just putting together a harem," he slurred back. I almost responded, because I certainly didn't see any women around him. Booze and money were the only things he probably ever had any fun with. Still, he did have some pretty impressive skills as a black-smith. There might have been something there, maybe even the possibility of a harem, if not for . . . what? His personality? If he was just a bit more serious about his forging, I wouldn't be surprised if some people actually started to take a liking to him.

"All those women wouldn't have ended up like that, either, if they'd just picked their side with a little more care," Motoyasu II mused.

"I would have thought you'd be against the killing of women, even as enemies," I commented. We'd executed a large number of them from Takt's forces. I'd expected Motoyasu II to complain about that. The old coot's eyes glazed over for a moment, and then he looked back at me.

"I understand the nature of such things," he replied. I wondered if that was really something to boast about. "I've been involved with more than my fair share of horrible women. You can't worry about the fates of them all, or there'd be no end to it."

"You really can pick 'em," the old guy agreed.

"Shut it," he snapped back. "I prioritize the women I know over those I've never seen before. That should go without saying. Those Takt bitches took the life of sweet, courageous little Atla and brought suffering to women across the world."

"Women across the world, huh?" I said, unable to stop myself.

"Half the world is women!" he shot back. "How many of them do you think would suffer if someone like him took power?" Still, this was hardly the place for such a conversation. I was starting to see a bit of a different side to Motoyasu II, however. His awareness of women was a little different from the old Motoyasu, at least.

"What if you had been friends with some of Takt's women, then?" I probed, perhaps foolishly.

"What do you think? I'd have told you not to kill them," he quickly replied. So he'd protect the women he knew—an easy-to-understand answer, and not a bad one.

"Anyway, what brings you here, wasting my time?" he barked.

"Master, can you back off a bit? If you talk with the kid for too long, it's just gonna get you all riled up again," the old guy countered.

"Whatever!" Motoyasu II spat back as Imiya's uncle led him back into the depths of the shop.

"So, kid, I'd love it if you could show me some Kirin materials right about now. Any luck?" the old guy asked.

"I'm sorry to say we are still investigating what happened to them, even in Faubrey," I responded. We were talking about the materials from the Kirin that Takt had defeated, which were currently still missing in action. I'd really wanted to secure them and have the old guy make some gear to prepare for the upcoming battles.

"The word is out to give us the lion's share if and when they are found. So if they show up while I'm away, just get started," I instructed him.

"Away? Where you off to?" he responded.

"Right. That's really what I came to tell you," I recalled. I proceeded to tell him about the upcoming trip to Kizuna's world.

"I see. So you want me to tinker with your gear so it can still be used over there?" he asked.

"That's the short of it. Think you can manage it so quickly?" I replied.

"The armor you are using now is pretty good with that kind of compatibility, so it shouldn't take too long. If I swap in those parts you brought me last time . . . I reckon I can pull something off without the cursed parts," he stated. I was glad to hear that. "Will Spirit Tortoise materials function over there?" he asked.

"I used the Spirit Tortoise Heart Shield, so they should be fine," I replied.

"Then it should all work out. When you came back last time, I checked it out, and the materials used for those parts . . . well, though not entirely legal, were similar to the demi-human materials from the four benevolent animals," the old guy explained.

I wondered if it was connected to the four holy beasts. It corresponded to the main races of Siltvelt.

"I mean, if you asked, I'm sure the demi-humans would happily provide them," he said.

"I would never ask, though, and never take them," I responded. This was bad. I thought I'd worked through the stuff with Atla, but my hands started to shake. I really wanted to say that the four holy beasts and the demi-human four benevolent animals were two different things.

"Yeah, of course," the old guy said after an awkward pause. "I shouldn't have said anything. Sorry, kid."

"No need to worry about it. It's just not something I'd do," I responded. Maybe the one thing I definitely would never do. The old guy understood that and had apologized. We were good.

"If you need any work doing, I'm sure a blacksmith over there will be able to help you out. Once you're all finished, come on back and bring something nice with you to show us, okay?" he said.

"That I can do," I replied. We had him making armor for all of the heroes now. He was like our personal blacksmith.

"I wanted to have a shield from the Phoenix materials ready for you by now," he mentioned. "Sorry about that."

"I'm sure the Spirit Tortoise Shield can still get the job done," I assured him. Based on what I'd seen from Ren's sword, a shield made with Phoenix materials would probably be pretty similar to the Spirit Tortoise one anyway. Just from the numbers, the Phoenix would be better, but the modifier I received from Ost's protection really muddied those waters.

"Kid, I know it won't be easy, but do your best. The little lady is waiting for you," he said.

"Raphtalia has always been there to support me. I have to do the same," I responded. Then I waved goodbye to the old man and left the store behind.

Chapter Three: Party Selection

The eve of our departure to Kizuna's world finally arrived. It was decided that the heroes would gather in the village mess hall and determine the plans for the trip. The main topic of conversation was who was going to join the party to visit Kizuna's world tomorrow and who was going to stay behind in this world. Of course, I would be going.

"Basically, the shield has given me permission to do it, so I'm going to Kizuna's world," I stated. "Can you guys cross over too?" I asked Ren, Motoyasu, and Itsuki.

"Don't ask me," Ren replied.

"A different world from this one?" That was Motoyasu's starting point.

"The only answer is, we don't know," intoned Itsuki. The issue was that the four holy heroes were part of the fundamental support system of this world. Would it be possible, then, for them all to leave at once? When I thought about it logically, without special permission—like what had happened with Ost—they probably weren't going anywhere.

As the four of us bickered, the gemstone on my shield glowed a number of times.

"What was that?" I wondered. Then the gemstones on the

other heroes' weapons also glowed. This was one of the most annoying things about our situation—no way to talk directly with the Shield Spirit. Sometimes it was like I could hear Atla, but this wasn't one of those times.

I didn't see any other choice. I approached the matter as I would when talking to a monster.

"Everyone other than me can't go," I stated. No response from the gemstone. "Is it possible for me to take at least one of the other four heroes?" Then it glowed. So it looked like that meant yes. "Can I take them all?" I continued. This time nothing. "Man, this is a pain."

"Naofumi, please give it a better try than that," Ren said.

"Okay, okay, I'm not done yet," I retorted. "I don't think we should all be leaving anyway. Our search for Witch hasn't turned up any results yet, for one thing." Witch had cast Takt aside and fled and was now hiding somewhere in this world, very likely—no, definitely—plotting some fresh evil.

She was wanted, dead or alive, not just in Melromarc but in every nation in the world. Once she was found, it had been determined that the heroes would go and deal with her. If Raphtalia hadn't been summoned to Kizuna's world, I would have been out searching for Witch myself.

To be quite honest about it, we really didn't have the time to go off and pull Kizuna's ass out of the fire. Yet it was still an issue that we had to take care of.

Q'ten Lo offered a good rate of experience, but without Raphtalia, the only way there was from the port in Siltvelt. We were already having Sadeena and Shildina help us with some nice experience gains under the sea, but Ren swam like an anchor, so he couldn't take part. He had been patrolling regions with powerful monsters and gradually raising his level that way. Itsuki had been patrolling the nearby oceans on a ship with Rishia, while Motoyasu had been racing around in the mountains with his filolials. Those who could swim should really be going under the sea!

Even now we were ostensibly working together, but we were still all over the place. The only advantage of that, perhaps, was that materials from all sorts of different locations were coming in.

"We still need to decide who to take along," I said. I proceeded to take a look around the assembled faces. "Trash."

"Yes?" Trash replied, turning his gentle gaze from Melty, Ruft, and Fohl.

"I'd like to refer to your opinion here," I told him. It certainly couldn't hurt to hear from the Wisest King of Wisdom—the one who had destroyed the Faubrey forces Takt led during the previous battle. The plan was to have Trash himself stay behind. In terms of intellect, there was no one more trustworthy than Trash right now. Even without me here, he'd be able to handle pretty much anything that came up. I almost wanted to take him along, to be honest, but that would seriously damage our defenses back here in this world.

"Based on what you have already told me, Hero Iwatani," Trash started, "if you go to that world, you are returned to level 1, correct?"

"That's right," I confirmed.

"But as the situation also requires a certain degree of haste, you won't have much time to raise your levels," Trash continued. Yes, that was a good—and painful—point. Ethnobalt had said that he should be able to bring us into a safe space after we crossed over, so hopefully we wouldn't suddenly find ourselves in the middle of a scrap. But there was definitely going to be an issue with time.

"Considering the threat apparently posed by the enemy you will be facing, it can be assumed that a hero other than just you will be required. That said, I would personally recommend forming up your party based on those you took with you last time, Hero Iwatani," he concluded.

"Okay. Which means . . ." I looked at Filo and Rishia. Filo was being shielded by Melty so that Motoyasu didn't spot her. Neither of them looked especially happy to be here, but considering the circumstances, it wasn't like they had a choice.

"I'll do my best!" Filo chirped. "Are you coming too, Mel-chan?"

"Filo, I'm sorry, but I have my hands full stitching this

war-torn world back together. I'd leave that to my father and come with you in a heartbeat, if I could," Melty bemoaned. Her father just laughed, but in a cloying, doting fashion that almost made my skin crawl. Seriously, since casting aside his issues with me, Trash had taken on many aspects I'd never seen in him before. He was like a totally different person.

"Don't you need me to protect you, Mel-chan?" Filo asked.

"I'll be fine, Filo. This time you need to be with Naofumi," Melty assured her.

"Okay! If you say so!" Filo responded.

"Very well. That counts Filo in—" I started.

"If Filo-tan is going, then I'll go too, I say!" Motoyasu interrupted, suddenly springing to his feet.

"Bleh! You stay away!" Filo ran from the room. Motoyasu made to chase after her, but Melty stood in his way.

"Cool it, Motoyasu!" I ordered.

"Wherever Filo-tan goes, I must follow! No matter the place, no matter the danger!" he proclaimed. Filo would never manage the trip with him along, and I was keen to quickly exclude him completely. But Motoyasu also brought a lot to the table in terms of being able to fight. In either case, if I didn't take action, Motoyasu was definitely going to be coming along.

I considered what it might look like if we did take Motoyasu to Kizuna's world. I immediately saw myself repeatedly having to chew him out for chasing Filo around. We would be facing all sorts of issues over there already, so just considering throwing Motoyasu into the mix, I felt like I had a stomach ulcer already.

Then I noticed disapproving glares coming my way from the three differently colored filolials under Motoyasu's command. If we took him, those three would be coming too, of course. Leaving them behind would put me on their bad side forever.

"Nope, Motoyasu. You aren't coming. It would cause all sorts of other issues, so you can just stay here. I'll have Ren or Itsuki keep an eye on you," I told him.

"What?!" Ren's brow furrowed in distress.

"But, father-in-law! I have sworn my most unbreakable vow that I will fight for the sake of sweet Filo-tan! Wherever my feathered princess goes, I must follow!" Motoyasu babbled. That might have been useful if he had shown up during the trouble in Q'ten Lo. Unfortunately, back then he'd done absolutely nothing—although I did give him credit for having protected the village.

"If you come, your three filolials will come too, correct?" I asked him.

"That would be the case," he replied.

"Then just give up. In that world, they will be transformed into a different type of monster," I explained.

"What?!" Motoyasu exclaimed. I recalled how Filo had been transformed into a humming fairy, a monster that changed appearance many times as it developed. But there were no filo-lials over there. The only time she could be a filolial over there was when that world was matched with this one during a wave.

"This isn't settled yet! I will be fine so long as Filo-tan is there!" Motoyasu persisted.

"Bleh! Stay away from me!" Filo retorted.

"Just calm down, both of you," I barked. "We've hardly started yet. The decisions will be made once we've heard from everyone. Just be ready to give up on coming along."

"But—" Motoyasu started again. He wasn't going to just give up. I needed to redirect the conversation.

"Motoyasu, is your love nothing but chasing after Filo? Defending the place that Filo will come back to—couldn't that be called love too?" I asked him. Motoyasu snapped back to himself with a look of realization on his face.

"Very well then, father-in-law! I will defend Filo-tan's territory with my life!" he proclaimed.

"Bleh!" Filo retorted. I waved her back, not wanting her to say anything else. She might trigger him wanting to come along again.

"Naofumi, you're getting better at handling Motoyasu," Ren said.

"I've had enough practice," I replied. I wasn't happy about that either. I almost preferred the old Motoyasu. He hadn't been easy to handle, but as someone a bit older than the rest of us, he also had an air of being in control. It was something that almost suggested . . . reliability. However, I'd only seen that version of him on the day we were all summoned.

Anyway, I thought, getting back on track . . . I'd consider everyone else first, and then if Motoyasu really was the only one fit for the purpose, I'd take him along. I had to do what was best for everyone, including Filo and myself.

If he did come with us, of course, we'd probably have to drag Melty along too.

"Naofumi, we might need to have a discussion about that look you are giving me later," Melty said.

"You're hypersensitive, Melty. Has anyone ever told you that?" I glibly responded.

"I can't say they have," she retorted tartly. "I've never thought about it myself." Yeah, Melty could handle herself. She was as sharp as a tack, that one.

"Kwaa . . . kwaa!" Now Gaelion piped up.

"Gaelion, calm down!" Gaelion and Wyndia were getting into it.

"Just because Filo is going is no reason to start making demands. If you go, who will perform class-ups here?" Wyndia reasoned. Gaelion immediately glared at Raph-chan, as though to say there was someone everyone seemed to prefer anyway.

"Raph?" Raph-chan questioned.

"Bleh to you!" Filo and Gaelion started staring each other down.

"Filo, stop taunting the poor dragon. I'll have Rat give you a physical," Melty warned.

"Yuck!" Filo protested.

"Kwaa, kwaa!" Gaelion squawked as he flapped over to me. Then he whispered in my ear.

"He really wants to go, but I'll keep him under control somehow. If you are going to another world, isn't there's something other than this dragon that you should be taking with you?" he asked.

"Like what?" I said.

"Have you forgotten already? The Demon Dragon core. That dragon core from another world," Gaelion reminded me. Right, of course, I recalled. That dragon core. It was the Dragon Emperor from Kizuna's world, after all. We'd really brought quite a dangerous item back with us. I hadn't been sure what to do with it since then either. Taking it back seemed like the best idea.

After relaying this message, Gaelion fluttered back over to Wyndia.

"Right then." I tried to keep things moving. "Apart from Filo, the only one here who I took along last time is Rishia." She'd made quite an impression on me too, fighting the good fight against Kyo. I'd thought of her as pretty weak up until that point, but when it came to the crunch, she'd been more like a main character than a supporting player. Her stats weren't awakened over there, but she had already learned life force. To top it all off, she was also the projectile seven star hero. She could more than pull her weight when compared to last time, and no one here could be said to be better suited.

"Fehhh . . ." Rishia looked at me and then at Itsuki. She was invested in the proceedings of the other world and was friendly with Kizuna and her allies already. That meant Rishia was up for the challenge. But she also probably didn't want to let Itsuki out of her sight. The curse on Itsuki had to be close to breaking completely, but his personality still hadn't come back.

Both Filo and Rishia would bring some muscle, but they had plenty of baggage too. Itsuki was as out of it as ever.

"If Rishia is going, I should probably go along too," Itsuki suggested. He seemed to have read the situation, for once.

"Ah," S'yne piped up, raising her hand.

"Hey, S'yne, that reminds me. While a wave is happening, this place becomes dangerous for you, right? Why didn't you leave during the last wave?" I asked her.

"Under those circumstances—" S'yne managed around the noise that always blocked out what she said.

"Is there any reason you are asking this now?" her familiar asked me for her. I guessed that leaving after another wave and just saying goodbye wasn't quite her style. "S'yne wishes to accompany you on this mission, Naofumi. It may be a world she has already passed through."

"Right, I hadn't thought of that possibility," I responded. S'yne was the holder of the sewing vassal weapon from another world. Her own world had already been destroyed, and now she was using the waves to pass from world to world. That meant maybe she had already increased her level in Kizuna's world. This issue with her was that, though she tried to hide it, her vassal weapon was on the verge of breaking, meaning she wasn't really all that strong.

Even so, S'yne was definitely suited to the mission. The enhancement and protections she received from my trust in her were likely boosting her stats a little too.

"Very well, S'yne. Welcome to the party," I told her.

"Thanks," she managed to say.

As the selection of party members continued, Raph-chan excitedly raised a paw.

"Raph, raph! Raph," she said.

"Okay, okay. Calm down. You're in, Raph-chan," I said to her. Raph-chan had been born over in Kizuna's world. Although she hadn't been outfitted with the concept of levels back then, the items we did enhance while there would surely still be effective. Which meant Raph-chan was coming too.

Not to mention that she could detect Raphtalia . . . and that there was no freaking way I was ever going to leave that cutie behind.

"Daful!" Raph-chan II was waving to Raph-chan. That suggested she planned on staying behind.

"Based on the advice from Trash, I think that's all the immediate combat strength we can hope for. Fohl, what about you?" I wanted to give him the option, but he shook his head.

"I do want to go and help out . . . but Atla left me this village to protect. That comes first," he explained. It might have worked to take him along, depending on circumstances, but if he didn't want to go, then I wasn't about to force the issue. Taking too many heroes away would leave things unbalanced on this side too.

"Okay. I will feel better having you protecting things," I told him.

"Brother . . ." he said. I did place quite a lot of trust in Fohl. His past, risking his own life and fighting so hard for his ailing sister in Zeltoble, had made a lasting impression on me. Both due to his reliable abilities and his mentality, I had wanted to take him along. But the opposite was also true. Fohl would protect the village by pure stubbornness alone, if it came down to it. While we were off in the other world, we could safely leave things here in his hands.

"Little Naofumi. Oh, little Naofumi! What about the two of us?" Sadeena and Shildina were looking at me with expectation in their eyes, pointing to themselves.

"Huh? You two want to come along? I'd rather you helped raise the level of everyone in the village," I said. The ocean was such a great place to raise levels that if they kept on raising levels even while I was away, then we'd be ready for the waves or any other unexpected circumstances.

"Little Naofumi, you know what I want, right? You really think I want to be safe back here while Raphtalia is in danger?" Sadeena questioned. She had a deep connection to Raphtalia's parents and a strong sense of wanting to protect Raphtalia. Now that Raphtalia had gone off to some other world, she didn't want to stay behind and wait.

"I have friends I can count on! Little Sasa and little Elmelo!" she said. Right, those two mercenaries. I'd thought I might get along with the panda. So she was planning to leave things to those two?

"You won't listen even if I try to stop you. Okay, Sadeena, you can come," I said.

"And me?" Shildina raised her own hand, looking at Sadeena in annoyance.

"You're staying behind. I need you to train Ruft and everyone else we can trust," I told her.

"Oh my! No! I don't want just Sadeena to go!" she said. I wanted to tell her to stop being so selfish, but her appearance belied her age—Shildina wasn't all that much older than Raphtalia and the others. She also had quite complex feelings about her sister, Sadeena, and so what she perceived as unequal treatment was bound to trigger this response. She had been raised under such pressure. It could be seen as regression to an infantile state, but maybe she was just getting accustomed to the village.

That selfish reaction made me recall my own younger brother. Maybe he had been quite uncomfortable around me too—although when it came to pretty much anything, studying or anything else, he had generally been my superior.

"Shildina . . . just calm down." Ruft stepped in. "The shield hero is leaving the village in your care. Doesn't that mean he trusts you more than Sadeena?" This was interesting. Ruft placed his hand on her shoulder as he talked her down.

"Oh my . . ." It seemed to be working. Ruft was pretty good at managing her.

"Oh my! Do you really think so?" Sadeena chimed in. Just when I needed her to shut up!

"Dafu!" Raph-chan II moved over and climbed onto Ruft's shoulder. Shildina immediately leapt up and moved to hide behind me. I really wished she would get over this by now.

"Dafu, dafu, dafu!" As though berating her for being self-ish, Raph-chan II was pointing at Shildina and squeaking.

"Okay," Shildina finally said. "I'll help everyone here and wait for sweet Naofumi to come back."

"That would be perfect," I told her.

"But we need to have lots of fun once you return," she confirmed.

"Sure, sure," I said. In that moment, some kind of light

flickered around Shildina. I wondered what it was. It appeared to be some light leaking from the anchor accessory Ethnobalt held. I blinked a few times and couldn't see it anymore, so maybe I was just imagining things.

Whatever. We were finally getting a party together, anyway.

"Bubba, bubba! What about me?" Keel was wagging her tail happily as she put herself forward. The last time we'd gone, we had to leave her behind because of wounds she'd sustained from one of the Spirit Tortoise's familiars.

"I don't want to take a whole army. And like I said, we might find ourselves fighting almost right away," I replied. If she really wanted to do it, I wasn't going to stop her, but I also didn't want to leave the village undefended. "Sadeena can handle herself even at a low level, right? And she gets strong really quick," I said.

"Yeah, that's true. I bet Sadeena is mentally strong even at level 1!" Keel enthused.

"But what about you, Keel? Do you have the confidence to fight at level 1?" I questioned.

"Hmmm. Okay! I'll stay here and support Fohl!" she said, quickly changing her mind and grabbing onto Fohl's arm.

"Sure, okay," he said unsteadily. I might have given it more thought if she had said something like, "You didn't take me last time, so this time I'm definitely going along!" But she didn't try that line.

I'd left peddling to Keel anyway, and it was going well. It wouldn't hurt for her to just continue along those lines. I'd obtained considerable territory and wealth, but for the sake of the future, I wanted to maintain patrols and keep the peace while also conducting sales.

"Just keep doing your best!" I told her.

"I will! I'll make so much money you'll make a new sweet treat for me!" she yipped. So it was a sugar injection she was after? Sometimes I really thought I'd screwed up the way I raised everyone in my village.

"That should be enough," I said, keen to get this stage of the process finished. Considering the situation over there, it was probably best not to take a huge number of people along anyway. There was strength in numbers, but taking too many for the sake of it could also lead to unnecessary deaths. After all, if we ran into someone that Rishia and I couldn't handle, most of those here wouldn't be any additional help. I needed to keep any losses down as far as possible.

So we were taking Filo, Rishia, Itsuki if possible, Sadeena, Raph-chan, and then S'yne. "Looks like we've got a party," I concluded. Ethnobalt and I would round out the group.

It both felt like too many and yet maybe not enough. But there were still the waves and all sorts of other issues to resolve in this world. There was little leeway other than this group.

"Okay. From the four holy heroes, I'll take Itsuki. Will

that work?" I asked the shield. It shone again. Looked like I'd received permission.

If possible, I really wanted to just meet up with Raphtalia, save Kizuna, deal with the vassal weapon holder who had caused the problem, and get the hell back here.

"That settles it," I said. "Everyone get ready to go."

We finally had our party for the trip.

The next morning, Ethnobalt focused his awareness on the anchor accessory, confirming again that everything was in order. Everyone else had made preparations and were ready to go. I'd also made enough soul-healing water for each of the heroes, so we could enhance them if we met with Glass.

"See you later, Bubba! Everyone!" Keel yipped.

"I won't be gone long, Mel-chan!" Filo said.

"I know, Filo. Just take care," Melty replied. Pretty much everyone from the village had come out to see us off.

"Ah . . . hoping for your safe return, I made this accessory. If you keep it with you, it may keep you from harm," Imiya said, handing me an accessory.

Two Spirit Charm (four benevolent animal protection, all stats up [medium], freely imbued random effect)
Quality: excellent

It combined materials from the Spirit Tortoise and Phoenix around a gemstone called a pastel diamond. It also looked like it could be imbued with magic. "Freely imbued random effect" was an effect slot that could be increased via magic. Each time it was imbued, the stats would randomly change. It was quite a powerful effect.

I was impressed. I'd been making accessories myself in order to combat status effects, but I wasn't sure I could turn out something quite like this. It really was the result of all the hard work Imiya had put into making accessories.

"Thank you," I told her. I accepted the accessory from her and then ruffled her hair. I could see her cheeks flushing. "I'm sorry about the misunderstanding before. I gave you totally the wrong idea."

"It's fine. No need to worry about it. Just please come back with Raphtalia and everyone else," she responded.

"Yeah. It's time to bring Raphtalia home," I said. Everything finally ready, I gave Ethnobalt the signal. More voices called out, telling us to come back safely. There was even a "dafu" mixed in. The assembled party gave everyone a wave.

"It was only a short visit, but thank you for everything. I will repay this kindness at a future date. Here we go," Ethnobalt said and raised the anchor accessory. It started to glow and a gentle light surrounded those of us who were making the trip. Then the world around us changed. It felt very much like after using a portal.

We set out for Kizuna's world.

Chapter Four: Arrival into Conflict

I looked around. It was like passing through a tunnel of light, exactly like the first time I visited Kizuna's world.

"Oh my?"

I heard a voice I was expecting.

"Oh my!"

Then I heard another that I certainly wasn't. I turned around amid general exclamations of surprise from the rest of the party. The one who had spoken was looking around with the same surprised expression on her face too.

"I thought we agreed you were staying in the village. What are you doing here?" I asked. As far as I recalled, she had been standing next to Ruft and waving goodbye with everyone else. "Don't tell me, as we departed you did a 'don't leave me behind!' and dashed into the light?" I asked her. Whatever the reason, Shildina was among our little group as we proceeded through the tunnel of light.

"Little Naofumi, I was watching myself. Little Shildina didn't do anything like that. In fact, when we set out and the light around us started to appear around her too, she looked just as surprised as Ruft," Sadeena explained, coming to Shildina's defense.

"That's true. I saw that too," Itsuki confirmed. I was impressed they had seen so much. I'd hardly seen anything with all the light swirling around me.

"So she was just caught up in the spatial transfer?" I asked. That seemed hard to believe. There weren't many people who could make that happen.

I looked over at Ethnobalt, but he vigorously shook his head.

"It wasn't me. I clearly stipulated those who the accessory should transport," he reported.

"Some mistake with your settings?" I suggested.

"I suppose we can't rule that out," he conceded.

"Can we just go back?" I asked. Ethnobalt just quietly shook his head. "Then we don't seem to have much choice," I said with a sigh. I looked at Shildina again and cautioned her while scratching my head. "I really did want you training everyone in the village, but if this was an accident, then no one is to blame. I don't want to hear any complaints, though, no matter what happens." I was worried about her terrible sense of direction. Even if this accident didn't happen, there had been plenty of potential for trouble anyway.

"Okay, sweet Naofumi! I'll prove myself more useful than Sadeena, at least!" she replied.

"Good, good for you," I managed in reply.

We proceeded through the tunnel of light.

We completed our passage through the tunnel of light and emerged on the same grassy plains that I had seen before. These were the plains where L'Arc's country was, close to the port town in which Kizuna made her home. Not a bad spot to have arrived in.

"Everyone, check your level and your gear. We don't know what's going to happen next," I warned them. With that, I also checked my own situation. My level was the same as when I last departed from Kizuna's world. The Barbarian Armor didn't have any scrambled text issues, but the status had fallen a little. I should just be thankful it was even functioning. Basically, it was all thanks to the efforts of the weapon shop old guy. The gear he had supplied to Itsuki and Rishia was in a similar condition.

In terms of shields, I had a nice surprise upon discovering that the Spirit Tortoise Carapace Shield could still be used. However, my level was a little too low to be able to change to it. I'd need to make do with a stopgap shield for a while.

"I'm fine," Filo exclaimed. I'd expected as much. Filo had checked her stats in her human state. Considering how things had worked out last time, Filo's abilities were suited to rear support.

"S'yne is fine too," S'yne's familiar reported for her.

"Level 58," she added.

"So this is a world you've visited before," I said. I was a little uneasy about that number, but it sounded about right for having moved with each wave.

"Raph?" Raph-chan sounded surprised.

"Oh my!"

"Oh dear!"

I looked at the killer whale sisters and found myself having to look down—look down quite a lot more than I expected.

Sadeena was fine. At a glance, she didn't seem to have changed at all—there was no way to tell visually if she had any text-corrupted gear she couldn't use.

The problem was Shildina. Back in our world, she had been almost the same size as Sadeena, but now . . . she had shrunk. She was currently in her demi-human form, so there was no doubting it. She was now just a little taller than Raphtalia had once been, and her clothing was all loose too. She even looked younger, like a little kid, with just a tinge of pink to her skin. Her voice was higher pitched too. She really did just look like a normal kid—or at least not like someone who had been a mature woman just a few moments ago.

"Fehhh . . ." Rishia was looking over with surprise on her face. Seriously, I wished she would grow out of making that annoying sound. It was hard to say whether she'd made any progress at all, really. Now Itsuki was the one keeping her calm.

"L'Arc did mention that Raphtalia got smaller when she came to this world," I said.

"I have heard about what happened with you. It made quite an impression, so I recall it well," Ethnobalt said.

"So I guess, just like how Filo and Ethnobalt changed to reflect each world, demi-humans get younger," I concluded.

"Oh my? What about me?" Sadeena asked.

"When Filo came to this world before, she was a humming fairy chick, correct? But when I went to your world, I became something close to an usapil, didn't I?" Ethnobalt said.

"Maybe age is reflected in there too. You grew pretty big too, didn't you, Ethnobalt," I reminded him. Raphtalia was in fact only around ten years old. Maybe that was why she had looked so young upon first arriving in this world. The same went for Filo. The reality of that matter was that Filo wasn't even one year old yet. In the case of Ethnobalt, it might be because he was a race that developed slowly . . . but that still left questions.

"Little Naofumi, did you want to see me when I was a child?" Sadeena asked.

"Not particularly," I responded. I recalled Sadeena saying she was 23 years old. She had spent time with Raphtalia's parents before Raphtalia had even been born, so it made sense she was older. She had that whole history as the water dragon's miko priestess and executioner in Q'ten Lo too.

"Oh dear," Shildina said.

"You're so cute, little Shildina!" Sadeena said, lifting her sister up from behind.

"Stop it. Put me down!" she protested, looking very unhappy at now being of carrying size. That made her look even more like a child. Appearances could be so confusing.

"I might prefer you like this. You look so cute, Shildina," Sadeena continued.

"I don't care what you think, Sadeena," she retorted. Shildina turned into her therianthrope form and started to whack Sadeena with her tail. I took a breath in admiration. A mini killer whale! She was like some cute aquarium mascot. As cute as Keel, almost—and a lot like the Sadeena doll that S'yne had made. Sadeena proceeded to hold the transformed Shildina out at me.

"Look, little Naofumi. Isn't little Shildina so cute?" she asked me. I gave a "hmmm," taking Shildina from Sadeena and lifting her up. She felt so light with the difference in strength due to our levels. Shildina just wagged—if that was the word— her tail without showing any signs of displeasure. Was this what Shildina had been like when she was a child? She was small, that was for sure. I'd been treating her like an adult, but I was going to have to keep a closer eye on her now.

"Up you go! Up you go!" I said, lifting her up in the air.

"Little Naofumi?" Sadeena looked at me in bemusement. Wasn't that what you did with a child? I'd done the same thing with Raphtalia when she'd been smaller too. I'd had my own issues back then, but Shildina would probably prefer being treated closer to her own age. I also patted her head.

"Oh dear!" Shildina didn't seem to know how to respond.

She was a child who had never been spoiled, clearly. Eventually, perhaps having run out of magic, or perhaps out of consideration for me, she turned back into her demi-human form.

"Why are you mothering Shildina, Naofumi?" Ethnobalt questioned, clearly puzzled. But there was no real reason why. I was just going with the flow. "There were quite a few childish people in your village too . . . I see." Ethnobalt seemed to have realized something—or thought he had. *Hey! There's nothing to read into any of that!*

"So this is what you'll be like once you have children, little Naofumi," Sadeena said.

"I should have expected that," I commented. A stranger walking by would probably read this scene as me holding the child of Sadeena and me. At that, though, Shildina turned her fists on Sadeena.

"I'm not Sadeena's child!" she protested.

"Oh my!" Sadeena gave a laugh, her eyes full of warmth.

"I'm going to get back to myself before you know it!" Shildina exclaimed. I was happy to see her motivated, but I hoped they didn't fight too much.

"Raph," said Raph-chan to attract my attention and then pointed toward a castle. There was a town around it, but it looked to be in pretty bad shape. There had definitely been a fire. The whole place looked much more rundown than before.

"Fehhh . . ." Rishia said.

"Stay alert. We need to work out the situation first," I said.

"Oh my. I hope little Raphtalia is okay," Sadeena commented.

"We just have to pray that's the case. Raph-chan, can you sense where she is?" I asked. Raph-chan had started out as a shikigami used to locate Raphtalia. I wasn't sure if that function was still working, but it couldn't hurt to ask.

"Raph," Raph-chan replied, seemingly understanding exactly what I had asked, and pointed at the town—at the castle. It seemed that was the direction Raphtalia was in.

"Right. Enough playing around. Let's get moving. However . . . be sure to take care. If you've got a low level, be extra careful," I cautioned them. I proceeded to cast support magic on everyone, and then we headed for the town around the castle.

In front of the town—in front of the castle gates—there was a battle that could only be said to be "raging." Troops in armor I didn't recognize were fighting those wearing armor worn by L'Arc's forces, each side hacking at the other, weapons in hand. It looked like we'd walked into an invasion of L'Arc's country.

As I fought through the ranks, I protected Filo and Ethnobalt and made my way to the front line. If I kept Shooting Star Shield up, there was no worry of someone catching a stray arrow.

A grunt attracted my attention, and I turned to see Glass

and Raphtalia with their weapons locked in combat against someone holding the scythe that should have belonged to L'Arc. Raphtalia was there! And she looked to be losing ground. From L'Arc I sensed a real tension, a kind of panic.

"Now! Defeat the arrogant King L'Arc Berg, former holder of a vassal weapon!" yelled a voice. This came from a woman standing at the rear of the enemy forces. She had an atmosphere around here that, at worst, could have been said to be like Witch. Meanwhile, Therese was fighting behind Raphtalia and Glass.

"You scum! Stealing my weapon and doing all of this! I keep telling you, this is not the intended purpose of these weapons!" L'Arc growled.

Someone else was there—a man retorted, "Hah! Why would we listen to someone whose weapon dumped him? This sweet little scythe doesn't want a goody-goody justice lover like you! It came to me because I'm the kind of owner it always wanted!" The man holding the actual scythe snorted at L'Arc's anger. He had the same atmosphere about him as Kyo and Takt.

"You lie! The scythe vassal weapon would never think such a thing!" Therese denied those claims, and Raphtalia and Glass glared the speaker down. The enemy with the scythe dropped back, launching a follow-up of countless magic and ofuda directly at Raphtalia and Glass. The two women fought them all off.

"Seriously? You can't do a thing unless you all bunch together! Pathetic. You can't hope to save this world, at this level," the enemy cackled. Things certainly didn't look good. For one thing, L'Arc had bandages wrapped around his head and arm. He didn't have his scythe vassal weapon either. It sounded like it had been stolen, much like Takt stole our weapons. Therese also had bandages wrapped around her arm and leg. From the way she was walking, she had suffered serious injuries. Glass didn't seem to have any particular injuries on her, but her clothing had definitely seen better days. They were clearly all worn down from a string of successive battles.

"Even I no longer have the patience to abide by Kizuna's wishes," Glass stated. "This is the time to truly bring an end to you and this foolish battle you have started!" She raised her fan and struck a fighting pose. "Raphtalia, if anything happens to me, I leave Kizuna and L'Arc in your hands."

"Calm down, please, Glass!" Raphtalia responded. Glass was attempting to gather all of her evil energy into herself. I had used the Shield of Rage myself, so I understood the feeling crackling in the air.

"If we lose this battle, Kizuna is not going to come back. I'll do whatever it takes—" That was when I leapt in front of Glass, cutting her off and calming things down.

"Calm down. We might be able to win this without any noble sacrifices," I told her.

"That voice!" It worked. Glass stopped what she had been doing. She'd been attempting to use a cursed weapon. That was why I stopped her.

There had been a reason why I didn't talk to Raphtalia and the others immediately after arriving at the battlefield.

"I, hero, command the heavens and earth! Transect the way of the universe and rejoin it again to expel the pus from within! Power of the Dragon Vein! Obey now orders from the hero, the source of your power, combining my magic with the power of the hero. Read again the way of all things and lend strength to them all!" I chanted. "All Liberation Aura X!" The highest level of support magic was cast across everyone within range whom I considered an ally.

"This is . . . incredible! I feel so light!" said Glass.

"My stats have been incredibly boosted! What a rush of power!" said L'Arc.

"Huh?" The one with L'Arc's scythe turned his gaze on me, clearly not happy with this unexpected new arrival. "Just who might you be?"

"Mr. Naofumi!" Raphtalia saw me, her eyes opening wide and her expression brightening. There were even tears in her eyes. But of course, the last time I'd seen her I'd been close to death myself. She hadn't even known if I was alive or dead, so this wasn't an overreaction. Honestly speaking, I wanted to enjoy the reunion myself, but first we needed to do something about these enemies.

"You started out as Kizuna's allies, right?" Ethnobalt had told me that it was a bunch of former allies who had launched a surprise attack and stolen L'Arc's scythe. "Didn't he tell you about me? One of the four holy heroes from another world?" If they had been allies, I was sure to have come up in conversation.

"So you're reinforcements, called in because we've got your little friends here bleeding out. Turn around and go back to wherever you came from, and I promise not to cut you down as you go," the man growled.

"You're not possessed by Kyo, are you?" I asked. He was acting just like that dick. Ethnobalt had made it sound like this guy and Kizuna had been pretty close. The sheer wall of over-confidence he presented totally rubbed me the wrong way. It told me one thing: he was my enemy.

He'd done so many bad things already, too, there didn't seem much hope for a peaceful resolution, as I had managed with Ren, Itsuki, and Motoyasu.

"You'd lump me in with that trash? Just look at me! I'm far stronger than he ever was," the man snarled back.

"Of course you are. And if you're strong, anything you do will be forgiven, right? I'm sick of hearing that shit," I replied. Chalk up another similarity with Kyo—thinking strength allowed him to do anything. Did it mean he was also a vanguard of the waves? "Who's pulling your strings, puppet?" I asked him.

"What's in it for you, asking that?" he fired back.

"Just tell me," I spat.

"You really think I'm going to talk?" he replied.

"No, you're right." Of course he wasn't. All of his ruffian friends were already making to attack me with magic, arrows, and an assortment of weapons.

"Mr. Naofumi!" Raphtalia cried out. If I tried any longer, Raphtalia was going to get mad. But seeing as I'd been unable to get Takt to talk, I thought this might be a good opportunity.

"If you push your luck . . . this will be worse than death for you," I cautioned. There had been Takt and what happened with him in our world, not so long ago. Regardless of the one who initiated it, once they let things get this far, once they were defeated, it was always tragic. I wasn't about to sugarcoat things. Taunts, insults, whatever they wanted to throw, I could take it. I was carrying too much on my back. For the sake of Atla and Ost and everyone else who had fallen along the way, there was no turning back for me—however filthy the path I had to tread.

"Don't egg him on," Glass advised, finally understanding the situation. "This whole battle just completely changed in our favor."

"Perhaps my interference wasn't welcome?" I asked her, one eyebrow raised.

"Not at all. This is not an enemy worthy of an honorable battle," she replied.

With a shout of rage, L'Arc closed in with one of the enemies at high speed and cut them down. The others just stood there, stunned, heads moving from left to right.

"You think these petty tricks are enough to win? I'm almost at a loss for words, honestly. Let me show you what I can really do!" the scythe guy raged.

"If you've got something to show me, go ahead. Defeat me, if you can," I calmly replied. Then I activated Attack Support and launched spikes at the enemy holding L'Arc's scythe.

"Glass, finish him off!" I shouted.

"Got it!" she replied. The Attack Support landed on target and—even faster than Raphtalia—Glass swiped her fan powerfully to the side, waist low and deep. The entire movement would likely be little less than a flicker to anyone not under the effects of my support magic.

"Circle Dance Slice Formation! Flicker!" Glass had sliced into the enemy from behind with her fan five times, then dropped away and was now standing with her back to him.

"As your former ally . . . I give you this final mercy. You will die without pain," she said.

"Huh? You seriously think you've defeated—" In the moment he turned to confront Glass about her declaration of victory, the guy with the scythe split into chunks, then simply turned into a red mist and was blown away.

Impressive. She hadn't left any trace of him at all.

Enemy women were looking around with shocked expressions on their faces. All the women who had been fighting alongside him started screaming. Among the noise, it sounded like some of them were shouting his name, but it was too distorted to hear.

I wondered for a moment if this was some kind of curse, some kind of ritual, that I had to go through. It had been much like this with Takt.

"Raph!" From her position riding on my shoulder, Raph-chan leapt down and whacked at the spot the enemy had been standing with her tail, sending something else flying.

"Isn't it a little merciless to also destroy his soul?" Glass asked.

"We don't want him coming back like Kyo," I reminded her.

"Good point. I apologize for my naivety," she responded. A moment later, a faint light appeared from the spot the enemy had been standing in and then flew toward L'Arc. Once the light vanished, the scythe vassal weapon appeared back in L'Arc's hand.

Then I noticed something. In the moment the scythe returned to L'Arc's hand, an accessory attached to it flew off. What was that all about? There had been a similar accessory when we were dealing with Takt.

"Your boss is dead! This scythe being back in my hand is

proof! Will you surrender or continue to resist? Choose!" L'Arc shouted. Seeing L'Arc proclaim victory, most of the enemy started to retreat.

"You'll pay for killing—" The name was again lost amid more cries as a number of women rushed in, screaming for revenge. Our forces quickly took them down. I noticed that Witch-like woman trying to make a break for it too, so I grabbed her by the collar to keep her close.

"Let me go! Do you even know who you are daring to fight against?" she spat.

"No idea. But if you're important, then we really can't let you go," I told her.

"Well done, Naofumi!" Glass proceeded to smack the woman in the stomach with the handle of her fan, making her pass out. "She's an ally of the ones we are fighting, supporting them. We've no idea what she might have done if we didn't catch her."

"Fair enough. Still . . ." It felt a bit anticlimactic to have wiped them out so easily. There were still more of them out there, apparently, but this looked like it was going to all be over more quickly than I had imagined.

"We need to form up a pursuit party and capture these enemies of the state in order to make our victory certain in this war!" L'Arc shouted. His forces roared back their agreement, and then they started to chase down the fleeing enemy.

"Raph!" Raph-chan pointed toward Raphtalia. She was dashing right toward me.

"Mr. Naofumi!" she cried.

"Raphtalia!" I responded, instinctively rushing toward her myself. I caught her in my arms.

"Mr. Naofumi?" she asked, surprised. I heard her voice, a little uncertain of what was happening. She smelled nice. I was happy, really happy, that she hadn't been caught up in anything as complicated as our last visit here.

"Are you all in one piece? I was worried about you," I said.

"That's my line. Not to mention that amazing, almost unnatural boost to our stats. What was that?" Then Raphtalia pushed me to arm's length and looked me over from head to toe. "Those wounds you took—what about those?" Raphtalia had stayed behind to let us escape from our first encounter with Takt, during which I had been seriously injured. All sorts of things had happened after that, but she had no way of knowing any of them.

"All fine. What about you, Raphtalia? If you need any healing, just let me know right away," I said.

"I'm fine too. No serious wounds. My katana teleported me before things got too serious," she explained. Raphtalia also looked relieved to see my shield. That was because, just before parting with Raphtalia, Takt had stolen my shield.

"My shield? You bet I got that back. In fact, it's like it was never even taken from me," I reflected.

"So was it stolen or not?" she asked.

"That's a tough one. How best to explain . . ." While we talked, L'Arc, Therese, and Glass came over.

"You saved us. Without your aid, we would have suffered hard for such a victory," Glass said.

"You did seem to be struggling. What if something had happened to Raphtalia?" I asked. I had to ask. I knew it wasn't their fault, but I still had to say it anyway.

"Mr. Naofumi—" Raphtalia started.

"I know," I cut her off. I knew her all too well. "Under these circumstances, you'd never run off and be safe all alone." If she did run for her life, she'd no longer be Raphtalia at all.

"Naofumi, it sounded like you were in pretty bad shape yourself," Glass said.

"My lady Glass, cool it. Look at what he just did—he clearly dealt with the problem," L'Arc responded. I was glad he was quick on the uptake.

"Anyway. Sadeena and some of the others are here too, so let's get them involved," I suggested. We proceeded to move away from the battle in front of the gates, meeting up with Sadeena and the others. We started to chat in the courtyard of the castle.

"Little Raphtalia! I'm so happy to see you again," Sadeena said.

As soon as Sadeena saw Raphtalia, she grabbed her and started hugging her.

"Sadeena, please. You're suffocating me," Raphtalia managed to say.

"Has that settled this problem? Is this the equivalent of defeating Takt?" I asked.

"Well, maybe. You have defeated one of the enemies. But, Mr. Naofumi, what happened with the Whip Hero? The queen was badly injured with you, wasn't she?" Raphtalia asked. I looked away at her question, falling silent. Realizing what that meant, Raphtalia also looked down.

"I barely survived myself, mainly due to my own vitality and the power of the Shield Spirit," I eventually said.

"I see," Raphtalia responded, subdued.

"Regarding the Whip Hero, Takt . . . Trash took over after the queen died, you see, and awoke again as the so-called Wisest King of Wisdom. Takt decided he wanted to take over the world, but Trash put a stop to his plans and achieved victory for Melromarc," I explained.

"Are we talking about the same king? I can hardly imagine it." Raphtalia only knew the old Trash, after all. It wasn't surprising she couldn't conceive of the change in him.

"I'd only heard the rumors myself, but he really is something else," Sadeena confirmed.

"I concur. He put up a fight more than worthy of the title

of Wisest King of Wisdom," Itsuki intoned. Of course, Itsuki and Rishia had fought alongside Trash's forces. That meant they probably had an even better idea of what he was capable of. Itsuki went on. "I just fought, doing as I was instructed, but before I even realized it, the Faubrey forces had been wiped out."

"I can vouch for that. It really was so fast," Rishia added, backing up Itsuki's words with a nod. They had just been following orders, so of course they hadn't seen the whole picture. I'd personally been off bringing down Takt, so I hadn't been part of the main battle either.

"I'm sure the departed queen would be most happy with the outcome," Raphtalia said. "But the king hasn't changed his name back yet?"

"He seems to have accepted the name 'Trash' now. He told me not to change it," I replied.

"That's a little sad, isn't it?" she commented. *Don't look at me!* I thought it was crazy too.

"It was so impressive, seriously. He's so charismatic. 'Trash' doesn't suit him at all. He led the coalition army, with inferior numbers and strength, and drove off Takt's Faubrey army," I said. I had called him Aultcray, and he'd given me a sharp look until I took it back and called him "Trash" again. I still wasn't sure why it had upset him so much. "I also took part in Trash's operation, and repaid Takt as viciously as I could."

"Viciously? Repaid? That doesn't sound especially pleasant," Raphtalia commented, furrowing her brow. I proceeded to explain the course of events that led to Takt's defeat. After borrowing the staff from Trash, I had used my stats boosted by the support magic All Liberation Aura X to completely overwhelm him. I had become so much stronger than him it had been hard to hold anything back, and so I'd ended up letting him also take the staff and then worked together with Fohl to kick the crap out of him. As a result, I not only got my shield back but also liberated all the seven star weapons. After stripping poor Takt of everything—his pride, his arrogance—I'd captured him.

"That pretty much settled it. For his plans to take over the world, he was executed along with most of his harem of women. There wasn't much helping it, considering the circumstances. But I can't say I really enjoyed the public execution," I told her. It wasn't an especially pleasant memory, but it was important to remember what had brought it about. Planning to take over the world, starting a selfish war, and then getting defeated were more than enough to earn such a conclusion.

"I have no sympathy for them. They were the ones who took Atla, and so many others, from us," Raphtalia responded.

"That's right," I agreed. If Takt hadn't seen fit to get involved in the fight with the Phoenix, that whole situation would have turned out quite differently. It had been an ugly, cruel execution, but I had no sympathy for those who were killed.

"In any case, they have been avenged, which is the best we could ask for," Raphtalia concluded. We had saved many more lives by defeating him. That was the attitude to hold. "I'm sure Atla would be pleased too."

"Actually, about that," I said. "When I was on the verge of death, I met Atla inside something like . . . I guess you'd call it the world inside the shield. She was still very much herself, anyway." I showed Raphtalia the shield, and the gemstone glowed. Was that Atla taunting Raphtalia from inside the shield? The light did look a bit mocking, if light could be said to do that. Raphtalia seemed to have noticed the same thing, and her brow furrowed.

"I am just glad to see you in good health, Mr. Naofumi," Raphtalia finally said.

"Atla said much the same thing. Still, I think the whole experience has made me a little more accepting than before," I replied. I wasn't completely uninterested in love anymore. I still had to put my duty first, but I could at least respond to the feelings from others now. "Once the waves are finished, in the time after completing my duty but before I go home, I'm thinking a little of the 'fun and games' that Sadeena alludes to might be acceptable."

"That was one of Atla's final wishes, and I can understand

it, but I'm still wondering exactly why things need to be like that," Raphtalia questioned. She made a good point. It was like me standing here telling a woman who trusted me that after I'd saved the world, I was going to screw my way through as many women as I could.

"Come now, little Raphtalia. Little Naofumi has made so much progress! This is when you need to put your best foot forward. Like I've done already. Take a look at this! I present to you the bundle of love created by myself and Little Naofumi!" Sadeena, really laying it on thick, grabbed the little hands of the pint-sized Shildina who was riding on her shoulders.

"What? That much time has passed in the other world?!" Raphtalia gasped. Exasperated, I was about to step in and nip this in the bud when Shildina did it for me.

"Stop turning me into your kid!" she wailed, whapping Sadeena on the head. Raphtalia looked at Shildina with a confused expression for a moment.

"Is that Shildina up there?" she finally said, working it out.

"That's right," I confirmed. "We'd been planning to leave her behind, but she got dragged along anyway. After crossing between worlds, she ended up like this."

"It's the same as when Raphtalia came here," L'Arc commented.

"Indeed," I agreed. "It seems those with an external appearance that relies heavily on their level are turned into one more suited to their age once they cross worlds."

"That did happen, didn't it?" Raphtalia recalled.

"I would have liked to see it," I commented casually.

"Why would you want to see me as a little girl?" Raphtalia questioned.

"Just to remember what it was like when you were smaller. See you and cherish you, that's all," I replied.

"You're not pulling the wool over my eyes. Talking about 'cherishing' me is embarrassing too!" she responded. Especially in my more accepting state, I wasn't about to denounce how cute she had been back then. Of course, I would never consider making a Raphtalia who looked like that into my girlfriend.

"Anyway, it sounds like you've had it pretty tough, Nao-fumi. Raphtalia and I were both very worried about you," L'Arc said, somewhat evasively, after hearing my explanation of events. When I thought about it, Ethnobalt had come seeking our aid, but we had been in a pretty tricky spot ourselves. Only after resolving that had we been able to come here and offer our aid to this world.

"I'm sure it sounds very cruel to you guys, but they did more than enough to deserve such punishment," I explained. The idea of leniency because someone was a woman was a mistake. My personal stance was to suspect everything women did, but then that was all thanks to Witch. I hated the idea that just because the alleged victim was a woman, absolutely everything she said had to be true.

"They ran around killing vassal weapon holders, attempted to kill the four holy heroes, and even killed members of the royal families from various nations. They surely got what they deserved," Glass said with a nod. She seemed to have accepted it.

"Oh? You approve, Glass?" I asked.

"I don't know what Kizuna would say, but there's no way to escape from punishment for such a list of crimes. No matter how you attempted to defend them, it would have to be the death penalty. The same goes in this world. Just like those women over there." Glass looked over at the captive women from the battle. "You have been wanton and selfish, you women. Even Kizuna would never find it in her heart to forgive you for all of this."

"Glass, my lady, I know that's true, but still . . ." L'Arc started.

"It is our duty to tackle the waves and protect the peace of this world. Yet they have killed the four holy heroes and disregarded their duties as vassal weapon holders. After all this undisputed damage they have done, you would still forgive them?" Glass rounded on him. "They stole your own vassal weapon!" Based on what Ethnobalt had told me, Glass and everyone here had been in serious trouble. That was probably what made her more sympathetic to understanding what we had been through in our own world.

"I mean, I can't deny that. We've had a rough time too," L'Arc admitted.

"So give me some details," I said.

"This battle here today was just like with Kyo. And that guy like Kyo was the one leading them all. So having lost their lynchpin, his nation will have no choice but to surrender," Glass said, breaking it down for me.

"All sorts of stuff happened. We've been training between each wave. And other than Kizuna, we've tried hard to contact the other holy heroes," L'Arc continued.

"Kizuna is pretty laid back. I bet she's off fishing somewhere, saying 'whatever will be, will be.' Or something like that," I said. There didn't come a reply. "Hey. You're not going to deny it?" *Seriously!* I'd known it already, but Kizuna always had a pretty positive outlook. She'd fulfilled her duty as a hero without losing it too, meaning this world was probably a softer one to end up in.

All things considered though, her laid-back nature was one of her good points. She was also strong too, even with the handicap of not being able to attack directly.

"We've also had a few chances to talk to other holy heroes. They weren't interested in what we had to say—not at all. But Kizuna said she understands what you went through," L'Arc continued.

"Sounds like things shake out the same in every world,"

Itsuki commented, still in monotone. I wasn't sure he was really one to talk about such things. But at least I'd hammered the power-up method into the other heroes, added them to my forces, and unified us against the waves. Maybe things weren't so bad, I conceded.

"I've been meaning to ask . . . You're—" L'Arc started.

"Yes, one of the four holy heroes from the same world as Naofumi. I am Itsuki Kawasumi, the Bow Hero. It is nice to meet you." Itsuki completed his self-introduction and displayed his bow.

"Right. We fought at the Cal Mira islands, no? I think I saw you in the Spirit Tortoise too, right?" L'Arc said.

"That's right," Itsuki said.

"Kiddo, is this guy right in the head? His voice sounds kinda flaky," L'Arc said. All he needed was the slightest opening to start calling me "kiddo" again!

"That's right. Itsuki had been through a lot. He sunk to the use of cursed weapons and ended up suffering from paralysis of his individuality and other emotions," Ethnobalt explained.

"I see. So this is the hero that Rishia talked so passionately about," L'Arc said. Itsuki remained silent. But did he look a bit embarrassed?

"Fehhhhh!" I just ignored Rishia, with her strange noises and bright red face.

"We had all sorts of issues, but I managed to secure the

other three heroes, and we are all sharing information now. Didn't Raphtalia tell you this?" I asked.

"Yeah, she told me. It sounds like it wasn't easy," L'Arc responded.

"I wish Kizuna had learned more from your example, Naofumi," Glass commented.

"But she hasn't been slacking off too much, right?" I checked.

"I mean . . . Kizuna did try her best when negotiating with them," L'Arc conceded. I took Motoyasu, Ren, and Itsuki into consideration, it seemed to take a certain breed of weirdo to get selected as one of the four holy heroes.

"I heard when Kizuna was talking with them, just like with you, Naofumi, they had some kind of advance knowledge," L'Arc explained.

"So the same thing here. It was called an 'update' or something. I guess that's what it was," I extrapolated. I'd thought Kizuna holding the negotiations might have helped things go differently, but it looked like things had turned out the same here as in my world. Capturing or holding heroes against their will could create international problems. The only way was to take it slowly, a little at a time . . . just like I had done.

There was also the issue that the four benevolent animals had indeed appeared in this world and started to cause chaos, but Glass and her allies had defeated them pretty quickly. That meant the four holy heroes in this world hadn't experienced many setbacks. I almost felt sorry for them.

"Then one day we received a report that the other three heroes, everyone apart from Kizuna, weren't responding anymore. We conducted an investigation. The vassal weapon holders revealed that they hadn't considered any of them suitable to be the four holy heroes and defeated them," Glass said. I had heard an outline from Ethnobalt, but L'Arc and the others were doing a better job of filling in the details. Appalled at the killing of members of the holy heroes, Kizuna had led a gathering of her allies and representatives from each nation. The main issue on the table had been the purging of the vassal weapon holders who had perpetrated the killings. It was a known fact that the four holy heroes were the pillars of the world to which they were summoned. Losing even one of them increased the threat posed by the waves. As the discussions turned to how those responsible had to be punished, someone who Kizuna had considered an ally—but also someone with a few personality issues—attacked L'Arc right there in the conference venue. Personality issues or not, he had also been a pretty good fighter.

After a tussle in close combat, L'Arc had dropped back and tried to unleash some skills just to incapacitate the attacker. Then his scythe had vanished from his hands and transferred over to the traitor. The enemies had then proceeded to show off the holy weapons that they had captured. There had been far more than one traitor too, and faced with overwhelming odds—and with key leaders from each nation taken hostage—the party had been forced to retreat. It was during that retreat that Kizuna had stepped forward in an attempt to buy the time for Glass and the other leaders to escape.

Although she didn't have the ability to attack people herself, Kizuna did have access to a forbidden weapon, and she had been forced to use that to protect everyone. She had combined her strength with Glass's. And though the cost would have been high, they had attempted to get through the crisis together.

However, the traitors had read even that move. They proceeded to capture Kizuna and use a mysterious teleportation technique to whisk her away. It sounded like L'Arc's scythe and Kizuna had been their only targets the entire time.

Glass and the others had planned an operation to rescue Kizuna. It had looked like all-out war would erupt with the traitor-controlled nation . . . but then a new problem had occurred.

The explanation was cut short there for a moment in order to get all these new facts in order. Packing in too much information at once could only make a situation even harder to understand.

"So the actual events are a little different, but it seems like a similar issue to what we faced in our world," I said.

"Yes, it does," Glass agreed. At that point, Therese, who had been silent the entire time, started to cry.

"Master Craftsman . . ." she sobbed.

"Please don't call me that," I told her.

"The item that you provided me with . . ." She trailed off and then showed me the broken pieces of her Orichal Starfire Bracelet.

"Right. When we were in danger, it was this accessory you created that saved us, Naofumi. Without it, I reckon we very well might have been killed," L'Arc said with a slightly pained expression.

"We managed to survive only because it chose to sacrifice itself by unleashing all of its power," Therese explained. During the battle, after the scythe was taken, it was apparently the power of the accessory I had made for her that allowed them to survive. Wasn't that a good thing if it meant the lives of L'Arc and the others had been saved?

"I am so sorry. Sacrificing such a work of art as this . . ." Therese continued.

"Hey, Therese, no need to apologize to me quite so profusely. Besides, I don't like the look in L'Arc's eyes," I told her.

"He looks a lot like you do sometimes, Mr. Naofumi," Raphtalia muttered, looking between our faces and comparing them. When did I ever look like that? I wasn't sure what the feeling in the air was, but it was almost like—even though I wanted no part of it—I was stealing Therese away from L'Arc.

"Indeed. He does look a lot like Naofumi," Itsuki commented.

"Fehhh! Itsuki, please be quiet!" Rishia hissed. I seconded her statement, internally, and with considerably more vigor.

"The gemstone is cracked, but I can polish it up again, change the shape and remake it as something else. I hope that will be enough for you," I told her. I wasn't sure why it was falling to me to console her. My suggestion did make her raise her head, however. It was the best from a bad situation, then.

"Really? You can do that?" she asked.

"Sure I can, if I can find a moment. It's basically your weapon, isn't it, Therese? So it's definitely worth it to make you something," I told her. Making accessories for Therese allowed me to experience the feeling the old guy must have all the time. Like the reforging of a broken sword, I would give some thought to how to bring new life to this shattered accessory. It probably wouldn't be easy, but it felt like it had some magic left in it.

"Thank you so much! I couldn't ask for more!" Therese bowed her head as she thanked me and then saw the accessory Imiya had made for me and froze completely. "W-w-w-w-w-w-what is that?!" she eventually stammered.

"This? This was made by someone who could be considered . . . well, both my apprentice and a fellow student," I said and showed Therese the Two Spirit Charm that Imiya had given me prior to my departure.

"Ah! It looks divine! So lovely!" Therese marveled. As though it were too bright for her to look at, Therese covered her face with her hands and looked away from the Two Spirit Charm. "It's quite incredible," she said, breathing heavily. "I never imagined such a fine piece could ever exist."

Being able to draw out the power of accessories meant that this would be quite effective if given to Therese. That said, Imiya had been thinking more of me when she created it and handed it over. *That said*, if holding this made Therese stronger, then maybe that was the greatest value it had to offer.

"Therese, I'm sorry, but I can't give this to you . . . but I could lend it to you, just until I go back," I said. Imiya had given this to me, wishing for the safe return of not just me but everyone in the away party. Making the best use of it seemed the best way to realize that wish.

"Are you sure?" she exclaimed.

"Yes. But it's just a loan. When I go back, I'll want to take it with me . . . I know. How about we say you can use it until I fix the broken one?" I compromised.

"Whatever you say!" Therese started to practically grovel on the ground in thanks.

"—and then—" Filo was doing her best to translate for Sadeena and the others, facilitated with notes from Rishia. Based on the "oh mys" coming from Sadeena, they were getting the gist of it.

How had it come to this though? Therese was practically worshipping me. L'Arc had that look in his eye again too—the same look I supposedly made.

I proceeded to give the Two Spirit Charm to Therese. The change was immediate. Her body started to give off a light glow, and the bandages on her arm and leg scattered into pieces and blew away. The curse marks beneath them then just vanished too.

"Interesting. I have seen this in anime and games before. It is when a unit is replaced or promoted. A new unit comes in to replace the broken one that was used up," Itsuki said. From where I was standing, he was barely making sense. I understood the nuance he was going for, but he really needed to work on his delivery.

"This is incredible," Therese said, thrilled. "I feel so powerful I think I might burst!" She had actually started to float off the ground. Wings of fire grew out from her back and it looked like she could fly now too! "I'll do my best to meet your expectations, Master Craftsman!"

"He healed Therese's wounds . . . Incredible . . . I can't compete with that . . ." L'Arc bemoaned to himself. *Hold on! You don't have to compete with me!*

So I told her, "Look after L'Arc too, okay? By which I mean don't cast him aside, understand? And definitely don't say stuff like, 'Whatever you wish, Master Craftsman!' Okay?" I pressed the point home pretty hard. *Please, for God's sake, don't let me end up on the route where I take a woman from L'Arc!* I had no interest in doing such a thing anyway.

"Whatever you say!" she replied, a little too close to my command for comfort. Still, it was nice to see her full of energy again. Maybe she'd be strong enough now to take down our enemies with one punch.

Imiya's accessory was something else, that was for sure. If Imiya could find the time, I'd get her to make something especially for Therese.

"Little Naofumi, little Raphtalia," Sadeena said, approaching us as we watched Therese power up. "At first I thought little Naofumi had brought us to a different country with one of his teleportation skills, but this really isn't the world I know," Sadeena said.

"Finally got that, did you?" I asked.

"It certainly is not. Why? Have you noticed something?" Raphtalia asked. What was she onto?

"Is there something here that's different from our world?" I asked.

"Well . . ." Sadeena muttered, looking from the courtyard out toward the town. "First, I don't have a clue what people are saying. Not a word. This isn't like a dialect or just a different language. You really are heroes, aren't you? Raphtalia included."

"I understand. I couldn't understand what people were saying until I obtained this katana," Raphtalia replied. The hero weapons all had a universal translation function. But for someone without any such special powers—someone like

Sadeena—it made sense she wouldn't have a clue what people were saying. The translation attribute was just another thing we had the hero weapons to be grateful for.

"In Zeltoble, that melting pot of peoples, I encountered some languages I hadn't ever heard before . . . but they weren't like this. This is totally different," Sadeena said.

"Rishia picked it up in a few weeks," I responded.

"Little Rishia is very smart. I won't be pulling that off, I can tell you," Sadeena replied. Maybe not. It had taken me a long time to learn the alphabet in Melromarc, and the magic alphabet too. It was unfair to use Rishia as an example.

"It would have worked out better if the analysis of that translation accessory S'yne enemies carried had made some progress," I said. I'd left that task to the accessory dealer, but the accessory in question was made from some kind of unknown material and couldn't be replicated. S'yne's familiar currently carried it. Without it, communication with S'yne would have been almost impossible. She seemed to understand what I was saying, but hardly anything other than strange noises emanated from her own mouth. It had been getting even worse recently, preventing us from conversing even on basic topics. If her vassal weapon broke down completely, she might not be able to talk at all . . . but I didn't think it would come to that.

"Hmmm," Sadeena pondered.

"Filo understands it too, right?" I said. She always seemed

like a bit of an airhead, but Filo was also kinda multilingual. She could learn new languages in a really short space of time.

I was starting to wonder exactly what "being smart" meant.

"Hey! You're thinking something rude about me, Master! I'm not a dummy!" Filo said.

"I wasn't thinking anything of the sort," I countered. "I was just pondering some of the mysteries of the universe."

"Mysteries of the universe?" she asked.

"Raph?" Raph-chan chirped too.

I was thinking about how mysterious it is that Filo seems to just understand some things. The language barrier seemed low but was actually quite high, and yet there were plenty of geniuses around here who just seemed to jump right over it.

"Hey, Naofumi. If there is going to be more fighting, then we had better get our levels and weapons in order quickly," Itsuki suggested. The situation was pretty dire over here, so I could understand his concerns.

"Do you have any earth crystals?" I asked. "People coming from our world can turn them into experience."

"Ah, of course. I heard about you using them last time you were here," Glass said. That was right. The special ore "earth crystals" were only found here on Kizuna's world. They could be turned into experience if people from our world used them. It depended on size and purity, but using them at a low level could be expected to provide a considerable boost. They wouldn't provide enough to reach really high levels, but it would be better than nothing. Then we could consider the situation and go hunting to increase our levels in short order after that.

"That's the situation, Itsuki. I know you'll feel uneasy until you can hold your own, but just have some patience," I told him.

"Very well," he replied. His monotone intonation didn't inspire confidence, but Rishia should have his back. She had done little but make her silly exclamations since our arrival, but she had actually been recently selected as one of the seven star heroes and could also initiate her awakened state on command. She had a strength that transcended just levels, and she was also a very trustworthy individual.

"We're getting off topic here. L'Arc, about those bandages—you've been cursed too?" I asked, checking on his condition. Seeing as he was still wearing the bandages even after having healing magic applied, I guessed the injuries had been caused by a curse or something similar and so the healing was delayed.

"That's right. The injuries the ones who stole my vassal weapon gave me aren't healing especially well," he replied.

"Liberation Heal X." I extended my arm toward L'Arc and incanted some magic. He made a soft exclamation in surprise as healing magic was applied. I focused on the spots wrapped in bandages. The X-class magic could even heal curses. The only issue was that it took a little time.

"Of course, Naofumi has the ability to lift curses with his healing magic. He healed me too," Ethnobalt chimed in. This was how I had healed him.

"Where did the 'X' come from?" Raphtalia asked.

"The staff power-up method allows you to spend points to boost the effects of skills and abilities. I put some into magic and gained access to the X. It's the spell I mentioned when I told you about how we defeated Takt," I explained.

"I see. That's quite incredible. I can see the curse fading even as I watch," Raphtalia replied.

"Even so, it seems to be rooted pretty deep. It's going to need multiple treatments to fully heal up," I said. After we worked out it had curse-healing properties, I had tried it on Motoyasu too, but it had done nothing at all to him. I wondered what was going on there.

Itsuki, meanwhile, was probably easier to handle in his current state, so I hadn't even tried it on him. I didn't need him to start frothing at the mouth about justice and have us end up on opposite sides again. Maybe I'd be able to get through to him this time, but he wasn't causing any trouble at the moment. He was fine for now. If he got badly injured, of course I'd use it.

"Wow, I feel so much better! I think I'm seeing the light at the end of this tunnel, thanks to you, Naofumi!" L'Arc enthused. He swung his arms around, proving how improved his condition was, a grin on his face. "Not sure how to thank you!"

"Don't worry about it. There are other people who need treatment too, right? I'll heal them later. Finish your explanation of what's going on here first," I told him. From what we'd been told so far, I still didn't know how Raphtalia had gotten involved or how Ethnobalt's ship had been stolen.

"Right, okay. Back on track. It was while we were forming up a party to go save Kizuna—although my injuries made it hard for me to do anything. Glass can probably explain this a bit better," L'Arc said, looking over at her.

"We had the rescue party ready and set out to save Kizuna while L'Arc and the others were healing up," Glass said, picking up the story. "On the way, however, we were attacked by a group who looked to be adventurers. I'd never seen anything like them before, from the magic they incanted to the attack styles they used." The first phrase that came to mind was "when it rains, it pours."

"Ethnobalt, you gave me the lowdown on that, right?" I confirmed with him.

"That's right. These new enemies also have the power to steal vassal weapons, and they were targeting Glass's weapon and my own," Ethnobalt replied.

"We faced unknown attacks and with inferior fighting strength. As a trump card, I used some soul-healing water and unleashed an attack, but they were highly skilled themselves. Finding ourselves in dire straits, Ethnobalt's vassal weapon was stolen. I barely escaped with my fan." That all matched up with what Ethnobalt had already told me. "Losing Ethnobalt meant our means of quick travel was gone, which comprised a major setback to our plans to rescue Kizuna," Glass continued. "We also had to fight to quell another one of the waves. And then, while we were fighting off an attack from the traitors—"

"That's when I was summoned into the middle of the crisis," Raphtalia said. Boy, it sounded like she'd really been called into a shit storm—although, from another perspective, it might have been perfect timing. "I fought while using magical illusions, but the enemy proved most powerful. As the fighting wore on, we were losing more and more ground," Raphtalia continued. The timelines didn't line up exactly, but crossing worlds likely caused this kind of discrepancy. "Mr. Naofumi . . . concerning the mysterious forces that Glass was just talking about . . ." Raphtalia looked over at S'yne, who of course had also come along. I instinctively knew what she was trying to say. S'yne seemed to have worked it out too, because she had a stiff and stern look on her face. "From the descriptions of their magic and the gear they were carrying, I believe them to be the same enemies as those S'yne had faced."

"I see," I replied. This just made the entire situation even more complicated. "Sounds like you've been beset on all sides."

They had really taken a beating, that was for sure. I was quite worried about what might have happened if we hadn't shown up when we did. We'd done so much to help them during our last visit, and this was the result? I was almost ready to accuse someone of negligence. That said, being attacked by someone like Takt without any prior information could easily lead to this kind of situation. I'd give them that one.

"Luckily, thanks to you, Naofumi, we made it through another crisis. You have my deepest gratitude," Glass said.

If we were looking at people trying to pull the same thing that Takt had been doing, we should be able to defeat them if we all worked together. I'd been hitting the Liberation Aura X hard recently. No need to stop now. A bit of aggressive muscle should get the job done!

"I'd better tell you something I found out," I said.

"What's that?" Glass asked.

"It was when I was badly injured myself," I continued. "The Shield Spirit told me that Takt was one of the vanguards of the waves. We still don't know exactly what kind of enemy is behind the waves, but please keep this point in mind. From Takt's attitude and how similar he was to Kyo, I should think Kyo was too."

"Are you sure?" Glass responded.

"Most likely. If they have the power to steal vassal weapons, then I'm sure those guys are connected," I stated. Such a major commonality as stealing weapons meant they had to be related.

"The waves have also been invading us like that. Does that mean they're more than just a phenomenon caused by the fusing of the worlds?" Glass was having trouble, understandably, grasping the size of the enemy standing against us.

"That, I can't tell you. Do the waves have intent of their own? Or is there another reason for all this?" I pondered aloud. Now I was just throwing out questions. The very fact that monsters appeared along with a wave was an unexplained mystery. The information we currently had wasn't enough to reach an answer, anyway.

"Let's get back on topic," I said, not for the first time. "There are ways through this situation . . . but is Kizuna okay? Is she alive?" I asked.

"I think . . . she probably is," Glass responded. "Kizuna can't attack people directly herself, and she's been considerably weakened by the curse. If they kill her, we could summon a new group of four holy heroes, so they are likely keeping her alive." If Kizuna died, it would be possible to summon a new group of four holy heroes. There had been issues with summoning heroes when it came to me, but it worked well for everyone else. The spirits of the holy weapons wouldn't respond to a summons from people who didn't have the best interests of the world at heart. That meant Glass and her allies, fighting for the sake of the world in order to stop the waves, had a clear advantage.

If a situation like this had been explained to us upon our own arrival, we might well have listened. If a group that was happy to use their game knowledge to fight some battles in another world were summoned, we would probably be able to convince them to join the cause too. The enemy wasn't going to risk increasing the forces arrayed against them so drastically. Rather, if they just kept the weakened Kizuna alive but imprisoned, they could push Glass and her allies further into the corner.

"So she's alive, but we don't know what's being done to her. One wrong move and Raphtalia could have ended up in the same position," I said.

"Tell me about it," Raphtalia agreed. I just hoped Kizuna was okay.

"Anyway, we've dealt with the traitors now. We need to send out a unit and secure Kizuna's safety as quickly as possible," L'Arc said.

"Agreed. As quickly as possible," I responded. Something stirred in the back of my mind. My otaku background made me think of those nasty games that involved rape. I thought we should also consider how terrible people could be. We should probably prepare some memory-wiping medicine to take care of serious mental issues Kizuna might face after the rescue. We weren't in some made-up story, and those who had been captured would definitely be tortured. "Still, I do wonder . . .

why are these vanguards of the waves all so selfish? How can they put themselves ahead of the needs of the world like this?" I pondered aloud. They were little different from the video game-playing otaku summoned as heroes—no sense of peril attached to their actions.

How to turn this all around, then?

"I split an ofuda with Kizuna that summons Chris, but for some reason Chris isn't able to locate her. I want to leave as quickly as possible," Glass said.

"Calm it, Glass. I know it's hard. I'll make sure we can leave today. Don't worry," L'Arc assured her. Glass gripped her fan tightly. Then she took out an ofuda and summoned her penguin familiar Chris.

"Pen!" Chris said.

"Raph!" Raph-chan greeted her. It was almost like a reunion between two old friends.

"Pen! Pen-pen!" Chris continued.

"Raph . . ." Raph-chan sympathized.

"Glass tried to attempt a rescue many times, even with everyone stopping her," Raphtalia murmured quietly to me. "It wasn't easy to stop her either."

"I'm sure it wasn't," I replied. Kizuna was to Glass what Raphtalia was to me. Having someone around who understood her had helped Glass stay calm.

"In order to be reunited with you, Mr. Naofumi, I took on

a number of waves, hoping to be able to return to the world I came from," Raphtalia told me.

"They didn't match up though, did they?" I said. The only wave in our world had been the recent one in Melromarc. That one hadn't matched with Kizuna's world, meaning Raphtalia had been without any way to get back.

"We just need to go and get Kizuna back, right?" L'Arc said. His voice was loud and high; he was hoping to ride this wave all the way to victory. "Great to have you helping out— you and your party, Naofumi—but what's the plan once we save Kizuna?"

"Well . . . as for these vassal weapon holders with the power to steal weapons, if I'm reunited with Kizuna, together we can instantly weaken them," I said.

"What?!" L'Arc exclaimed.

"I told you about Takt, the guy we faced in my world, right?" I confirmed.

"Yes, I heard you. But is it that simple?" L'Arc asked. I mean, I wasn't sure it would be that easy, but in light of the situation, it was clear what we needed to prioritize.

"The seven star weapons in our world are the same as the vassal weapons here in yours. Which means the holders of the holy weapons outrank them. They should be able to easily strip anyone who isn't fulfilling their duty as a vassal weapon holder of their right to hold the weapon," I explained. The removal of authority I had levied on Takt would only work on a seven star weapon. I couldn't, for example, use it on S'yne. I'd also tried it on Rishia, Trash, and Fohl, but it had no effect on those who were recognized to be using their weapon correctly. It looked like authority could only be stripped from those who had obtained the weapons in an unjust way or who had abandoned their duty.

But even if we could take them all back, we didn't know the location of some of the seven star weapons.

"It sounds like you haven't made much progress with sharing power-up methods here in this world. That's why we've probably gotten a bit stronger than you. Anyway, once preparations are ready, should we perhaps hunt down the vassal weapon holders first?" I suggested. One priority was definitely to get back Ethnobalt's vassal weapon. If the enemy started using that to get around, we would be in even more trouble.

That said, the movement skills found in the weapons here were fundamentally different from the skills we had—like Scroll of Return or Dragon Vein. If we were careful of teleportation interference, we could probably escape or come back without too much trouble.

"If you're willing to help, that sounds great to me," L'Arc said.

"Then that settles it. First things first . . ." I looked over at Sadeena, Shildina, and Itsuki. "Can you share some earth crystals with us? I want to boost the baseline levels of my allies, to be better ready for whatever comes next. We don't know when the enemy might strike, so it doesn't hurt to be prepared."

"Sure! We're starting to recover now! I just hope Kizuna will come back to us safe and sound!" L'Arc exclaimed. We proceeded to begin the preparations for her rescue.

Chapter Five: Inter-World Adaptation

"Little Naofumi, do we just have to grip this ore tight?" Sadeena asked. L'Arc had managed to get some earth crystals from a merchant. They were now being supplied to Sadeena and the others.

"That's right. After you raise your levels from the fixed experience obtained from the crystals, we'll go fight some monsters and raise your levels higher to prepare for the operation. However, the war has left the region unstable. Keep your guard up at all times," I cautioned them. I still didn't know how long there was until the operation was going to start, but there was no reason not to be prepared. "We also need to sort out our gear. We'd better go check in with Romina." We could probably get by with our current stuff, but it certainly couldn't hurt to check in with Romina.

"Romina is still working hard at being a blacksmith," L'Arc informed me.

"What about Alto?" I asked.

"He's off collecting information in another country," L'Arc replied.

"He was the merchant of death, right? Watch out. He's probably leaking all your secrets," I warned him.

"Even Alto knows how to handle himself in that regard. Lots of the other vassal weapon holders are selfish and difficult to talk to, after all," L'Arc reasoned. I thought for a moment and agreed with him. The very fact Alto was the merchant of death meant he was unlikely to do anything that might put his own life in danger.

"Let's go see Romina then," I said. We left Itsuki and the others who needed a level boost with L'Arc, and the rest of us headed to Romina's studio. Glass came with us. When we got there, I noticed that a mysterious dojo had now appeared next to Romina's studio. It definitely hadn't been there before.

"Yomogi and Tsugumi are based out of that dojo," Raphtalia explained. "They are assisting Kizuna." I made a noise to show I was impressed. I definitely remembered those two. Yomogi had started out siding with Kyo, but she was honest and serious and just a lovable dummy, really. She had been pretty vocal about Kyo's plans and constantly questioned him, which had led to Kyo tricking her into attacking us on what basically amounted to a suicide mission. Once she realized Kyo had tricked her, she had turned on him and joined us in a position of something like slave to Kizuna.

Tsugumi had been part of Trash #2's retinue. Trash #2 had wanted the katana vassal weapon and had attacked in order to kill Raphtalia and take it. She had turned the tables on him, though, cutting him deep with the katana and then warning him—multiple times—that he would split in two if he moved. He had still chosen to move and fell apart into pieces.

In order to avenge this, Tsugumi had joined Kyo's forces. After being physically modified, she had been sent to attack us on what was basically her second reckless suicide mission—this time with other members of Kyo's harem backing her up. But Kizuna had saved her. After that, she'd been pretty amenable. Her romance-fevered brain had finally cooled.

"Okay. So where are Yomogi and Tsugumi now?" I asked.

"They are off working to calm the waves in each region. They are very close with Kizuna now, so they're working hard to keep this place safe for her," Glass explained. As we stood around chatting, Romina came out from her studio and narrowed her eyes.

"Can you stop gossiping in front of my place of business?" she asked.

"Thanks for coming out to greet us," I said.

"Once Raphtalia showed up, I thought you'd be along sooner rather than later," she replied, taking my witty remark in stride.

"Glad you know what's up," I said.

"This might be the moment to celebrate our reunion, but I guess you want to get down to business first," Romina said. I felt a bit sorry about my attitude too. I did tend to consider things from a transactional perspective first. Then Romina gave a smile. "It's okay. Don't worry about it. I was just thinking things were starting to feel more like when Kizuna was here."

"Really?" I replied.

"I guess, even though this is a different world, you are both heroes. It's the atmosphere that both of you have around you," she said. I didn't really understand her reply. I had an atmosphere around me that was like Kizuna—perhaps that was the lesson.

"I'm not as carefree as her," I stated.

"But you have a different way of reassuring people," Raphtalia stepped in, scoring for completely the wrong side! *Stop it with the support attacks against me!*

"Whatever. If you need something, get in here," Romina said. We proceeded to follow her inside. "Showing up at my studio means you want some weapons, correct?" she confirmed.

"Yeah. I want to beef up our gear a bit to help get Kizuna back," I explained. "I've also got some stuff I want to show you, Romina." I showed her the materials the old guy had given me, along with the Barbarian Armor and everyone else's gear. It was all functioning, but without some tweaks it wouldn't be able to exhibit its full potential. "This too," I finished, tossing the Demon Dragon core over to Romina.

"Hold on. This is the dragon core I used on your armor, right? So how do you have another one?" Romina asked.

"That's the one you guys swapped in. It caused some issues

for us too," I stated. Then I explained to her the trouble the Demon Dragon core had caused.

"Wow. This dragon core caused that much fuss?" she asked.

"It did. A whole heap of trouble." I made sure to rub it in.

"But the weapons made with the Demon Dragon materials were great," she countered.

"I'll give you that one," I eventually admitted. They were really versatile, that much was true, and among all the finicky shields in my collection, it had proven exceptionally easy to use. I certainly didn't want to wear a whole set of that dangerous Demon Dragon stuff though. Forget that.

"Roger. What about these other materials? They look a bit like something I recognize," Romina pondered.

"They come from some of the four benevolent animals in my world," I explained.

"I thought as much," she said. Romina proceeded to check the Spirit Tortoise and Phoenix materials, nodding to herself all the while. Purely based on her skills . . . she was at least better than the old guy had been prior to going into training. But I wouldn't say she was at the level of Motoyasu II. "They look a lot like some of the material fragments we found after defeating Kyo. These look purer, though, and probably tougher to use," Romina evaluated.

"Can you turn them into gear we can use in this world?" I asked.

"Probably not impossible," she responded. "But how quickly do you need them?"

"I mean . . . as quickly as possible, to be honest," I replied. It should be easy to portal back and forth to collect them. Even when I factored that in, there would surely be a few days before we were ready to go and get Kizuna.

"Can you start with the easy ones?" I inquired.

"Okay. I'll kick things off with adjusting the gear you carried over with you and get to making new stuff later. Sound good?" she replied.

"Sure thing," I confirmed. "Anything else?"

"Maybe you could try to hammer a little more accessory-making skill into L'Arc?" she said.

We were going to try this again, were we?

"He holed up in my studio for a while, determined to make something better than you can make," Romina revealed.

"I taught him the basics, after all," I commented.

"He's so . . . clumsy . . . I guess is the word. And yet he was trying so hard. But he just couldn't get any better. Eventually his face became more and more like you, Naofumi, and he fell asleep while making a new accessory. In his sleep he was muttering 'he'll take her from me . . . he'll take her,' whatever that means," Romina continued.

"Talk about obsessed. He sure worries a lot about dumb stuff," I observed. Encountering L'Arc at night in this shop would be like something from a horror movie. "When you teach him, I'd like an accessory made for Therese, so give him some of the four benevolent animal materials," I told her. Romina worked directly for Kizuna, so she should have some pretty good materials. Quite a lot of time had also passed since we were last here. They could have quite a stockpile of good stuff. For the sake of Itsuki and my weapon, it was also worth having four holy beast materials in the mix. Even if the stats themselves were low, they had an unlock bonus.

"L'Arc managed to buy back some of those that went out into each region, so we should have some. We can use these materials too, I guess. I'll get everything ready," she said.

"Gotcha. You think you can restore functionality for my armor?" I asked.

"The one who made this armor has really increased his skills." Romina quietly made an impressed sound as she examined it. "It's much finer work than the last time you were here. I need to up my game." I wondered if she could really tell that much. Some kind of craftsperson sense? "It is designed with adjustments in mind, so I should be able to pull this off pretty quick. I can also add some parts I've made to maybe boost its abilities."

"You're not going to get me cursed again, are you?" I asked.

"I've reflected on that incident a lot, I assure you. I'll make sure everything goes smoothly this time," she assured me. I just hoped that was the case. "If I have anything left over, I can maybe make some weapons as well."

"Even just as a backup, if you could get a harpoon and katana ready, that would be great. I've got people who could use them," I told her. Sadeena and Shildina would need weapons. The equipment L'Arc provided to the knights of his realm would probably be sufficient, but it would be better to have custom-made gear. The Water Dragon's Harpoon wasn't functioning, as I'd expected it wouldn't.

"Okay! A harpoon. Think a lance would work too?" she confirmed.

"I think she could make that work," I replied.

"A harpoon for Sadeena, right?" Raphtalia said.

"Yeah, that's right. On pure skill alone, she might have the edge even on you, Raphtalia," I replied.

"It hardly seems fair to compare me to Sadeena or even Shildina. They both have quite a few years on me," Raphtalia responded. Those two . . . It would be a while before she could best them on a technical level. Atla might have learned to beat them after a couple of fights.

"They sound quite powerful," Romina said. "I'll have to see what they've got later."

As we chatted . . . "Jangle-jangle!" Completely oblivious to the situation, Filo got her morning star out from her wing and dropped it on the counter. I'd completely forgot she was there, for a moment.

"There's something wrong with my jangle-jangle," Filo said.

"Hmmm. I see what you mean," Romina commented. "But it looks to have some fun tricks up its sleeve. Can I toy with this too?"

"Not a bad idea," I said approvingly. "It's like Filo's hidden weapon." She often threw it out to catch enemies by surprise. She had originally picked it up at the Zeltoble coliseum, and for some reason she still really treasured it. It felt like a while since I'd seen it though.

"Yeah! Make it all shiny for me!" Filo said.

"It does look interesting . . ." Romina said.

"Can you use that in this world, Filo?" I asked her. Since she was unable to use her powers as a filolial in this world, I was mainly intending to keep her as rear support. She'd really just be singing and activating magic. She made a thinking noise though, suggesting she wasn't sure if she could use it or not. That said, it probably wasn't a good idea to leave her unequipped. It might be worth getting something made for her too, I guessed.

"She's a humming fairy, right? Maybe I'll try modifying it into a weapon she can swing around while flying," Romina pondered.

"Thanks. How about some armor for her?" I suggested.

"A convertible shoulder pad, maybe. A scarf might be good too. I'll try making some more armor for monsters," she said. We finished up with Romina and then left the studio.

Chapter Six: Hidden Abilities

After finishing discussing our gear with Romina, we headed straight back toward the castle. The sun was getting pretty low. Still, we'd taken one of the enemy down on the day we arrived, so that was definitely something.

Now I needed to get on with making some combat accessories.

"L'Arc, shall we do this?" Therese said.

"Ready when you are!" came the reply. Therese proceeded to unleash the same magic she had used when we first met, aimed directly at L'Arc's scythe.

"That feels good. I think I've got quite a bit more than that too!" Therese appeared to have made a full recovery. "Using the power of the accessory that Master Craftsman lent me as a medium, I have increased the range of translation," she explained to me proudly. She really did seem to have a thing for me. It made me think of Motoyasu for a moment. She seemed even more aware of me than before. "I'm actually quite incredible, being able to do this much."

"Is that so," I said, playing down her achievements. Then Sadeena came up with an earth crystal.

"Little Naofumi, this mineral is most interesting. I've

leveled up in no time at all," she told me.

"Glad to hear it. Shame it only works on those coming from the other world," I said.

"Oh my," Sadeena commented.

"Are you a high enough level to be able to fight now?" I asked her.

"My only possible reply to that is . . . I don't really know," she replied. She'd never been to this world before, after all, and even I didn't know that much about it. She could still use her therianthrope form though. If she didn't take too many risks, I suspected she would be fine.

"You call these ladies 'therianthropes,' correct?" L'Arc said, pointing at Sadeena and Shildina. So accustomed to seeing her transformed, I almost did a double take.

"Oh, it's so nice to be referred to as a 'lady'! I'm so happy!" Sadeena gushed.

"Looks like you've got your work cut out for you, Naofumi," L'Arc commented, pulling away a bit. Sadeena did come on a bit strong, even for someone like L'Arc.

"She's definitely the biggest joker in my party," I confirmed. I thought her jokey, easygoing attitude was quite similar to L'Arc. She always kept some leeway—a reassurance about her, backed up by everything she'd achieved in the past.

"I see. She definitely doesn't leave any openings. I'll have to keep an eye on her," he said.

"Did you hear that, Little Naofumi?" she said.

"He's talking about you," I reminded her. Sadeena really had a way of controlling the conversation.

"What about you, little Shildina?" Sadeena asked. Shildina said nothing, her stomach rumbling. All that leveling up had made her hungry.

"Shall we get some food?" I asked.

"Are you cooking, little Naofumi?" Sadeena asked.

"No, I don't have time. Get some of L'Arc's men to make it," I told her.

"I think food little Naofumi makes would be more effective," she said, displaying her cunning again.

"Eating nutritious food may be another good way to get stronger," Ethnobalt proposed. This progression of events was definitely proceeding toward me having to do some cooking.

"I want Master's food!" Filo chirped. Raph-chan and Chris spoke up too, all the small animals chattering for a feeding. Seriously . . . it was a pain, but just giving in would be easier than trying to resist it.

"Okay, okay. Take me to the castle kitchen. Just this once, understand?" I said.

"Oh, I want a drink too! Let's try some booze from another world!" Shildina added.

"That's a negative. You can't give booze to a baby," I replied.

"Oh my," Shildina said.

"I'm going to drink! Booze from another world, bring it on!" Sadeena said.

"Oh?" That caught L'Arc's interest. "Can you drink, my lady?"

"If Sadeena is drinking, I'm drinking too!" Shildina trilled.

"Killer whale sisters—quiet!" I shouted above the clamor. "L'Arc, these two women drink—if you'll excuse the phrase—like fish. They have drowned countless men in booze. You will need serious commitment before you take them on."

"Heh. You don't know what I can do," he bragged. Oh, I knew enough. I knew he wasn't as hardened as he thought he was. I was amazed he was showing this much confidence; he couldn't even beat Raphtalia.

"If you can win, Sadeena will surely take a liking to you. She likes men who can hold their liquor. Do your best!" I told him.

"Oh my. My heart already belongs to you, little Naofumi," she quipped.

"Whatever," I replied.

"Heh. Kiddo, you're about to experience the terror of potentially losing a woman you love," he crowed. I trusted Sadeena, that much was true, but I didn't recall falling in love with her. The feelings L'Arc had toward Therese and the feelings I had for Sadeena were not the same thing, surely. I guess I'd support him in this.

"Good luck," I said, although my delivery was pretty wooden. Maybe this experience of crossing worlds would turn Sadeena into a non-drinker . . . but the hope of that seemed slim.

"L'Arc, you like that woman now?" Therese asked, having taken her sweet time getting to the question, her head tilted to one side.

"Therese! No, no I don't! I'm not serious! I just want the kiddo to experience the same feeling I have . . ." L'Arc stuttered, rushing to dig his own grave.

"You're not serious? That's quite rude of you," Sadeena said. Motoyasu, in his past life, probably had more luck than this. It was only hearsay, but he'd apparently picked up his fair share of women. When I looked at him now, of course, he was just a pathetic, filolial-obsessed moron.

"Anyway! I'm just going to teach you all that I can handle my drink!" L'Arc raged. "Once I do that, kiddo here can experience the same terror that I've been going through!" After that outburst, Therese gave him a gentle, and at the same time pitying, look.

"L'Arc, everyone has things they can do and things they can't. It's still not too late to back down. Okay?" she told him.

"Why are you trying to get me to stop?" he replied. "I won't know unless I try!"

"I'm trying to get you to stop because I already know what

will happen. I'm the one who'll have to pick up the pieces after she drinks you under the table," Therese said pretty sharply. I mean, it definitely was a pain to take care of a drunk. I had some experience with that myself.

They were a noisy bunch though. I'd give them that much.

"I'm sorry you got asked to cook almost as soon as you got here," Raphtalia apologized to me, but I just waved it off. No need to worry about that. I cooked pretty much every day back home. It was habit by now.

So we ended that day with an impromptu outdoor party in the garden at the castle.

"Everyone! Let's have lots of fun today!" Filo shouted out. In order to cheer everyone up, she had started singing with some of the other gathered musicians.

"Raph," said Raph-chan. She was in command of the visuals, using her illusion magic to set off fireworks.

"Pen!" Chris was backing her up, waving a mysterious glowing stick like he was at some kind of idol concert. Filo was putting all her training from Melty to good use, and the whole venue was filled with a gentle and relaxed atmosphere.

"Wow. I wish I could share this scene with everyone working so hard out there for us now," L'Arc said, looking out across the scene with a smile on his face. Then he started to eat my food. "Kiddo, you've really upped your game in the kitchen." He just made pointless small talk, stuffing his cheeks with my pilaf. I was really getting sick of him calling me "kiddo" too.

How hard would it be for him to learn my name, like a civilized person?

"All sorts of stuff has been going on, boy. I've increased my skills in regard to making all sorts of stuff," I said.

"What? Are you saying you've increased your accessory-making skills too?" he accused.

"Don't look so horrified," I said.

"Right!" L'Arc was getting all excited again, and then he charged over to the wine cellar. "Time to see who can hold their drink! Hey! Bring out the good stuff!"

"Oh my!" Sadeena and L'Arc were both excitedly awaiting the liquor. I'd finished serving most of the food and started to eat as well.

The drink arrived soon afterward, and L'Arc and Sadeena started to drink. I was expecting him to at least put up a fight, but it seemed like only moments before he was hiccupping and slurring his words.

"Oh my? Are we finished already?" Sadeena asked.

"L'Arc, please just give up. If you don't, I'm pretty sure you will die," Therese said. She took the collapsed L'Arc away and put him to bed. Just as I'd expected, he hadn't stood a chance. Using healing magic to cure the effects and let him keep on drinking had been an option. It might have let L'Arc win. But the moment I tried it, Sadeena probably would have worked it out.

Realizing this was all a waste of time, I decided discussing our next steps with Glass would be a better idea. I went over to the outside table where Raphtalia, Rishia, and Itsuki were eating with Glass.

"Glass, can I have a moment?" I asked her.

"Of course," she replied.

"Making preparations is all very well, but what's the frequency of the waves like in this world? Couldn't Kizuna escape during a wave?" I asked her.

"Regarding the waves, they have been occurring more frequently due to the deaths of the other three holy heroes," she explained. "Roughly every two weeks." That was pretty short, especially if they were occurring in each nation. They must have been using Return Dragon Vein to travel around and keep a lid on things.

"Isn't that a bit much?" I asked.

"We've actually made some technological progress of our own. We've created a tool that can be registered to a dragon hourglass, just like a hero's weapon, allowing for teleportation to the location of each wave. We've been using those to divide up our forces and handle each wave accordingly," Glass continued.

"Interesting," I commented. That sounded like something we could use. I'd get the details later, including how to make it.

"Seeing as we hadn't made all the information public yet,

and because the enemy vassal weapon holders also don't consider the waves a threat, the situation is just . . . continuing, basically," she went on. Takt hadn't been worried about the waves either, I recalled. A common characteristic of these lunatics. Even Ren, Motoyasu, and Itsuki had only really considered the waves events to make them stronger for the future. I felt like I was getting to the heart of things. Now we knew that the waves weren't a natural phenomenon. That cast suspicions on the knowledge of the heroes. When I followed that line of thought, the summoning of someone like me—someone with no knowledge of a game that played like this world—had allowed for the sharing of power-up methods to go much more smoothly. And yet they continued to summon people with game knowledge. That knowledge had proven a barrier to becoming stronger.

It was as though game knowledge itself was some kind of impediment.

"In regard to Kizuna's capture, we don't know what kind of measures they are using to hold her, but she has been unable to escape due to a wave summons," Glass concluded. I grunted.

"Some things haven't changed then." When we met, she had been captured because she didn't fully understand the waves. This felt like it was becoming a bit of a habit with her. "So they haven't chosen to attack, using Kizuna as a shield?" I asked.

"They probably didn't think it was necessary to go that far," Glass presumed. They had to be pretty confident, then. When we fought Takt, his retinue had been happy to try and use Raphtalia as a hostage. In this case, Glass had struck down their leader before he even had a chance to try such a tactic. But that guy hadn't had as large of a retinue as Takt either.

"Now is the time to turn things back in our favor. Once this meal is finished, I plan to set out myself," Glass said, full of energy. Then I felt eyes on my back. I turned around and Itsuki spoke to me.

"I like this mood. Upbeat. Is this because you are here?" he asked.

"Not sure about that," I replied.

"Itsuki . . ." said Rishia. The curse should have been almost gone by now, and yet he was still expressionless in aspect and monotone in delivery. We could only hope Rishia would finally find some peace someday soon.

"I also want to help everyone feel better," he continued, right out of left field.

"Help how? What can you do?" I asked.

"This looks like the time for . . ." He didn't finish. He just got up and went over to Filo and the musicians.

"Itsuki?" Rishia went with him. Then he started talking to the musicians. One of them went over to their spare instruments and proceeded to hand one to Itsuki. It wasn't a guitar or a violin, or even a ukulele, but something similar, and crystal-tipped. Itsuki plucked a few things, checking the sound they made.

"Here we go," he said. Then, insanely, he started to play it. He just joined right in accompaniment to the song Filo was singing. It didn't sound out of place at all. In fact, he expanded the breadth of the music—while both song and music had previously just been background noise to brighten the mood, now everyone present naturally started to give it their full attention. Filo already had a great singing voice, and the synergy of all of the elements created a scene people were unable to turn away from.

Filo, too, had looked a bit taken aback by the sudden interloper at first, but soon she started to sing along with a smile on her face. Even I had to admit that he had a pretty good sense of rhythm. The song that Filo had been ad-libbing soon ended. And after only a beat, Itsuki immediately started to play a different piece.

This one I had heard before somewhere. It was likely a piece of classical music. So Itsuki could play after all. The very first time I saw him, I'd thought he looked like a piano player or something like that.

"The bow guy is incredible!" Filo said, offering her informed opinion on Itsuki's playing now that her singing was finished. Melty could play pretty well herself, and I'd seen her assisting Filo's singing during the festival. Itsuki was at least as good—no, maybe better than she had been. Even as I pondered his playing, he finished the classical piece and moved onto something a bit more rhythmical. If I had to place it, I would have thought it was the opening to some anime or game.

A moment later, a strange light started to glow across the venue, creating an illusory scene centered around Itsuki. The other musicians tried to also take up the music, perhaps not wanting to be shown up too much. But their attempts produced nothing but a brief cacophony of noise. As though warning them off, the light turned into little spikes and flicked out close to them. The only one who seemed allowed to harmonize—the only one who could—was Filo.

I'd listened a lot to Filo's singing, Melty's playing, and the playing of other musicians, but when ranking Itsuki's current performance, it would be much faster to count down from the top.

"He's pretty good," I eventually said.

"Indeed. Better than some national musicians, I bet."

"This is quite something," Glass murmured, obviously impressed. "He isn't imbuing any magic in his playing, and yet he is triggering magic."

"That light? That's some kind of magic that exists in this world?" I asked.

"Yes. It's the same as what Filo uses as a humming fairy,"

Glass explained. Right, of course. Coming to this world had allowed Filo to attack using her songs. I remembered her using it when her other magic had been sealed away. And during a concert to cheer me up, she had sung a suspicious song that put Motoyasu and the rest of her fans under a charm spell. "With the level of skill he is displaying here," Glass continued, "he would only need a little instruction from a specialist in the field to produce results equal to Filo—if not greater," Glass continued.

"Sounds like a good idea," I replied.

Once Itsuki finished playing, he came back over to us.

"Itsuki, that was amazing!" Rishia said. Seemingly a bit embarrassed, Itsuki took her praise without saying anything and sat back down.

"You look like someone who can play something too, Rishia," I commented.

"That's true. I can play a little. But I don't have the confidence to pick up something I've never seen before and just start playing it," she said. That made sense to me. Just because you could play the piano didn't mean you could play the guitar.

Unless you were Itsuki, of course. What was going on there?

"It looked like Itsuki played that weird crystal thing without any complaints," I ventured.

"So many instruments are basically the same, once you get

down to it. I bet you could play too, Rishia," he intoned.

"Fehhh," said Rishia. I mean, there was something to what Itsuki was saying. But nine times out of ten, they would surely be too different and it wouldn't work so well.

"How was it?" Itsuki asked.

"I think you've really improved the atmosphere. Itsuki, everyone is looking at you now," I told him. Itsuki took a look around, showing hints of embarrassment.

"There is no need to be polite. This is mainly thanks to Filo," he replied.

"I've always thought you could probably play, right from when I first met you," I told him. Itsuki tilted his head to the side, face expressionless.

"What are you talking about?" he asked. That response . . . I had seen it before somewhere. I needed to think back and compare it to my own memories.

Raphtalia was looking over at me.

"Isn't this like you and your cooking, Mr. Naofumi? You can't remember Imiya's full name, but you can remember recipes no matter how long they are," she said. Yeah, that was a thing too, I conceded. In my case, it was the evaluation of everyone around me that made me "good" at cooking, but it did feel kind of similar.

I decided to probe the topic further.

"Itsuki, tell me . . . can you play any piece of music after hearing it just once?" I asked him.

"Why are you asking such an elementary thing?" he replied. He really did think that was a question too obvious to even answer! I knew I wasn't capable of such a thing, at least. I might be able to hum something I'd heard a couple of times, but I definitely couldn't play it note for note.

"Itsuki, you remember when you said I might have the Nullify Sickness ability?" I asked him.

"Of course. What of it?" he replied.

"Do you think maybe you also have some talent relating to music?" I suggested.

"I've never been told such a thing . . . but I did used to play as a hobby," he said.

"Maybe you have some supernatural power that makes you good at playing music," I continued, pressing the point. He was using magic much like Filo but without any special training. This could really boost his support abilities if he got some practice in.

"I don't think so," Itsuki said, tilting his head and muttering almost to himself. "A talent for something isn't a supernatural power. Those with supernatural powers controlling sound can do far more than me, even at lower ranks. For example, those who can control sound waves can use them to paralyze the semicircular canal of an opponent, and they can play music without the assistance of an instrument." As always, he talked about supernatural powers as though he was discussing making coffee—likely, this was partly because it was something he understood well and partly because of the curse.

Still, the phrase "without the assistance of an instrument" stuck with me. He made playing a violin sound like it was as easy as taking training wheels off a bicycle.

"Those with supernatural powers are evaluated based on their applicable uses. Even if I have a talent for music, it would not be evaluated highly under such criteria," Itsuki continued with a gentle smile on his face. Sometimes his attitude just made me want to hit him. I'd never realized before how someone being humble could really make you want to punch their lights out. Maybe I acted in a similar way sometimes. I'd need to be more careful when people were talking about my cooking or not getting drunk.

I was also struggling to accept this degree of humbleness coming from Itsuki, who had always been so vain before. I almost told him to brag a bit, having found something he could actually be proud of. Sure, that would be annoying too, but probably better than this.

"I'm not sure, but something about all this rings a bit false," Glass said, coming out with exactly what I had been thinking. Itsuki looked surprised and tilted his head.

"Yeah, for me too," I agreed. "There must be all sorts of ways to use that ability, but I just feel like slapping him on the head."

"Fehhh!" Rishia exclaimed.

"Mr. Naofumi, calm down! I understand your anger, but the Bow Hero doesn't mean anything by it," Raphtalia said.

"I'm not really angry, don't worry. Just tell me, Itsuki, are you doing that on purpose?" I asked him.

"What do you mean?" he intoned. It looked like he really didn't understand why he was rubbing us the wrong way. If he had no self-awareness, then there was no helping it.

". . . Itsuki, this seems like a good opportunity to learn the magic that activates when performing music, like Filo sometimes does. It might prove useful," I told him.

"Very well," he agreed. With that, following my orders, Itsuki went over to the musicians to start learning the magic. I hadn't expected to uncover another one of Itsuki's talents after coming to another world. It just went to show that you could never tell what was going to happen.

Maybe all four of the holy heroes had this kind of hidden ability. Mine was related to cooking, and Itsuki's was music . . . so what about Ren and Motoyasu?

I absolutely had no idea.

From my first impressions, I'd thought Ren was pretty cool, and Motoyasu looked like a normie with a non-otaku life. Any hints there, then?

Nope, nothing.

Motoyasu looked good at picking up women, but at the

moment he was obsessed only with bringing in more wild filolials. It would be almost impossible to search for a talent the
owner had no idea they possessed. You could ask them anything and everything, and they still wouldn't know.

"Huh?" As I sat thinking about Itsuki's hidden abilities,
I noticed that Shildina and S'yne had started playing cards. I
decided to go talk to them next.

"Ofuda? Was there such a convenient weapon in this
world?" Shildina was asking.

"It seems so. They can act as the trigger for weapons and
magic in this world. Ah, S'yne has won," said her familiar.

"I lost, but these cards do seem fun. I want to learn more
card games. When I get back to the village, I'll play them with
everyone else," Shildina said.

"How's your hunger?" I asked. "Are you feeling better?"

"Huh? I've still got some space left," she replied. "Your
food is so delicious, Naofumi."

"Glad to hear it. Eat lots and grow up big," I told her. She
nodded, a little embarrassed, as I patted her head. She was just
so amenable. If Shildina would just stay this size, rather than
turning back into Sadeena's size, she would be so cute . . .

"Hey, Naofumi. I've just been told that cards are a weapon
in this world," she told me.

"Right. I had Rishia use those. They have all sorts of magic
contained in them," I recalled. When we were here last time,

Rishia had used ofuda and provided backup from the rear. When I thought about it now, she'd shown an aptitude for projectile weapons even back then. Not to the same extent as Itsuki, perhaps, but she had provided excellent support from the rear.

Now, of course, Rishia was the projectile hero. Ofuda, used as a thrown weapon, might actually be effective for her.

"I want them too! Tell me how to make them!" Shildina just loved card games. She still carried her holder of cards around with her. She'd used them as part of her oracle powers, so maybe she could make use of them with her own unique abilities.

"If you want to learn more, why not see if there's someone among Glass's allies who can use this technique?" I said. I turned to look at Glass, just to see her actively put some distance between herself and Shildina.

"What's wrong?" I asked.

"I'm not sure I really understand it myself. Shildina, was it? I just feel something telling me not to get too close to you," Glass explained.

"Oh my!" Shildina wasn't quite sure what to do either, being told that to her face.

"Don't worry, sweet Naofumi. I've heard far worse than that before. I'm used to it," she said to me.

"That's nothing to be proud of," Raphtalia told her, not unkindly.

"Oh my," Shildina said again, still not really sure how to respond. It might be better to call Sadeena over, I mused. Getting this kind of reaction from people due to being a former executioner was probably something only someone from the same line of work could hope to understand.

Not to say I didn't have any experience with persecution myself. However, in the most recent instance when Takt and his women had been laying into me as I beat them down, I had to admit I'd really rather enjoyed it.

Of course, those feelings had all turned a bit more complex once we started killing them.

"I'm really sorry," Glass said. "I know that was a nasty thing to say."

"Rare to hear something like that from you, Glass," I commented.

"I know," she replied. "Shildina, do you have some kind of secret or something?"

"A secret? Is that your warrior instincts speaking?" If it was, she had a pretty keen observational eye. From a combat perspective, Shildina had strength to match that of Sadeena.

"No, I wouldn't quite say that . . ." Glass replied.

"Well, she's the younger sister of that drunkard over there and pretty much just as strong. She's got good combat abilities, and her magic is basically off in a realm all of its own," I explained. She was high spec, I had to admit, hearing it all again now. But these events had also revealed just how close in age she was to Raphtalia and that she still required my protection.

Shildina was practically puffing out her chest at my words. She still hadn't returned to a normal body size, and in her child-like state, she had the same kind of cuteness as Filo. Maybe better than when she was an adult.

"She also has abilities as an oracle," Raphtalia added.

"An oracle?" Glass asked.

"Well, to put it simply, she can trace the abilities of the owner of an object from the residual thoughts within it. Then she opens a hole in her soul and puts those thoughts into it," I explained. Shildina raised her hand toward Glass without saying anything.

"That's it. Can you stop doing . . . whatever that is, please? It feels like I'm facing a soul eater, and I just can't calm down," Glass said.

"Sure, okay," Shildina replied.

"What did you do?" I asked. It seemed Shildina had worked out why Glass was on guard around her.

"There are people in this world called 'spirits,' right? They are similar to the thoughts that I can summon using my oracle powers. Because I can capture such thoughts, these spirits are instinctively afraid of my presence," Shildina explained.

"Like you're their natural enemy?" I asked.

"A little different. But a spirit may feel it that way," she replied. An unexpected effect, for sure. But if I recalled correctly, the hole in Shildina's soul had been blocked, considerably reducing her oracle powers.

"When it's as clear as this, I can perform the summons even without having to force open a hole. That would make certain things much easier," Shildina continued.

"Certain things? Like what? That sounds a bit unpleasant from where I'm sitting," I said. I was getting worried about what Shildina might do to Glass. Could she eat her soul, like a soul eater? Sadeena, on the other hand, didn't have any of these kinds of powers and wasn't an oracle.

"Should I experiment a little?" Shildina asked.

"I would rather you didn't. Human experiments only cause problems, in my experience," Glass said. I had to give her that one. Even if we tried it with a spirit other than Glass, we had no idea what it might do to Shildina either.

"Getting back to the previous topic," Glass said. "Ethnobalt knows a lot about ofuda." I'd had a feeling he was knowledgeable on the topic. They had diverged a little now, but he was originally an intellectual type, just like Rishia.

"Did you call?" Ethnobalt, who had been helping L'Arc and the others, came over.

"Yes. Shildina would like to know how to make and use ofuda," Glass explained.

"I see. You did so much for me in your world, so it would be a pleasure to teach you whatever I can," he replied.

"Great!" Shildina exclaimed.

"First things first, you need to select the material to make your ofuda from. If you don't start with careful selection of your basic materials, you won't achieve a good final product. Then you use some ink that's melted using magic—" Ethnobalt led Shildina aside, keeping her out of the way of the others. I'd ask about how to make them myself later—although we didn't know if they could be used in our world.

Still, Ethnobalt was certainly smart. This was a library rabbit in action.

"Little Naofumi! No one is willing to entertain me," Sadeena complained. She turned her back on the bunch she had already drunk under the table and wriggled around as she called out to me. She was acting exactly like normal then, even in this world. Everyone was just doing whatever they wanted.

"Sadeena, don't cause too much trouble," Raphtalia said. It was okay to ignore her. Raphtalia had it covered.

"Oh my. There's all this rare liquor here but no one to drink it with. That makes me so sad," she said. She clearly wanted me to drink with her.

"We'll be finished eating soon. Then I'll chat with you, so just wait a little longer," Raphtalia said.

"Very well, little Raphtalia. I'll tell you how hard everyone in the village has been working while you've been away," Sadeena said.

"Yes. I'd like to hear that," Raphtalia said, placating her. Even though they weren't related by blood, Sadeena and Raphtalia were like sisters. They started to chat together.

"Well then, I'm heading out to rescue Kizuna. Watch out for raiders while I'm gone," Glass announced. The meal and discussion finished.

"It's a hassle, but we'll join you. No idea when enemies could attack," I said.

"That would be appreciated," Glass said. For that night, those who had attained a certain level came along with us. Once Itsuki had raised his level, he and Rishia would come after us, also aiming for the country of the traitors who were holding Kizuna.

Chapter Seven: Finding Kizuna

"Raph!" said Raph-chan.

"Pen!" said Chris. We were in the carriage, heading to the country where Kizuna was being held. The two little ones were having some kind of conversation, while Raphtalia and Glass looked on.

"Pen! Pen-pen!" said Chris.

"Raph, raph!" said Raph-chan. I wondered what they were talking about. If Filo had been there, she probably could have translated, but I'd sent her to help Sadeena and the others. Ethnobalt was training Rishia, and L'Arc was working to rebuild the nation.

I realized that I had hardly spent any time together with just Glass. Kizuna had always been there between us. Raphtalia seemed to have spent longer with her than I had.

"Raph," said Raph-chan.

"Pen," said Chris. The two of them seemed to have reached some kind of understanding, like an earthling and an alien touching their index fingers in what looked like a sign of friendship. Then a faint light started to shine out from where they were touching.

"Pe, pepepepe—!" Ah! Chris fell flat on his back and it

looked as though he was having some kind of seizure.

"Hey! What are you doing to Chris?" Glass shouted, immediately noticing what was happening.

"Yes! What are you doing?" Raphtalia helped Glass pull the two critters apart.

"Raph?" Raph-chan asked.

"Pen . . ." Chris managed. Raph-chan looked at Raphtalia while tilting her head, while Chris looked a little disappointed.

"Seriously . . . just what was that? You need to train your shikigami better, Naofumi," Glass said.

"Train her? Raph-chan has never done anything wrong," I said.

"You bet she has!" Raphtalia retorted, choosing this moment—for some reason—to come at me with her brow furrowed. Raph-chan doing something wrong? Like what? If she'd tried to pull something when I wasn't looking, I'd have to have some words with her, of course.

"What, then? What did she do?" I asked.

"The Raph species!" Raphtalia immediately replied.

"I'm not sure that really counts," I countered. The monsters in the village had wanted to become members of the Raph species, after all. They had done great things not only in the Phoenix battle but also when defeating Takt, and Raph-chan II more than pulled her weight. They were like the leaders of the monsters and the guardians of the village.

More than anything, they could get really big and were so soft and comfortable to lean on. I mean, I loved the Raph species.

"I really wouldn't class that as being bad," I continued. I hadn't told her about Ruft yet. We could save that one for after the two had been reunited.

"It seems our opinions have diverged on this matter, Mr. Naofumi," Raphtalia said.

"You said they were convenient!" I countered.

". . . I admit to saying that," she acquiesced. Deploying the Raph species against Atla had led to an unprecedented victory. They also got on really well with everyone in the village.

"I'd love Raph-chan even if she turns Chris into one," I said.

"What are you planning to do to Chris?! I won't be held accountable for my actions, depending on your answer!" Glass raged. So she was on Raphtalia's side. I didn't like her tone of voice either.

"Raph, raph!" Raph-chan jumped on my shoulder and started hitting me on the head. I guessed she wanted me to stop giving people the wrong idea about her.

"Pen!" said Chris, also directed at Raph-chan. Just what were the two of them trying to do?

"Just what have you been doing with that shikigami anyway?" Glass asked.

"Not much. Researching her with my monster specialist back in the village, a woman named Ratotille. That and raised her mutability a little, that's all," I told her.

"That's all? Increasing her mutability might turn her into who-knows-what kind of dangerous monster! How could you do something so reckless?" Glass exclaimed.

"Even if Raph-chan did turn into a dangerous monster . . . Raphtalia is the only one who would be put out," I said.

"Why are you bringing my name up in that context?" Raphtalia asked.

"Because you're the only one who doesn't like any of this," I said.

"Raph," Raph-chan said. Then Chris leapt down from Glass's arms and started waving a flipper about, trying to explain. I thought for a moment it was just shadowboxing, but no. After punching an imaginary foe, Chris pretended to take damage, then spun around on the spot and collapsed.

"You're weak and you hate yourself for it?" I ventured.

"Pen!" Chris pointed at me, indicating I'd guessed correctly. I was smart when I needed to be. Then Chris pointed at Raph-chan and struck a pose, arms flexed.

"Raph-chan is strong, so you're learning something from her?" I guessed again.

"Pen!" Chris leapt around happily, indicating another correct answer.

"Mr. Naofumi, your skills at communicating without language have really improved recently," Raphtalia said.

"I guess so," I replied. It felt like he was making sense. I actually enjoyed conversing like this!

"You're not allowed to do anything!" Glass put her foot down. "If something happens to Chris, we're the ones who'll be sad! I'm sure Kizuna would feel the same way!" She made Raph-chan sound like some kind of virus or infection. Still, if that was her stance, then it couldn't be helped. I'd just stay quiet about Raph-chan and Chris having already done this numerous times behind Glass's and Raphtalia's backs. They seemed to have split whatever ritual it was up into numerous parts.

"In which case, maybe I'll make an accessory for Chris to try and provide a bit more confidence," I suggested.

"And will it really just be an accessory?" Raphtalia asked. She and Glass both had accusatory eyes. It looked like I had to prove I wasn't involved in the ritual Raph-chan and Chris had been performing.

A few days later, I handed an item over to Chris that I had created in collaboration with S'yne.

"Here you go, Chris. I did consider making you some armor or something, but I think this suits you best," I said.

"Pen!" Chris replied. I had given Chris a red hat with a pointed design—the kind of thing you would see Santa wearing.

"That's just like a pekkul! Mr. Naofumi, are you playing around?" Raphtalia accused.

"No, I'm not. Kizuna told me that Chris was born around Christmas, right? So my design plays into that backstory," I told her. It wasn't what you said but how you said it, I had always thought. "You make good use of that hat, you hear me?"

"Pen!" Chris replied, full of energy, almost giving me a salute.

"Raph!" said Raph-chan. Ah, she was jealous! I would have to make something for her later.

"I'm not sure I like this. It feels like Chris is getting more selfish," Glass said.

"This isn't being selfish," I told her. "Chris is eager to take action."

"Noninterference isn't the same as taking care of something," Raphtalia commented, striking at an unprotected spot. Not long afterward, Glass complained to me that Chris had started to keep things in the hat. Was it so wrong to make effective use of potential storage space? Still, it really felt like Chris's pekkul transformation was proceeding apace.

Our journey with Glass continued. We reached the country that traitor we defeated had been in league with, just to hear that Kizuna—who we had been hoping to rescue here—had already been captured by a different vassal weapon holder. Our plan to meet back up with Kizuna slammed right into another brick wall.

"What's going on here? Is Kizuna some kind of poor princess, continually getting kidnapped in each new destination?" I bemoaned. We had to return to L'Arc's castle, find a room, and discuss what to do next. I'd thought we'd save her easily, just to find her captured by someone else. Confounded by another trope!

"So? Which of the other vassal weapon holders is responsible for taking Kizuna?" I asked.

"From the information we acquired, it sounds like it is the musical instrument vassal weapon holder. If I recalled correctly . . . they are a summoned hero," Glass explained.

"So someone summoned from another world is causing havoc again," I said. Just doing whatever they liked. Like the other three I'd come in with—back at the beginning.

"This is just a guess based on the weapon they had, so I can't be sure," Glass continued.

"One thing . . . I don't think I've ever asked this before, but how many vassal weapons do you have in this world?" I questioned. This was another world, and I hadn't really felt the need to find out, but it seemed like a good idea to confirm the number right now.

"I have heard there are eight," Ethnobalt informed me, opening up a book and checking its pages.

"Eight, huh? Can you tell me all of them? Just in case. You'd better tell me about the four holy heroes too," I said. We had the seven star weapons in the other world, meaning they had one extra here. I couldn't quite explain it, but something felt off about all this. Like, maybe there was a secret eighth seven star weapon in our world too. When I was in the shield world, I had counted the lights and seen eight, if I recalled correctly, so the possibility seemed pretty high.

"Very well. I'll explain everything we know in order," Ethnobalt said.

"Sounds good," I confirmed.

"So we have Glass's fan, L'Arc's scythe, and the ship that I held. Then there's Raphtalia's katana," Ethnobalt said. Those were the allied vassal weapons. "Next there is the book that Kyo had and the mirror Albert held." Albert . . . I didn't know much about him. I didn't know what kind of guy he had been, but from what I'd heard, he had been surrounded by women. I couldn't get past the feeling that he had been a Kyo II.

"Then there's also the harpoon and musical instrument vassal weapons. We've found the owners of each one . . . and are currently opposed to them," Ethnobalt said. That meant we had the fan, scythe, ship, katana, book, mirror, harpoon, and musical instrument. All of them sounded pretty funky.

"What about the four holy heroes?" I asked.

"There's the hunting tool, held by Kizuna, and then the

jewels, the blunt instrument, and the ofuda," Ethnobalt revealed. I shook my head. A bit of an odd menagerie. The vassal weapons sounded more promising, to be honest! Jewels? A "blunt instrument"? And ofuda were one of them too? Those could be made. A lot of mysteries around these four holy weapons, I thought. Ofuda and jewels both sounded kind of magical.

"You've got a pretty abnormal selection in this world," Itsuki stated, choosing this moment to unleash his caustic tongue.

"Itsuki!" Rishia quickly shushed him. "They might kill you for insulting the four holy heroes, for all you know!" Both Ethnobalt and Glass showed discomfort on their faces.

"I'm not really sure what you mean. Are they that strange?" L'Arc questioned.

"Based on the Japanese standards I am used to, the only answer to that is yes. Didn't Kizuna say something about this?" I asked.

"Huh . . . You know what? She did, but it was a while back now," L'Arc recalled. I'd expected as much. Being able to change her own weapon into a variety of forms probably meant it wasn't too bad for her, at least.

"I bet this 'blunt instrument' gives access to some pretty gray-area stuff, like axes and sword maces—just like how the Bow Hero can turn his weapon into a gun," I surmised. I looked over at Itsuki, and he obliged by turning his bow into a gun.

"I'm sure you are right. There's not much we can say for sure," Ethnobalt said.

"The weapons in our world are closer to what Japanese people are used to thinking of as weapons. They are definitely a bit easier to understand," Itsuki said. I was pretty glad we'd got normal weapons for our four, I had to admit. The shield though . . . That one was definitely out of place. I wondered if there was some way to turn the shield into something else.

No. Best to just think about something else entirely.

On a separate track, it might be worth asking S'yne about this stuff, through her familiar of course. Find out what the holy weapons were like in her world before it was destroyed. It would be funny if they had a sword vassal weapon.

"Getting back on topic, that means there is a total of twelve weapons in our world," Ethnobalt concluded.

"I see. And this musical instrument vassal weapon holder is the one who nabbed Kizuna?" I confirmed.

"That seems to be the case," Ethnobalt replied.

"No chance of a diplomatic solution?" I ventured.

"We have sent messages of protest, but they claim to have no idea what we are talking about," Glass explained.

"We might have been able to have more of a discussion if they had demanded a big pile of cash," I pondered aloud, wondering exactly what it was they wanted. I was starting to want to find these enemy vassal weapon holders and just cut them down where they stood.

I pressed on with getting the situation in order.

"The book—we defeated Kyo, but have you found the new vassal weapon holder?" I asked.

"No. Both the book and the mirror are still missing," Ethnobalt replied. I didn't really like the sound of that, but that was also a matter for later consideration. It would be a pain, of course, if one—or both—of them suddenly showed up in opposition to us.

This meant that the three other holy heroes had been killed, and we still had to deal with enemies holding the musical instrument, harpoon, and Ethnobalt's ship.

That was fewer enemies than I had been expecting, perhaps. When I took their mobility into account, though, the group with the ship vassal weapon holder was going to be a pain to deal with.

They were also the ones who seemed to have S'yne's enemies pulling strings.

"If we know where to point our weapons, we need to start pointing them. Itsuki, Sadeena, Shildina, how are your levels coming along? Report, including the state of your level raising," I ordered. I'd spent most of my time with Glass and L'Arc and so hadn't been following the progress of Sadeena and the others. Raphtalia had tagged along with them and provided all sorts of support.

"The monsters in this world provide quite a lot of experience. I've been pleasantly surprised," Sadeena said.

"Yeah, they have a lot of experience. Strong though," Shildina added.

"I see," I commented. When I was here before, I vaguely recalled thinking the monsters offered better-than-normal experience. But Kizuna had been in the party then, and she was strong when fighting monsters, so maybe that confused the issue.

"But the ocean offers more, right?" I asked.

"I'm not sure. I can say the monsters on the land compared with ones in the oceans of this world don't offer much difference in experience," Sadeena said.

"Yeah, not much of a difference," Shildina added.

"Okay then," I said. The reason was unknown, but it looked like in Kizuna's world there wasn't much of a gap between experience on the land and experience in the ocean.

"You asked about our levels. I've reached 82, and so has Shildina," Sadeena reported.

"Wow, good. That was fast," I said. I was still only 90, meaning they had caught up pretty fast.

"We can push it a lot higher yet," Sadeena said.

"Yeah. I've finally got some of my height back," Shildina added. She still wasn't back to her full height, but she was growing taller every day.

"That's great to hear. Carry on raising your levels. I'll take part too," I told them.

"Sure thing!" Sadeena cheerfully replied. Then I looked over at Rishia, and Itsuki nodded.

"I've kept up with enhancements and raised my level to 80. I'm easily getting the same kind of experience as we got from the Cal Mira islands during an activation period," Itsuki reported.

"Do you think it's easier to raise our levels because this is a different world?" I asked. It felt like there had to be a reason why experience was lower on our world.

"Each world—" S'yne said.

"S'yne is saying that there are differences in experience in each world, and these differences change depending on how frequent the waves are," her familiar explained. She had visited many worlds, so she was likely to know. This world, then, had three dead holy heroes and vassal weapon holders who were underestimating the waves. We should've probably been thankful that it hadn't been destroyed by the waves already, I mused.

S'yne had pushed her own level to 81.

"We are defeating the monsters relatively safely thanks to the magic Itsuki cast," Rishia reported. The discussion turned to the combat itself. Itsuki took the opposite approach from me, using support magic that debuffed all of an opponent's status. If we shared a battlefield and both used our respective support magic, it was quite a thing—the enemies got weaker and we got stronger. I was already using Liberation Aura X, which boosted our allies multiple times. If the massive reduction that Liberation Down X offered was then also applied to the enemies, it was hard to calculate the gap in status that would be applied. I practically had zero attack power, and even I might be able to defeat such foes.

Under those circumstances, the thing we really had to watch out for were status-rating attacks, like those Kyo had unleashed. If that happened, we should just use our boosted status to avoid them or use the power of Hengen Muso Style life force to escape.

There were plans in place . . . was my point.

"The forces seem pretty locked in place . . . The issue is travel time," I pondered aloud.

"Yes. Return Dragon Vein is sealed off too, meaning we have to take the fight directly to them," Glass responded.

"More wasted days on the road. Just keeping the waves under control is trouble enough already," I said. We were helping with the waves in this world with Glass, L'Arc, and Raphtalia, but they came at high frequency now. With backup from Itsuki and me, the fighting itself wasn't presenting much of an issue . . . yet. Our biggest issue was information warfare. We weren't facing complete idiots. If it started getting around that the guy who stole the scythe vassal weapon had been wiped out in seconds with the aid of support magic provided by a group coming from another world, they were going to put their guard up.

The issue there was the potential for Kizuna's abduction to be used against us. It would be for the best if we could get her back first and then go about wiping these guys out.

In any case, we needed to move while the wind was at our backs.

"First things first, we need to work out where Kizuna is being held. Chris, you can sense where Kizuna is, correct?" I asked.

"Pen . . ." Chris said.

"He should be able to," Glass confirmed, "but that didn't apply when Kizuna was trapped in the never-ending labyrinth. The same problem seems to apply this time . . ." Kizuna definitely had a thing for going missing—even if I knew she wasn't doing it on purpose.

"Pen!" Chris had been looking forlorn, but then he placed his flippers together and started to concentrate on something. A moment later, he opened his eyes and pointed in a certain direction.

"Raph!" Raph-chan was looking pleased with herself. Did this mean something she had done to Chris had boosted his precision in finding Kizuna? Chris proceeded to take out what looked like a world map from the hat I had given him and then drew a circle around a corner of the continent.

"Is that where Kizuna is?" I asked.

"Pen!" Chris confirmed.

"Wow! That's amazing, isn't it, Master!" Filo was in her monster form. Perhaps due to her further increase in levels, she was showing off what she could now turn into. She was a higher class of monster from the humming fairies in the field guide. I thought for a moment and the name came to me— humming cockatrice. I'd thought a cockatrice was a monster with the power to turn people into stone, but this one was a bit different—with the power to control sound waves.

It was basically a big chicken. But appearance-wise, she had feathers a bit of a different color from her filolial queen form. She could fly like that too, which I couldn't get my head around.

Enough about Filo, anyway.

"Now that we have a read on Kizuna's location, should we prepare to set out?" I asked.

"Indeed. We should proceed with as much secrecy as we can afford," Glass said.

As the discussion continued, a ball of light appeared in the room.

"What's this? Did someone cast some magic? Raphtalia?" I asked. She could use light magic, so it would be easy for her to create a ball like this.

"It isn't me," she replied. So it looked like it wasn't her. If this was some kind of attack magic, I had to be ready to defend against it. Even as I considered my options, the light scattered apart.

What it left behind was . . .

"A mirror?" Glass said. That's exactly what it was. A mirror, which I remembered seeing when I was here before. It had appeared in the middle of the room.

"What's the mirror vassal weapon doing here?" someone shouted.

"Don't ask me," I replied. The mirror showed no intent to attack us. It just floated in the air for a while and then started to unleash a blinding light.

"What's going on now?" I asked.

"I've seen this before!" L'Arc said. "When we came to get you, the mirror did the same kind of thing!" Right. That was after we defeated Kyo, when Kizuna and the others had come for us. I blinked a few times and then looked around . . .

"Where are we now?" We were together in an old, extremely dusty-looking room. I looked out the window. It looked like some kind of house. Outside the window, the surrounding area was quite overgrown, suggesting no one had touched this place for a while.

Back inside the room, there was an old mirror on the wall. So the mirror vassal weapon had the ability to transport things using other mirrors as a medium. That seemed pretty conventional and convenient—one advantage of having a funky weapon, perhaps.

In the room with me was Raphtalia, Filo, Sadeena, Shildina, Rishia, Itsuki, S'yne, Glass, L'Arc, Therese, Ethnobalt, Raph-chan, and Chris.

"Where are we?" I repeated.

"No idea . . . but the way the mirror vassal weapon appeared like that, I think it wants to lend us a hand," L'Arc said. That made sense. The legendary weapons seemed unlikely to try and get in our way without good cause.

"We should be careful, but take a look around," I responded.

"I'll use some illusion magic and take a look," Raphtalia suggested.

"Raph!" Raph-chan wanted to go too. The pair of them together could handle anything that might come up while scouting.

"Should I go too?" Filo asked.

"Just because you can fly, don't drop your guard. Be careful," I told her.

"Sure thing!" she said.

A short while later, Raphtalia finished her scouting and returned. The place was apparently an abandoned house deep in the mountains. There didn't seem to be anyone else here.

"Let's get moving and try to find some people," I said.

"This is pretty exciting!" L'Arc was in good spirits, as always. Now that he had the scythe back, he was probably spoiling for a fight.

"If the mirror vassal weapon helped us get here, I would think this is close to the location that Chris indicated," Ethnobalt said. I agreed with him. That definitely sounded right to me. That said, the vassal weapons could sometimes pull some odd stuff too. We definitely needed to proceed with caution.

Regardless of how strong we had become, we didn't need to just butcher anyone we came across. That would make us no different from Takt. The best move would be to remain undiscovered, just take down our target, and get Kizuna back. We could retreat easily enough using a portal. If our retreat was impeded in some way, we'd work something out.

As I was considering our situation, my shield arm started to tingle. I checked it over a couple of times but didn't find the cause. So was I just imagining things?

We left the abandoned house and headed toward civilization.

Chapter Eight: Subterranean Maze City

We arrived in civilization—a town in a certain nation. The buildings had a definite Western style. Things were also a bit steampunky, with various machines on display. It seemed pretty rare in this world of mainly Japanese-styled nations.

We decided to head into town after Raphtalia put some illusion magic on our faces, just enough to stop anyone from potentially being recognized. Checkpoints were a fixture in Kizuna's world, but it looked like we were already inside.

The gate at the entrance to the town looked like it had been left open. It didn't look like there were many guards either.

"There's a guild that services this nation, right? Let's find out exactly where we are," Glass suggested. Then she headed with Ethnobalt toward the guild to check things out. They returned pretty quickly.

"As expected, this is the country where the musical instrument vassal weapon holder is," Glass revealed.

"Incredible. It brought us to a town close to our destination," L'Arc said. I mused for a moment about how great it would have been if we'd been moved to the closest town to Kizuna immediately after defeating the guy who stole L'Arc's scythe.

Anyway. I looked over at the killer whale sisters.

"Sadeena, Shildina, make sure to look as close to human as possible. No going therianthrope when there are prying eyes around," I warned them.

"Oh my," Sadeena said. "But prying eyes are the best!"

"Why are you saying this?" Shildina asked.

"Don't you see? The demi-humans in this world and the demi-humans in our world are slightly different," I said. The ones here were more like elves or dwarfs. Those like Raphtalia, with animal ears, were much rarer. "Make sure to keep your characteristic ears and tails hidden. Raphtalia, you've been undercover before, right? You know what to do," I said.

"True, but this miko outfit probably stands out," she replied.

"Good point. Can't you use magic to make it look like you're wearing normal armor?" I asked.

"I don't understand your obsession with this miko outfit, Mr. Naofumi," Raphtalia said.

"Raph," said Raph-chan.

"I'm sorry, dear lady Raphtalia, but I can see his point of view. Kiddo here has clearly taken quite a liking to that outfit of yours," L'Arc said, providing some completely unexpected support. I mean, he wasn't wrong. I was just a little embarrassed to admit it.

"I do understand why you are asking, but if the magic is

noticed by anyone and it puts them on guard, then it will have been pointless," Raphtalia said. Maybe she was feeling a little embarrassed too, because her cheeks were flushed slightly red.

"Oh my, we are quite jealous over here," Sadeena said.

"We have our own ethnic costumes we can wear!" Shildina added.

"If you could stop that bickering, that would be great," I told them. I was trying not to let it get to me, but talk about ethnic clothing always made me think of Atla.

"Very well. Oh, little Shildina, how inconsiderate of you!" Sadeena chided.

"Shut it! Okay then, sweet Naofumi, how about you tell us what to wear?" Shildina replied.

"I mean . . . you two don't look especially demi-human so long as you don't go therianthrope, and your clothing probably won't stand out much either," I reflected. Maybe it was just that they had slightly different skin. It just looked like their hair was a tail, but that could be considered a strange fashion choice.

"L'Arc, do you think we could explain it away by saying they have odd tattoos?" I asked.

"Huh. Yeah, I guess so. If they want to keep exposing so much skin—something I'm all for, by the way—we can cover it easily by saying they are using a fashion accessory called an imitation jewel, which lets you become a Jewel," L'Arc explained. There was a race called "Jewels." They had all sorts of different gemstones as their cores. They probably came in all sorts of different colors. Saying that would be enough to cover up the appearance of the sisters though. It indicated some serious blind spots in my understanding of fashion in this other world.

Then I recalled that there had been similar fashion in Silt-velt—fake tails, if I remembered correctly. Demi-humans who didn't like the shape of their tail wore an accessory a bit like a wig to give it more volume. I also recalled thinking it might have been nice to give Raphtalia and Raph-chan fluffier tails.

"Therese probably knows more about that. She's a Jewel, after all," L'Arc said.

"Leave it to me. Yes . . . from their external appearance, I should think most people will presume them to be Jewels," Therese explained.

"Something else we definitely have to watch out for is language. Speaking an unknown tongue is definitely going to get eyes on you. Say as little as possible. Also, Shildina, you stick close to Sadeena at all times," I said.

"Why?" Shildina retorted.

"Because your sense of direction sucks," I reminded her. In just the last few days, Shildina had gotten lost in L'Arc's castle numerous times. That was exactly the main reason why I had wanted to leave her behind. "If we get split up here, we'll never be able to meet up again! Would you be okay with that?"

"No!" she exclaimed.

"So there you go. If you don't want to stick with Sadeena, you can stay close to Filo instead," I told her.

"Filo? Okay!" Shildina replied. Filo had experienced all sorts of troubles when she found herself alone in this world. She knew the deal. She could also fly up and spot Shildina from the air if she had to.

"Oh my," Sadeena said.

"In any case, killer whale sisters, you must not become therianthropes when there are other people around," I impressed upon them again. "Understood?"

"Oh, little Naofumi." Sadeena gave a laugh and a nod at my cautioning, like she did when she was messing about. "Women sometimes like to be restricted. If you wish to gaze upon our demi-human forms, I can resist my other urges."

"Yes, yes, whatever. You need to read the situation and keep a low profile, understand?" I told her.

"I understand!" she replied.

"Raphtalia, just keep your ears and tail hidden as much as possible," I said.

"Okay," she agreed. There wasn't much to worry about for Rishia and Itsuki . . . and then the rest of the group was originally from this world.

"Do we have money to prepare everything we need for the infiltration?" I asked.

"Naofumi, hold on." With that, L'Arc took out a coin from

inside his clothing. It reminded me of the silver coin-like cur-
rency I had seen when first being summoned. Then Glass and
Ethnobalt also took out their own money.

"It might be hard to buy really nice stuff for everyone, but
we've got this much," L'Arc said.

"That's right," Glass added, both of them holding up silver
coins with holes in the middle.

"Why do you have that with you?" I asked.

"Before the waves occurred . . . we visited many different nations and so carried various currencies with us," Glass
explained.

"But we kept the cash away from Kizuna," L'Arc commented. She sold things for cash whenever she needed it. Just
taking her personality into account, I decided it was better to
leave the money in the hands of her allies. She was probably
pretty wasteful.

"That said, we won't be able to rent lodgings with this
many people," L'Arc clarified.

"Just take a portal back. Anyway, getting back Kizuna is
our priority. We'll make some money when and if we need it.
Okay?" I asked.

We left the town without sticking out and headed toward
the spot where Kizuna was being held. We had to follow Chris's
directions, but every now and then, Chris would tilt his head
with a puzzled look on his face. Sometimes he seemed unsure
of the way to go.

Following the unsteady direction of Chris . . . after two days, we reached a hill from which the castle and accompanying town of the enemy country could be seen.

I wondered what was going on with the castles in this country. They built a platform, like a steel frame using truss towers, beyond a massive castle gate and then built the castle elevated on that. They had a pretty cunning design, quite different from the architecture seen in Melromarc, Faubrey, or Siltvelt. Getting inside looked like it would be a real pain.

"Why didn't the mirror vassal weapon drop us closer to Kizuna?" I pondered aloud.

"To avoid throwing us right into battle, maybe?" L'Arc responded.

"Hmmm." Not a bad answer. That said, with our current strength, we should have been able to handle it. *Right?*

My shield arm had been tingling for a while now. I really just hoped it was because Kizuna was getting closer.

I was also starting to get a nasty feeling about all this. I decided we had better stay even more alert.

"Kiddo Naofumi," L'Arc said. Now he was trying to apply his "kiddo" in the same way he often used "lady" for a woman. He really thought he could get away with it.

For a moment, I thought about seriously trying to take Therese off him.

"Naofumi?" he addressed me again. Having noticed the

look in my eyes, he gave a gentle cough and adjusted his form of address.

"Yes?" I finally replied.

"After we save lady Kizuna, what then?" he asked.

"What do you mean 'what then'? Aren't you planning on putting an end to this upstart of a vassal weapon holder?" I said.

"Not that. I mean, how do we escape?" L'Arc asked.

"Right, that," I said. This might not be the same as the Takt situation, in which chopping off the head of the leader would necessarily cause the military of this nation to surrender. In Takt's case, the coalition army led by Melromarc had already wiped out the Faubrey army. And even in the case of defeating the guy who stole the scythe, L'Arc's forces had proceeded to wipe out any remaining resistance. There were all sorts of possible plays, including just muscling our way through or taking out their leadership and calling for a surrender. But there seemed a high possibility of something going wrong this time.

"What is the reputation of this musical instrument vassal weapon holder in this nation?" I asked. "It will make a difference if the holder is the top of the food chain or a lower-ranking general or something like that."

"They hold a position known as the successor to the king, if that means anything," Ethnobalt explained. That meant dishing out some punishment would probably cause others from the nation to retaliate in revenge. It wasn't like we had a big party along. If they thought they could crush us with numbers, I mean, they were probably right.

"L'Arc, do you want to occupy the nation of the musical instrument vassal weapon holder?" I asked him.

"Doing that would definitely damage the trust placed in us by other nations. We just kind of restored that, but we're still facing a lot of opposition, so I'd rather avoid that if I can," L'Arc confirmed. They had Kizuna and a number of other vassal weapon holders, after all. That could definitely make them a threat, from the perspective of military force. If I took an example from my own modern society, it would be like trying to sue for peace by threatening an opponent—even if that did feel necessary in peace negotiations sometimes . . .

"Why don't you aim to unify the world?" I asked.

"That's the same idea as some of the problematic vassal weapon holders, Naofumi," L'Arc said, an edge in his voice.

"Yes . . . I guess that's true," I replied. We were acting to punish those attempting to achieve world domination. We weren't about to go and try the exact same thing. The stance held by Kizuna and Glass was to punish these vassal weapon holders who prioritized their own greed at this time when everyone should be coming together to fight for the sake of the world. They wanted to take a route that would leave their nation unimpeachable. That seemed like a hard position to maintain in the face of the deaths among the four holy heroes. But humans were not simple enough creatures to just accept something in the face of such circumstances.

"We don't have time to be fighting amongst ourselves. If there is an issue, we may need to make threats to contain it or we will be defeated by the waves and wiped out," Glass said. She seemed to have a better handle on that side of things.

"Still, I'm just trying to make sure we can secure an escape route for this many people," L'Arc said.

"It's a fair concern," I conceded. "After the rescue though, I'm pretty sure we'll be able to get out with portals that Itsuki and I will provide." There wasn't going to be some annoying barrier like in Q'ten Lo. So long as we could use the portals, we'd be fine.

"Before that though . . . Ethnobalt, what are you training for at a time like this?" I asked. He was using what looked like dumbbells to work on his arms. The other day, I had seen him doing circuits of the castle garden while walking on his hands. His training with Rishia was showing considerable results, and while not a hero, he was definitely awakened.

"Ah, I'm sorry. It's just become a habit," he explained, abashed. Why was it that every intelligent friend I made slowly turned into a muscle-brain? It was an annoyance to have to caution him about it too. I decided to just prioritize the operational meeting with L'Arc and the others.

"First things first, even if we want to take action, shouldn't we start by investigating exactly where lady Kizuna is?" L'Arc reasoned.

"I'd love to just charge in there head-on . . . but I guess that's not an option," I said. Once you experienced enough combat to truly believe being strong meant you could do whatever you liked, that was when you started to overlook the important details. I could see how the heroes often got self-conceited. I needed to be careful of that.

If we just rushed in and Kizuna got killed, all of this would be for nothing.

That might allow us to call in new heroes, but losing someone we knew was too painful. That had to be avoided at all costs. It sounded like Kizuna was in a pretty weakened state too.

"So before instigating the main operation, we need to do some scouting. We don't have any time to waste, so I'll go locate the building where Kizuna is being held. L'Arc, you go and check out the dragon hourglass. Everyone not joining us, avoid being alone. Just pretend to be regular people and scout the region," I ordered.

"That works. I'll go and take a look at the dragon hourglass first. Seeing as she doesn't understand what people are saying, I'll take a drinking sister along with me," L'Arc said.

"Oh my! I would rather go with little Naofumi, if possible," Sadeena said.

"This place is a key position. Sadeena, I really need you to use your sound waves to check out the defenses around the dragon hourglass," I asked her. I was pretty sure we could escape via portal, but we also didn't know what might happen. We needed as many options as possible.

"If that's what you want, little Naofumi, then no problem. You just keep little Raphtalia safe," she told me.

"I will," I promised. Then Shildina put up her hand.

"What about me?" she asked.

"You want to get lost that badly?" I asked her. She slumped her head.

"I'll stick with her!" Filo said cheerfully. She was gripping the morning star that Romina had modified for her—it was now more of a bolas—and looked ready for action. I was willing to bet she could just charge into battle and smash her bolas into the enemies as she passed them. According to Romina, it was now a pretty convenient weapon, able to both be copied as a projectile by Rishia and by Kizuna's weapon too. Three birds with one stone—now that was good work.

"If anything happens, I will be there," S'yne said. She stuck a small pin into my armor. She was suited to this, being able to both check out our escape and the enemy terrain. With that, then, L'Arc was going to take Therese, Sadeena, Shildina, Filo, and S'yne and go check out the dragon hourglass.

"We'll gather information around the taverns and guild,"

offered Itsuki, taking Rishia and Ethnobalt along. That left me, Raphtalia, Glass, Chris, and Raph-chan.

Divided up into three parties, we headed into the capital of the enemy nation.

"Pen!" Chris said. The entrance to the town looked . . . less guarded than expected, actually. The place looked like a peaceful castle town, totally free from the threat of the waves. I looked up at the big castle built on top of the iron towers. It definitely blocked the sunlight down here a bit. Having a castle on top of what was basically loads of Tokyo Towers was a pretty bizarre construction, all things considered.

We proceeded through the town. Chris led the way with his Kizuna-detector ability. We had to be pretty careful not to attract any attention, but I was pretty sure we'd be okay. We were just using a peculiar shikigami, that was all.

We made it through the main street and passed through the back alleys, then along a side street. Chris's detection still cut off every now and then, but maybe because we were getting closer, he quickly picked the trail up again.

"I was worried maybe she'd fallen into the never-ending labyrinth again, but it doesn't look like that's the case," I said.

"At least if that was the case, we would know she had a way out," Raphtalia commented.

"When you came here before, you found yourself in a bit

of a tight spot, right?" I asked her.

"I did. Thank you for reminding me," she said, heavy on the irony. "My escape was pretty thrilling, I must admit."

"Seeing as we're talking about Kizuna, she might be stuck there again," I said.

"I don't know. The history of this nation does state that the town was built on top of an underground maze," Ethnobalt explained. This sounded a lot like the nation that had sealed away the Spirit Tortoise.

"I've heard that the underground maze was once a place that adventurers explored," Glass added. From the way she phrased that, I guessed it had already been cleaned out.

There was the never-ending labyrinth anyway and also the labyrinth library to which Ethnobalt belonged. So that suggested this world had its fair share of labyrinthine buildings. In our world, there were apparently a lot of old ruins called dungeons, or dragon's nests, that had gradually been expanded in size. Wyndia, Rat, and Gaelion had told me about such places.

"Itsuki and his party can check out those things. We need to locate where Kizuna is being held," I reminded everyone.

"Of course. Chris, what are you sensing?" Glass inquired. Chris proceeded to make a protracted "pen" noise, placing a flipper on his head and moaning before indicating the direction to take.

Following the directions, we reached a block in the northwest of the town. It almost looked like a factory area. Everything was cramped in with lots of the metal supporting the castle above. There was lots of wire mesh too. It was almost making it hard to tell if I was in another world or my own modern one. The air looked pretty dirty, with smoke billowing from factory-like chimneys.

"Raphtalia, how are you doing?" I asked her. She'd been sick in the past. Polluted air like this could cause her to cough. Now that she had recovered from the sickness itself, she would probably be okay. But it didn't hurt to check in with her.

"I'm okay, for now," she replied. "This air looks horrible."

"Tell me about it. It doesn't look like many people come through here either, which means soldiers might get suspicious if they see us hanging around," I realized.

"No need to worry about that. I also have concealment skills. With Raphtalia here, we should be able to perform a search without standing out." Glass proceeded to spread her fan and then mutter the name of the skill. "Circle Dance: Mist Veil." We were buffeted by the same feeling as when a concealment skill or magic was activated. I hoped this would be enough. These kinds of skills and magic often didn't work very well on monsters—although with their level, or Raph-chan or Raph-chan II, it was possible to achieve complete concealment.

We'd just have to proceed as cautiously as possible.

We carefully pushed our way through the wire mesh and

began poking around. It didn't take long to find a suspicious-looking entrance to some kind of underground facility. There were guards on watch too.

"Pen," said Chris. His flipper was now pointing diagonally down at the ground. Looked like he wanted us to go down from here.

"If we can determine the spot directly above Kizuna, it might be fastest if we all just dug down together," I suggested.

"I can't believe you'd even suggest something so dumb," Glass said, shaking her head.

"You were trying to get us to agree to that?" Raphtalia added, looking appalled. What was wrong with that idea? At least I was making suggestions.

"So? That place does look super suspicious. Are we going in there right away?" I asked.

"We could . . . but it would be risky if we got spotted," Glass reasoned.

"If we get spotted, don't underestimate the magic of Raphtalia and Raph-chan," I told her.

"I'm happy to hear of your faith in us, but I also feel that we need to be careful," Raphtalia said.

"You think?" I asked.

"Yes. I just have a feeling that if we charge down there, we're going to get caught," she said.

"Raph!" Raph-chan added, nodding, seemingly in agreement.

With their transforming powers, I wondered if this was some kind of hunch unique to their talents. I did feel it would be dangerous to charge in there myself. If Raphtalia and Raph-chan felt the same, we should definitely fall back.

"Gotcha. Let's try this again when we're all back together," I decided.

"I think that's for the best," Raphtalia agreed.

"Still . . . you think we're looking at an underground maze?" It did sound a bit adventurous, I had to admit. The gamer in me was excited by the prospect. We observed the enemies a little longer and then left.

When we reached the meeting point, a tavern, L'Arc and the others were already there, waiting.

"Naofumi, how was it? Did you find anything?" L'Arc asked. It looked like Sadeena had started drinking already. She'd been told not to speak much, so she looked pretty bored and listless. She was so cheerful when she talked. I was surprised by how much she looked like S'yne, with this new attitude. Did that suggest that S'yne was actually super talkative and we just couldn't hear her?

Soon after us, Itsuki and his party arrived too.

"Shall we move?" I said. We proceeded to a place below something like an elevated bridge, where I hoped there wouldn't be many people to potentially overhear us. Trolley-like conveyances were passing overhead.

This all felt pretty modern. If the trolleys were running on electricity, I could almost mistake this for Japan.

"Based on Chris's directions, Kizuna is being held underground. The exit looks to be pretty heavily guarded," I explained. What we really needed was some kind of rear entrance or somewhere else that was connected to the maze.

"That does sound dangerous. I don't have any better news either. The dragon hourglass has restrictions placed on it. They don't even let people get close. We were saved by these two and their ability to check things out from outside the building," L'Arc responded.

"We were a vital part of the mission!" Sadeena said. Both she and Shildina looked pretty pleased with themselves. Surely, they needed to turn into therianthropes to use that ability. I wondered if that side of things had been okay.

"They've got pretty tight security," I said.

"They want to stop the vassal weapon holders from other nations getting in here, of course. The information on how to replicate the Return Dragon Vein leaked out too," L'Arc said.

"From you guys?" I asked.

"We have a filter, so we're fine," he replied. So they had that kind of ability too? That sounded pretty convenient to have around. "Lady Sadeena and her sister seemed to suggest the guards were in the middle of experimenting on the dragon hourglass. We collected some info from people living here, which suggested they've been up to something recently."

"I think you already know this, but we can't check it out that deeply," Sadeena said.

"I wouldn't have thought you could," I replied.

"For something involving digging, Imiya would be much better suited to helping out," Sadeena commented.

"No point in bringing up people who aren't here," I said. If she was here, of course, she would have been digging already. For sure.

"S'yne says she casually attached a pin to someone entering the building," her familiar revealed.

"Should we try the same thing at the entrance we discovered?" I suggested. The problem was that we hadn't seen anyone actually going in or out. The guards had been stationed at a smaller building on the ground level, and there was no one actually going inside. Security really was tight.

Having Sadeena check the vicinity with her sound waves was another option.

"However—" S'yne said.

"Yes, I understand. She said that she did place a pin on someone entering the building but then experienced jamming at some point after that. She has a bad feeling about all this," her familiar relayed. Jamming? That was strange. S'yne's teleport skill had the effect of being able to check the state of the destination site. I hadn't heard of her being unable to use it for anything other than physical interference at the site itself. There was a chance that S'yne's skill was just incompatible with Kizuna's world, but the fact that it was being jammed suggested something more sinister was at work. The whole situation made me think of all sorts of nasty possibilities.

"Itsuki, how about you and your team? Did you find anything out?" I asked.

"Some things, yes," he replied. "The area you were investigating is top secret and so regular adventurers can't find out anything about it. But we did obtain information on part of the underground maze," he said. With that, Rishia and Ethnobalt brought out a copy of a map of the underground maze.

"It appears there's a maze below this town, with the layers closer to the surface having already been reasonably mapped," Ethnobalt explained.

"Hmmm. Based on the location of the castle town, I'm thinking around here . . ." I traced over the map. We also had to consider an infiltration through the maze . . . Then I noticed something.

"The first three levels have been significantly developed, creating an underground city. The state management block is not on the map, however," Ethnobalt explained.

"Control of information, huh? That sure sounds suspicious," I said.

"Shall I explain what else we discovered?" Itsuki asked.

"You have more?" I asked.

"Yes. Some other suspicious points," Itsuki continued. Rishia and Ethnobalt looked at each other, seemingly unsure of what he was talking about. "First, I'll tell you about the musical instrument vassal weapon holder. He is also from another world—apparently, he's Japanese. His name is Hidemasa Miyaji."

"Okay. So he's like one of your problematic holy hero types, huh?" I said.

"I think so, but that isn't the issue," Itsuki replied.

"So what is?" I responded.

"I think the route by which he became a hero is strange. Please confirm this for me, Naofumi," he said.

"Go ahead," I told him. Itsuki prompted Ethnobalt to take over. Among the gathered members, Ethnobalt was the one who could read the best. Rishia was almost genius-level smart—it was true—but not enough to even read a language after such a short time.

"We found an article telling how the musical instrument vassal weapon holder Hidemasa came to be selected. According to this, he was just a regular person who got caught up in the summoning when the four holy heroes were called," Ethnobalt explained. What did "caught up in it" mean? Did he get caught up when the heroes selected by the holy weapons were summoned?

"Is that true?" I asked.

"I can only say that it does appear to be the truth. However, he doesn't appear to have any connection to the heroes of the holy weapons or anyone back on their original world. Various stories seem to back all this up," Ethnobalt replied. There were all sorts of ways to get summoned to another world, that much was true. All I had to do was read a book, while Ren, Itsuki, and Motoyasu had all been about to die when they were summoned. Kizuna had just thought she was playing a game and ended up in a whole different world as a result. "He vanished the same day he was summoned," Ethnobalt continued, "and the next time he appeared, he had the heavily guarded musical instrument vassal weapon. Then he pulled the musical instrument vassal weapon out in front of everyone. When he did that, he also explained that he was from another world."

"Still, this is all very odd," I said.

"Indeed . . . very odd." Itsuki nodded at my comment. "When a hero is summoned, they obtain their weapon immediately after being summoned, correct?" That was right. That was how it had been for me and the other four holy heroes. It was how it had surely been for Kizuna. When people from another world were summoned, they already had their weapons by the time they arrived. Which meant this Hidemasa Miyaji character had not only been caught up in someone else's summons but arrived without a weapon.

The weapon was the thing that translated the language, right? Without a weapon, he wouldn't have even been able to understand what the people here were saying.

The order of events was all wrong. I hadn't heard of a situation of someone getting caught up in a summons either. The weapons selected an individual and summoned them, right? So how was it possible for someone else to get caught up in that?

I could see why Itsuki thought this was all a bit fishy. Hadn't the people of this country thought the same? Still, he'd managed to pull out a weapon that normally you needed to be selected to use, so they had probably passed it off as just being a good result.

"These sources on this story could be in error," Ethnobalt stated, playing it carefully. "We cannot state for a fact that this happened."

"Still, do you think the guy can be reasoned with?" I asked. At my question, both Ethnobalt and L'Arc tilted their heads. After snatching Kizuna away from her original captives, he was now playing dumb about it. If he could be negotiated with, he wouldn't be hiding the fact he had her. If we were going to have a discussion with him, we could do it after we got Kizuna back.

We could also have Kizuna use her arbitration power to determine whether he was worthy as a vassal weapon holder. If he had been selected justly, then the vassal weapon should remain with him. If it departed . . . then something else was going on here—an increased likelihood of him being a vanguard of the waves, for sure. So after the genius, now we had someone from another world who had been caught up in a summoning? I really hoped he was someone we could talk to.

"Where is this Mr. Hidemasa to be found, anyway?" I asked. I hoped he was like Kyo, off doing something or other in the hinterlands or elsewhere in his territories. Maybe he was out fighting monsters and wouldn't be back for a while. That would be nice. Still, it seemed unlikely he would capture Kizuna and then just waltz off somewhere else.

"We have witnesses who place him in the castle today," Ethnobalt responded. It looked like maybe we'd got unlucky with our timing. I really want to take care of things without bumping into the guy.

"Something else . . . Ah, no, it's nothing. Never mind. It's impossible, after all," Itsuki said.

"Now you have to tell me," I responded.

"When we were searching a tavern back there, I thought I heard some familiar voices mixed in among the patrons," he said.

"Familiar voices?" I prompted. Itsuki looked over at Rishia for a moment.

"Fehhh . . ." She just made her usual useless sound—so she probably hadn't seen anything.

"Who did you hear?" I asked again.

"It sounded like Mald," he finally replied. *Who?* I'd heard that name somewhere before . . . Had to be a friend of Itsuki's and someone he was close to . . . from the way he said the name. Maybe it was that one guy he'd had under his command . . . Armor, right? Maybe "Mald" had been his real name.

In any case, it definitely had to be Itsuki's imagination. This was Kizuna's world, after all. The worlds hadn't been connected by the waves, so I couldn't see any way he could possibly be here. All of those guys had been missing since they manipulated Itsuki in Zeltoble, anyway.

Thinking about it now, they had sided with Witch and yet hadn't been with Takt. It was far more likely they were still in that world, up to no good. But I also couldn't really imagine Itsuki lying in his current state.

"Maybe it was just, you know, someone who sounded like him," I said.

"Yes. I think that has to be it," Itsuki agreed. I understood why he wouldn't like it to be him. He did nothing but cause trouble.

"Okay. We've collected quite a lot of information. Now we have to decide what to do with it," I said. There were all sorts of ways to run away, but getting in there was going to be a lot harder. Raphtalia's and Raph-chan's instincts suggested that we'd still be spotted even if we used magic and concealment skills. That said, there was a limit to what we could do by just creeping along and hiding.

"The sun is setting. Not a bad time for some sneaking," I said. If we could use the cover of darkness to sneak into the secret facility where Kizuna was being held, steal her back, and then immediately portal away, that would be that. If things went smoothly, we could also "discuss" the matter of Kizuna's abduction with the vassal weapon holder. And if we didn't like what we heard, well, we'd take care of him too.

I hoped it would all work out . . . but we couldn't just stand here wringing our hands either. Ideally we would find a safe route and take back Kizuna without them even spotting us. The biggest threat was having the musical instrument vassal weapon holder spot us and take Kizuna hostage. If he brought her out in front of us, like Takt had done, then all sorts of problems to save her presented themselves. It was better not to presume he would be that stupid. That was definitely something to avoid.

I still couldn't shake the feeling that there was a trap here we just weren't seeing. But I also felt that, whatever the trap was, we could break through it using Liberation Aura X. If these vanguards of the waves were all like Takt, unable to bring out the full power of their vassal weapons, then however hard they tried, we would still have the advantage.

And yet . . . I was hardly the Wisest King of Wisdom, but I definitely had a bad feeling about this. I was scared of something happening like when we fought Kyo, with L'Arc and the others summoned away by a wave right in front of our eyes.

Then there was the issue of Itsuki's old comrades. All sorts of materials fanned the flames of my unrest.

"Did you find out what weapon power-up methods the musical instrument vassal weapon holder knows?" I asked.

"Well . . . when Kizuna made contact with the other three holy heroes, we sat down and had a chat . . . and found out quite a lot then," Ethnobalt said.

"Glass, what about you? And, Raphtalia, you too," I asked.

"The other three, apart from Kizuna, were pretty stingy, it seems . . ." Raphtalia said, giving a roundabout answer. It was true that Kizuna wasn't the best type of person to be handling such negotiations. She'd probably offered up her own secrets in exchange, or something like that.

"The allies of the other heroes were pretty vocal with their distrust. Kizuna shared hers, to try and win them over, but she was the only one. Then there are probably leaks from Yomogi's old allies and the traitor who stole L'Arc's scythe. We can't be sure he hasn't heard about some of them," Ethnobalt analyzed. I guessed it was lucky that none of the other three holy heroes had shared their power-up methods. But there was always the chance they had been forced to talk before they were killed, of course. Perhaps it was through the use of more hostages.

This all meant that the enemy might have knowledge of more power-up methods than we did. Even if that was the case, though, I was pretty sure they wouldn't be maximizing their potential.

"Whatever the trap is, we aren't going to make any progress until we spring it. Rather than sitting around waiting, we are better off charging in before we miss our chance completely. Even if the enemy does use Kizuna as a hostage, they can't afford to kill her," I reasoned. The ironic thing about hostages was that they only had value for both parties when they were alive. If Kizuna died, then we would surely just rip them to pieces.

We weren't dealing with a moron here. Takt hadn't understood that at all. *He* had been a moron.

"Leave the intimidation to me," I said.

"You are unpleasantly confident. With you on our side, Naofumi, it almost feels like we're the bad guys," Glass said.

"If they use the hostage as a shield and won't respond, I'll intimidate them to make an opening. Then we grab Kizuna. We can think about classifications of good or bad after that," I responded. I could be evil, and Kizuna could be good. I was only a guest in this world, after all. I could shoulder a negative persona. No worries about that.

"I don't like to rely on you so heavily, but if it comes down to it, I also think you can handle anything that comes up. Very well. Intimidate away, if you have to," Glass said.

"That said . . . sometimes I have to make cold, hard decisions. Don't expect too much from me, Glass," I added. We weren't dealing with a foe who would respond to a diplomatic appeal to free the hostage. They wouldn't go for anything we dangled in front of them, be it money or weapon power-up methods. If we shoved proof of their crimes right in their face, they would just fall back to using Kizuna as a hostage. I had real trouble understanding how they were being this selfish when the world was in such danger.

Ren, Itsuki, and Motoyasu might have been wanting to have some fun using their game knowledge, but they hadn't considered taking over the world. If we couldn't settle this with discussion, we would have to use force. That was probably exactly what they wanted too.

"I understand," Glass replied. "I am prepared for that eventuality."

"Let me break down what I consider a good plan, then. First, Raphtalia, Rishia, and anyone else good at concealment will sneak into the facility to take back Kizuna. If that works out, we just escape right away," I said. That was the first stage and the best possible operation. If Trash was here, maybe he would have a better proposal. "If whatever Raphtalia fears is what causes them to be discovered, we will charge in to help. If that happens, L'Arc will lead a team at the same time to attack the dragon hourglass and cause confusion among the enemy. This is a gray area—about as close to black as you can get. But if we can get evidence of their wrongdoing, we will be in the right. Don't worry about the diplomacy side of things until afterward," I said.

"Sure thing! We just need to take them down, right?" L'Arc said.

"Yeah. You'll be acting as a diversion too, so make it as loud and noisy as you can," I said. Even if the musical instrument hero appeared over there, that would still suit us. That could buy us the time we needed to save Kizuna.

"Just to prepare for the worst . . . what if an enemy appears who can steal vassal weapons?" Therese asked. That was a good question.

"As a pre-operation preventative measure, I'll cast Liberation Aura X on everyone. That worked wonders against Takt. First use the element of surprise to quickly capture the dragon hourglass. If the effects of the aura run out, consider retreating, depending on the situation. Use Return Dragon Vein to escape if you have to, and go get reinforcements," I said. There were no rules saying we couldn't attempt the same moves that Kyo and Trash #2 had tried to use. L'Arc could use Return Dragon Vein to bring in a horde of his own soldiers, if he had to. There was a chance of weapons being taken. But with the boosted stats, L'Arc might be able to avoid having his weapon stolen. Or he might have gained some resistance to the attack after having experienced it once already. Since the increase to Liberation Aura X, the length the aura lasted had also significantly increased. If they couldn't take the dragon hourglass before the effects ran out, then the operation would basically be a failure.

The joint operation would be a good way to smash through enemy defenses. Even if one of the parties failed, success for the other one would still have a positive effect.

"If anyone looks like they are going to pull such a move . . . Therese." I drew my thumb across my throat. "Prove how much stronger that accessory has made you."

"I will! If you so order it, Master Craftsman. I will defend L'Arc and the others while defeating our enemies!" Therese even gave a salute as she responded. I wasn't especially comfortable with that, and it didn't look like L'Arc was either.

"Oh my . . . I think we have our work cut out for us, little Raphtalia," Sadeena quipped.

"Indeed we do. We'll have to up our game," Raphtalia replied.

"Let's start the operation," I said. Everyone started moving to put the operation into action.

Chapter Nine: Outsider Theory

Hidden by the cover of darkness, we started to follow the plan I had laid out.

First, those skilled at concealment or light on their feet—that being Raphtalia in the first instance, Rishia in the second, and then Raph-chan, Chris, Glass, and Sadeena—would go ahead in concealed status to enter the underground facility where Kizuna was likely being held. As the backup unit in case anything went wrong, Itsuki, Shildina, Filo, Ethnobalt, and I would wait outside. At the same time, L'Arc, Therese, and S'yne had gone to launch the diversion and capture the dragon hourglass.

"It's time," Raphtalia said.

"Go ahead," I told her. Of course, I had cast Liberation Aura X on everyone before they left. L'Arc and his party had definitely set off for the dragon hourglass with a spring in their step. I'd just told them to get the job done.

Raphtalia and her party looked at me. I nodded.

"Hey, what's going on here?! Uwha—!" Raphtalia quickly suppressed a guard that looked up at the light as she opened the door by knocking him out, binding him, and rolling him into the shadows. Then she proceeded inside the building.

She made it look easy, to be honest. I recalled other times when she used her infiltration abilities to save people. All sorts of problems had occurred during those incidents, but we always made it through.

About five minutes into the operation, searchlight-style beams came from the castle. At the same time, the Raph-chan icon appeared in my field of vision. Was Raph-chan asking to be called back?

"C'mon, Raph," I said.

"Raph!" Raph-chan said, popping out in front of my eyes. "Raph! Raph, raph!"

"Something happened?" I asked.

"Raph!" she confirmed, nodding. Just then, some huge firework-like lights went up in the direction of the dragon hourglass. S'yne was using her ability to watch both Raphtalia and me from a distance, and she was relaying the information to L'Arc. The firework-like magic was the signal they were starting the attack on the dragon hourglass.

I glanced behind me to check on everyone else, then dashed to the entrance to the underground maze and went inside. Itsuki and the others followed behind.

The underground facility was a well-maintained—no, especially "fantasy"-like—concrete building. It looked like it was just corridors.

"Any observation devices . . . have already been destroyed

by Raphtalia and the others," I noted. The remains of magical devices of some sort could be seen scattered about. This was a time for emergency measures, so it didn't matter if we triggered any such devices anymore. I deployed Shooting Star Wall and we plowed onward, simply ignoring any traps.

We'd only waited for about five minutes, so it hadn't been that long yet. I was sure we'd catch up with them pretty soon.

Even as I had that thought . . . "Raph!" Raph-chan said, calling us to a stop in a place, presenting us with the choice of going down another level. There was a door in front of us. It was silent.

"Raph, raph!" Raph-chan said. She was telling me not to touch the door, clearly.

"Is there something on the other side?" I asked.

"Raph! Raph!" she said emphatically. Then she pointed at the ground and repeatedly jumped up and down. "Raph! Raph!" This time her intonation was different. Like she was saying . . . "portal shield"?

"A teleportation trap, perhaps?" Itsuki muttered, almost exactly at the same time I thought of the answer myself.

"That's right. Upon entering this room, they were immediately sent somewhere else," Ethnobalt said. *If you understand what she's saying, maybe speak up sooner!*

"That's right!" said Filo, adding insult to injury.

"Okay then. I'd thought we could muscle our way through

whatever traps came up, but a teleportation trap is a different matter," I pondered. If this had been a pit trap or something like that, it wouldn't have given Raphtalia and her party any trouble. We didn't even know if her instincts had worked here, or if they had failed her.

Still, with the sirens ringing out like this, Raphtalia and the others must have been stripped of their concealment and the trap teleported them away.

"Here goes nothing," I said and reached to open the door.

"Raph?!" Was Raph-chan surprised by something? That meant . . . the trap was responding to us. It was likely designed to activate across a wide area and catch up everything within its range.

The ground flashed, and in an instant everything around us changed.

Fair enough. Pretty much the only way to deal with this would be to run from the effect of the trap the moment it was activated. But that was hard to do in a narrow passageway.

"Mr. Naofumi!" I heard someone shout. I looked in the direction of the voice. There was a Japanese-looking guy holding a weapon like a violin, five women, and Raphtalia and Glass standing opposed to them.

"So you're the hero with a holy weapon from another world," the guy with the musical instrument muttered. He was wearing clothing that was mainly black, black hair, and had an uppity-looking attitude. He was likely in his teens. Rather than the youthful coolness of Ren, he had a slightly more mature-type cool about him.

To put it more nastily, I didn't like the look of his face at all.

These guys always liked black. Were they all mentally stuck in middle school? My experience up until now was telling me he was going to be immature. This looked like it might be a bigger pain than expected.

"And you must be this Miyaji guy, huh? The one selected in this world by the musical instrument vassal weapon?" I said.

"My, my . . . an honor to meet you. I am Hidemasa Miyaji, the musical instrument hero," he replied, bowing his head. He just came off as false and slimy. That look on his face, like he saw through everything, really got me riled. Kyo had been similar, with his belief in his own intelligence. But this one looked to be feigning politeness even harder. He started to speak. "I was aware of you since your entry to this underground facility. Fighting a whole bunch of you at once would be most inconvenient, so I decided to split you up," he said. I looked around. We should have all been teleported together, but there was only Itsuki here from my party.

That meant Shildina, Filo, Raph-chan, and Ethnobalt were missing. That also meant Raphtalia and Glass had been split off from Rishia, Sadeena, and Chris. Damn! This complicated things.

"Sneaking into my nation based on some selfish sense of your own justice, and infiltrating key areas without authorization—not to mention your attack on the dragon hourglass—even for a vassal weapon hero, I think these are crimes too serious to forgive," Miyaji said to Glass. "Don't you think?"

"How dare you! We already have proof—proof that Kizuna was brought to this nation. Thanks to a search by a shikigami Kizuna created. We also know that she is being held here," Glass replied. Miyaji gave a high-and-mighty smile at her words, then took a look at the women around him.

"Even if we say we have no idea what you mean, I suspect you won't just give up and go home. I am here, trying to prove my innocence in all sincerity, and this is how you respond? As I suspected, Kizuna Kazayama and her allies think that being heroes gives them the right to act however they please."

"You took part in the murder of the four heroes, and now you're playing the victim—" Glass began.

"Hold on, Glass. I'll handle this." I stepped up in front of her.

"You, a hero from a completely unrelated world, have some opinion? Do you believe you have any right to speak here?" Miyaji said. Wow. In a past life, I would have let that go with a smile and just backed away. *Don't mess with me*, I wanted to say. *I've fought plenty of phonies like you already.*

"Kizuna and I are allies in that we were both summoned

as heroes from another world and are fighting in order to quell
the waves. We've built up a relationship of trust that you know
nothing about. You can't write me off as being unrelated to all
this," I replied. What he was really saying was something a lot
simpler. He was saying this had nothing to do with me, so I
should back off. My response was the first step in the process
of dealing with someone like him—to hit him with the reasons
why I was very much involved: she was an ally of mine.

"However you try to twist it, you aren't responsible for this
world, are you? Whatever an outsider like you says, I don't think
you can influence a hero of this world," he replied. Just as I
suspected, then. He wanted to push the claim that I was just an
outsider, unrelated to the situation, and stop me from getting
into the middle of things. I was only speaking sense, and yet he
had no intention of listening to me.

From this, I could determine he was the same type as Ren,
Itsuki, and Motoyasu. That meant I needed to proceed to step
two.

"Unfortunately for you, I am related to all this. The katana
vassal weapon hero who you see here is originally from the
world I'm responsible for, you see. If this world gets wiped
out, it's going to cause trouble for me too. That's because she's
a resident of the world I'm responsible for and one of my dear-
est companions." I pointed at Raphtalia, making my point that
I was very much invested in this world. Under his logic, that

should change me from someone unrelated to all this to someone who was here to protect someone. "If you want to talk about being unrelated, you might start fulfilling your duties as a vassal weapon hero and stop all this selfish messing about. If you don't, some very related parties are likely to have a problem with you." I turned this talk of being related right back at him, playing things right by the book. I knew this type of person wasn't going to respond to talk, anyway. I'd just have to go on the attack before he replied. I continued. "You could talk with Kizuna and the others and work with them. Or you could try to handle your hero duties in your own way. Why are you choosing to stand against them? If you have a reason, speak. If it's a good one, we might even help you." If he was going to talk about heroes being involved in this world, after all, that presupposed him to actually do the job of one. And yet this Miyaji had resisted making contact with Kizuna and her allies and just run around doing his own thing. I'd wanted to run away from the responsibilities of a hero myself, to start with, so I could even understand where he was coming from. If I'd been able to kill Motoyasu when he attacked me in order to achieve that, I probably would have done so.

"You can certainly talk the talk, can't you?" Miyaji said.

"I could say the same about you. Why are you doing this? Why are you being so hostile?" I asked. Circumstances demanded that we work together, and yet he made no contact with anyone else, holed up in his own nation, seemingly planning something—it was to be expected that we found him hostile. If there was some reason behind all this, like some kind of trauma in his past, we could discuss things.

"I got dragged here against my will, and now you think I should just play nice at being a hero? You have to be joking," he snapped.

"Trust me, I feel exactly the same as you about that," I told him. I'd come a long way perhaps, but there was definitely still a part of me that felt that way. In Miyaji's case, he had been caught up in someone else's summoning, so it was probably even worse for him.

"Naofumi!" Glass was glaring in my direction. I knew what I was doing. This was all just wordplay. I gave a small signal in Raphtalia's direction, and she realized what was going on and calmed Glass down.

I'd decided to fight, and Raphtalia, Atla, and the others helped me. I wasn't going to complain about my lack of choice in being summoned anymore.

"You just want to live it up in another world, do you? I understand that feeling too, but there's no world in which everything will simply go your way. If you have people you care about, you need to work as hard as you can to stop these suspicious waves that are attacking us. And in order to do that, working together with the other heroes makes things a lot easier on everyone. Especially if you were selected by your weapon," I told him. I didn't care especially about him underestimating the waves. That was one point of view. But when the damage the waves did was considered, that surely created all kinds of reasons to fight. Earthquakes, tsunamis, famines, and more; there was no shortage of disasters created by the waves. Certainly, it was no reason to just go off and do whatever you pleased.

He had to think about what people expected from us and why we had to fight. I presumed the people around him were residents of this world. When that same world was in danger of being destroyed by the waves, this was no time for games.

Speaking of games though, maybe that was the problem. The other three heroes had mistakenly thought the waves were just "updates."

"If you sit watching things burn on the opposite shore, wouldn't you think those sparks may eventually reach you—may eventually burn your own stuff down?" I asked.

"I'm not looking to join your merry little band," Miyaji retorted.

"And that's not what I'm asking you to do. You just have to do the bare minimum. But if you start to actually interfere with what everyone else is doing, well, that's when Kizuna, Glass, and the others from this world are going to have to get involved—and you can't complain," I replied. Glass gave a nod at my assertion. She had a stern look on her face. Just because you belonged to the same organization didn't mean you had to be best buddies. Indeed, having lots of people who all thought differently was probably more convenient. But anyone causing trouble for that organization was going to find themselves wiped out.

"Look at you, talking down to me. You have no manners. I'll say that for you." Faced with my impeccable logic, Miyaji just went and shifted the goalposts.

"You expect to be treated with respect? When everything you have said has been rude and ignorant?" I responded. I really wanted him to stop it with the affected airs when he talked, for a start. His own vapid nature was clearly showing through. At least Ren, Itsuki, and Motoyasu had some personality and their own ideas. They had been easier to talk to than this. I continued. "The holy weapons rank higher than the vassal weapons. That's just a fact. Glass and the others are on the same level as you, and you didn't even treat them with respect. This is hardly the best approach for you to take," I warned him. Once we finally met back up with Kizuna, it was definitely worth stripping this guy of his right to his weapon. If a vassal weapon holder was causing too much trouble, their vassal weapon should choose to abandon them. "You're the one who thinks you can just do whatever you like," I quipped. Being a hero wasn't a free pass, and there were consequences for denouncing the deeds of others.

"Shut up. Enough. I don't need to hear anything more from you," Miyaji replied. It didn't look like he was going to respond well to discussion after all. I hadn't even really gotten started yet . . . He was just a kid pretending to play the bigshot.

"You said something about acting in all sincerity, right? That's certainly not what your attitude looks like to me," I told him. I hoped he saw what I was getting at. I wanted to make clear what was different about him and those he was having trouble with.

The vassal weapon heroes had killed the four holy heroes, so I had been told.

If it had just been one of them, Glass and the others would have identified and pinned them down. The holders of the mirror and book vassal weapons were unknown. But this musical instrument hero, Miyaji, was clearly also under suspicion for having killed the three holy heroes. What Glass had just said made that clear to me.

"What you need to do is share some information with us. If you don't know what's going on, then you need to explain why we might suspect you. Tell us what the shikigami has sensed. Explain the reasons for this. Understand? And if you did kill the three holy heroes, and have a reason for that, then you need to share that too," I told him. A reason like when Ren, Itsuki, and Motoyasu had been cursed. What if the dead heroes had declared war on the world and demanded he join them? Fighting back under those circumstances would be quite understandable.

"They were trash, so I killed them!" he replied. That didn't sound good.

"But why were they trash? Were they trying to take over the world or something?" I tried anyway.

"They were getting all full of themselves, thinking they were so strong. So I had to put them right." He wasn't making a convincing case.

"I'm still not seeing your point here. How were they any different from you? There was no need to kill them, right?" I reasoned. Killing people simply due to concepts of strong and weak . . . I hardly knew what to say.

"The weaker they are, the more they yap. If you have a problem with me, you can share it after you've defeated me," he said. He was drunk on his own perceived power, thinking he could do whatever he liked. If he was one of the four holy heroes, I would try to make him see sense and to face the waves with the seriousness they required. But by killing those heroes, he was going in the exact opposite direction of what a hero should do.

"It is a mistake to think being strong allows you to do whatever you like," Itsuki muttered, choosing that moment to join the conversation. I glanced over at him to see him looking at Miyaji with disgust in his eyes. "Power without justice is merely violence. Tell us why you persist in believing that strength is everything?"

"Excuse me, dumbass! What are you rambling about? I've had enough of this, so now I'm just going to shut you all up! Strength is justice! That's all there is to say!" Miyaji replied.

"I see. Then allow us to abide by your rules and deploy our own strength in order to respond to your violence. We can discuss this further after you have been defeated. Do you agree, Naofumi?" Itsuki asked.

"That was the plan all along," I replied. "It looks like it's what he wants, after all." With a nod, Itsuki started incanting some magic. Raphtalia, Glass, and I all readied ourselves too. The effect of Liberation Aura X was still going.

"I, Bow Hero, command the heavens and earth! Transect the way of the universe and rejoin it again to expel the pus from within! Power of the Dragon Vein! Obey now orders from the hero, the source of your power, combining my magic with the power of the hero. Read again the way of all things and lend strength to them all!"

We paused for a moment and stayed alert for any initial attacks from Miyaji and his crew while we waited for Itsuki to start the battle with his magic. In that moment, however, Miyaji gave a chuckle. He took out an ofuda and gripped it in his fist. In that same moment, something passed by us from behind.

If I had to put a name on the sensation, it would have been the curse skills that Motoyasu had unleashed, Ressentiment and Temptation! In the next moment, with a mighty crash, my hand with the shield on it was dragged violently forward.

I gave a grunt of surprise. Itsuki was experiencing the same thing with his bow, which was currently still a gun. I barely had time to wonder what was going on, and faster than I could think, I felt something being . . . removed from me. I looked at the shield.

It was already off my arm, spinning in the air. Then it turned into light and returned to my hand, becoming a small accessory.

What the hell is going on?!

"Oh my!" Miyaji was laughing his head off. "What a stupid look you have on your face, dumbass! I simply can't hold my laughter in!" He laughed even harder, pushing back his hair with one hand.

"Mr. Naofumi!" Now it was Raphtalia shouting for me. Her face was pale.

"What?!" I replied.

"The support magic you applied to us has run out!" she responded.

"What?!" I exclaimed. I checked my status. It was true. The effect of Liberation Aura X had been completely cleaned away. Nullified, perhaps. We had experienced support magic being removed when fighting S'yne's enemies. This could very well have been the same thing.

"Naofumi," Itsuki said, his brow furrowed as he looked at his own hand.

"My incantation of Liberation Down got cut short. I'm trying to start it again, but I can't," he said.

"What?!" I said a third time. Thinking this was some kind of joke, I gave Liberation Aura X a try myself. But there was no sign of the incanting even starting, let alone the magic activating.

"He's sealed off our magic?" I asked.

"No, that's not quite it," Itsuki replied. "When magic is sealed, you simply can't concentrate when you try to cast it. This is something else . . . It isn't incantation interference either . . ." There was no weapon in Itsuki's hands.

"My, my, even I didn't expect such a stunning result! I really wasn't sure it would work until I saw it for myself," Miyaji said. I hated to have to ask him, but it seemed like the only choice. I wasn't even sure he would reply.

"What have you done to us?!" Glass questioned. Thankfully, she beat me to it.

"I heard some arrogant vassal weapon holders had called in aid from another world. That demanded I take steps myself," Miyaji revealed, pointing his musical instrument weapon at us. In that moment, I noticed something—an accessory on his weapon. Takt's weapon had been fitted with the same one. That definitely suggested a link between them. That said, I didn't have the time to think about that now.

I checked my status. Just as when my shield had been taken

before, it had dramatically changed. I had become super weak! Again!

I tried to get my head around the situation.

The strange feeling from a few moments ago had come from the direction of the dragon hourglass. Based on the information received from L'Arc, Sadeena, and the others, this was likely the effect of whatever experiments they were performing with the dragon hourglass.

Was this also why my shield arm had been feeling kind of numb since we arrived here?!

"Well, it would be a shame for you to perish without understanding why. I was able to take your weapons because the holy weapons of this world finally listened to and finally understood what I was telling them. Holy weapons from different worlds are not allowed to interfere with each other. Yet here you are, breaking that rule and rambling on about who should be doing what. You don't have that right! This is the reason why we are in the right, and you have nothing to do with this situation." It was like Miyaji's mouth had suddenly become a machine gun. Takt had been like this. Exactly like this—wanting to explain just how strong he was.

Miyaji had claimed to have gotten the holy weapons to listen to him. Somehow, he had managed to secure the weapons from the dead heroes and now had them doing his bidding.

This was looking like a bit of a crisis. I had no idea of the range on this effect, but I was definitely starting to worry about the party members who weren't here.

"Mr. Naofumi! Are you okay?!" Raphtalia shouted.

"Not really!" I replied. It wasn't like our levels had been reset or anything like that, so we could still fight—or at least I wanted to believe we could.

We couldn't use magic, that much was for sure. I could probably get some life force going and use Muso Activation, but I didn't have a weapon to use. It looked like getting Raphtalia or Glass to pass me some items and support from the rear was maybe all I could do.

"Eat this!" Miyaji placed his bow against the strings of his violin-like musical instrument and started to play. A sound like an explosion immediately rang out with what looked like musical notes being fired toward us at high speed.

"Watch out!" Glass spread her fan large and stepped in front, protecting us by taking the attack. With a shout, Raphtalia also stepped forward, chopping down the notes with her katana. That was all they did, and they both already had pained expressions on their faces and grunts of pain on their lips.

"There's plenty more where that came from! You girls, go!" Miyaji ordered.

"As you command, Master Hidemasa!" one of his women said, and the five of them rushed forward. All of a sudden—

"What?!" another of them exclaimed in surprise.

"Looks like there's panic everywhere." S'yne and her familiar teleported in and engaged the women. Perhaps the technically superior fighter, she clashed with one and then pushed her back. She dashed in on Miyaji, but he immediately fired off more notes, driving her back.

"Where did you pop up from?" Miyaji asked, still at ease. "Are you sure springing such an ambush was a wise move?"

"Yes, I think so. I've had enough of chatting with you," I replied. I meant it too. Really meant it. I had expected him to unleash some kind of trap, but not to stop the shield functioning completely. I just hated the precision behind such an attack! Now we had to fight against the odds again.

"S'yne, what about L'Arc?" I asked her.

"He's fin—" she started.

"He is safe," her familiar said. "Your support magic was removed, but he can still fight, and Therese is giving a good account of herself. I think they will be able to secure an escape route if necessary, just as planned." That was good to hear.

"You still think you can win? How? Without your weapons? Without your strength? This is why morons who try to solve everything by force are such a hassle! I'm disgusted by your inability to imagine a future in which pure strategy defeats you," Miyaji said. I wasn't sure what he was so pleased with himself about. This fight wasn't over yet!

"My, my. You have impressed me again, my dear Hidemasa!"

The statement came from a voice of someone who had just come into the room from a door behind Miyaji. I gave an instinctive, wordless shout upon hearing it, unable to believe my ears and feeling rage fill me.

Raphtalia was the same.

This was the woman who had stood behind Motoyasu and laughed at the sheer despair on my face. The woman who could have just stayed quiet and still manipulated an entire nation into believing terrible crimes had been committed but got personally involved nonetheless and made further claims of rape against me.

As Riyute was rebuilding, she had used her authority as governor to take over, levy a heavy tax on the people, and have her way again, but that plan had failed. She had then tried to manipulate events by pitting Motoyasu against Filo. At every turn, she seemed to be there, trying to turn things to her own ends, and always with a focus of messing with me.

She had even taken advantage of a chaotic situation to try and take the life of her own sister in order to further secure her own position.

"Oh my, what are you looking so shocked for?" she said. She had shown no remorse when punished for these crimes, betrayed Motoyasu—who had trusted her from the bottom of his heart—tricked Ren, corrupted Itsuki, and finally sided with Takt, making her a coconspirator in the death of her own mother! The criminal who was wanted all across our world!

"Darling, you won't get to have things your way this time. Not while we are here. It would be a mistake for you to think a single thing will go your way," she purred.

What the hell was she doing here?!

The scene almost seemed removed from reality, as though I was having a bad dream.

"How? Why?" Raphtalia wasn't taking it well either.

"Since you vanished again, I knew you might pop up anywhere. But I admit—I never expected to see you here," I told her. Things had definitely taken a turn beyond even my wildest imagination. I'd thought she was still just over there, planning evil stuff in our world!

This witch of a former princess, and witch of a woman!

"What do you say, Hidemasa? Have we impressed you by predicting the cowardly strategy adopted by this Shield Fool and showing you the appropriate steps to take?" she said. I was still stunned. After slipping away at the end of the Takt debacle, here she was, looking at us with an unsettling smile on her face. Witch!

Chapter Ten: A Familiar Face

"Indeed. The information you provided is why things have gone so smoothly. I am grateful for your cooperation," Miyaji said and gave his own unsettling smile as he moved over to Witch.

"What are you doing here?! Witch!" I shouted.

"You still dare call me by that silly nickname?! Hidemasa! Do you see now? That's the kind of person he is! Going around calling people by silly nicknames!" Witch raged.

"Nicknames? What are you talking about? That's your real name, as approved by your own parents!" I told her. Every single thing that she did, that she said, just infuriated me more!

"Giving people silly nicknames! Is that something a rational person would do?!" she shouted.

"Let me turn your own logic on you—Outsiders, stay out of this!" I retorted.

"What did you say?!" she raged back. As we sniped back and forth at each other . . .

"Mald . . ." Itsuki, brow furrowed, looked at his former underling, a guy in armor who appeared next to Witch. So he had been right when he thought he heard Mald's voice in the town.

"Don't you dare say my name, you imposter! The evil that seeks to impede our true justice shall leave the stage here!" Armor said, arrogantly dismissing Itsuki.

I could just about understand what they were saying. With the shield removed, I was barely making it through the conversation. I still had an issue with something though.

"Leave the stage?" I repeated. Was this guy kidding?!

"Still . . . how about this, Bow Imposter. If you slay the shield demon standing there, we will accept you as our true ally once again," Mald offered. No! That wasn't good! Itsuki couldn't really think for himself right now. He was getting better but still had a tendency to do whatever people told him to do. Right now, Itsuki and I were about the same strength. I didn't want any needless fighting here.

"Unfortunately for you, I have found something I wish to defend for myself. Mald, I will not obey you," Itsuki said. Interesting! He rejected the orders! Maybe he was coming back to himself at last. Or perhaps it was Rishia's teachings working their magic.

In either case, this was a good—and timely—change.

"Tell me, Mald! Why are you here?" Itsuki asked.

"I have no words to bandy with evil! I would be a moron if I told you how we came to be here!" he stated. I mean, I had to agree with the guy. I'd never heard of a self-proclaimed ally of justice explaining how they got somewhere.

"Let me change the question," Itsuki said, obviously trying again. "Why do you ally yourself with these kinds of people?"

"Why do you think? Because we share the same spirit of justice!"

"Mald, that person standing at your side is the very one who took in that megalomaniac Takt and attempted to use him for her own ends. There's no justice on your side," Itsuki said.

"Takt? He was just a sacrifice to form the foundation of our justice. His violence was purely intended to prove that we are just. We had every intention of swinging that justice hammer, but then you stepped in," Mald replied.

"How many people suffered for your opportunity to deliver that justice? The world does not exist for your selfish justice," Itsuki responded. That was the kind of thing a character would say from the kind of story Rishia probably loved. It was a common trope in manga too, a man of justice trying to correct the mistaken path an ally had taken—by force if necessary. Surely it wasn't actually possible in real life. Armor hadn't said much yet, but his attitude spoke volumes, and he definitely didn't seem like the type to listen to what others had to say.

In any case, it was nice seeing Itsuki being able to hold this kind of conversation. That was definitely progress. Back when we started out, Itsuki himself had been saying things like, "I won't listen to the words of evil!"

"Hah. Whatever you may say, I will never listen to your

false justice!" Armor replied, as arrogant as ever, and then stared me down. "Brainwashing even the Bow Imposter? Your list of crimes only grows!"

"You just look like a bully to me! Your victim won't listen to you anymore, so you're just lashing out at the one who helped them move past you!" I said.

"The impudence! You shield demon! We shall bring you to a fitting end!" This guy sounded like he'd swallowed the complete works of Shakespeare, seriously.

"What have I ever done to you, anyway?" I asked, thrusting a finger at Armor. I was far more concerned about Witch in this situation, but I actually didn't have any idea why Armor would have a problem with me. He certainly seemed to, but probably just because we didn't really see eye to eye. We'd had very little contact, after all.

"As if you don't know! You use your brainwashing power to impede our mighty justice!" he responded. Huh? I had to take a moment. He had jumped so many steps I was having difficulty understanding him. Just what was this guy and his "justice" attempting to achieve?

"Brainwashing? That's what Itsuki was trying to pull with his cursed weapons. I've never tried that," I eventually replied.

"Lies! You, Shield Demon, have taken over the world by brainwashing its people!" Armor ranted.

"What scum! It was bad enough having an outsider come

in and start lecturing me, but now it turns out you have already taken over your own world and so are seeking to do the same here!" Miyaji cut in, jumping more than a few steps himself. I wanted to shout at him to stay silent but managed to maintain what composure I had left.

"If you call gradually achieving good things, building trust with the people, and then bringing reassurance to a nation by defeating a moron proclaiming world domination 'brainwashing,' then sure, that's what I've been doing. However, it's only someone like yourself who would call it that!" I retorted. This wasn't brainwashing. It was trust! Acquired by shouldering my role as a hero and doing whatever I could to spill as little blood as possible while carrying it out. If trust was brainwashing, then anything could be brainwashing! Anything at all!

"Which is exactly why our justice shall crush your evil ambitions!" Armor declared. Exactly why . . . what? All they had done was throw in their lot with this coward and come out to crow about it when the tide turned in their favor.

"Let me ask you this one time. What *is* your justice?" I asked. I wasn't expecting much of an answer.

"Our justice is to create our ideal world of peace in which evil does not exist. Therefore, we will use our strength to end all evil!" Armor replied. I was honestly surprised to discover the existence of someone who actually believed in such textbook-like dictator rhetoric. He had no idea that justice wasn't even on his side, did he?

Itsuki's negative legacy was still here, rooted deep. From Armor's point of view, Miyaji probably wasn't a dictator at all. Armor probably blamed the four holy heroes for everything, including the loss of his reputation due to Itsuki's mistakes, not being able to receive the blessings of being a hero's companion as a result, and not being able to remake the world as he desired. Not to mention, my promotion of the betterment of Melromarc through trade being evaluated as a good thing was clearly pissing him off. His rage seemed purely based in being unable to obtain authority for himself.

I'd had enough of dealing with these crazy idiots. I just wanted to punch them and keep punching until they fell silent.

"Shield Demon . . . no, Shield Demon King and your minions, we true heroes will defeat you!" Armor shouted. Looked like I'd been promoted to a demon king. That did seem fitting for the opponent of heroes, but these guys weren't up the task of defeating such a monster.

Then, with some appropriate clanking and clacking, Armor pulled out an axe set with a dull gemstone.

"That axe! I've seen that before!" It was identical to the axe that Takt had taken out and attacked me with! Why did this guy have one of the seven star weapons?

"You seem surprised," Witch said with a chuckle. "That womanizer was hording all the weapons, so I decided to liberate some of them from him. You're the foolish demon king who let me get away with it," she taunted. My conversation with her had been cut short thanks to Armor, but now I returned my focus to her.

"Witch, what are you doing here?! How did you obtain that axe?" I asked. She belonged to a different world. There should be no way to move between them without a wave—not unless she had some other means, like we had.

"What good will telling you that do? You can't expect a woman to give up all her secrets," Witch replied, smiling as though she had already won this battle. Of course, I recalled that I was dealing with the type of bitch who never, ever told the truth. "That womanizer treated people like property. He was so condescending. The women around him were fawning and annoying. He deserved to die, but we were supposed to be the ones to do it." This "womanizer" she was talking about had to be Takt, of course. She had somehow learned of his defeat and pulled her own vanishing act.

It also sounded like she had been planning to kill him. From my point of view, she had just looked like another one of his harem members. But she made it sound like she'd been setting a trap for him, just like she had with the other heroes.

I didn't think Witch was capable of that, but the background to all this also concerned me. She could move between worlds now. There was something—or someone—behind her, for sure.

"Seriously . . . you could have just let that excitable woman-izer kill you. You made things so inconvenient for me. You are so persistent, so annoyingly persistent! Just seeing you makes me want to throw up," Witch said.

"Right back at you . . . In fact, due to my hatred of your very existence, I can comfortably claim to dislike you more than you dislike me. We have to stop meeting like this—and I intend to make this the last time. So be ready to die," I told her. Her very existence disgusted me to the extent I could be sure my hatred for her face exceeded any malice she bore toward me. I was going to eradicate her from this world as painfully and horribly as possible . . . No, I was going to shred her very soul.

That was the only way to avenge the queen.

"Do you know these two?" Glass asked.

"Yeah. This woman is the one who caused the friendly rela-tionships between the four heroes in my world to completely break down, and the armored guy is one of Itsuki's former allies and a traitor," I replied. They were both former allies of the four holy heroes, that much was true. "To be honest, they are both so horrible there is no defending anything they have done," I explained. "They're just like the companions of the one who stole L'Arc's scythe. The same as them," I told Glass. Understanding the situation, her face hardened further.

"I see. So there's no need to hold back," she replied.

"You've lost your precious weapons, and yet you still think

you can win? You're going to be pathetically defeated again, just like last time," Witch crowed. She really knew how to piss me off, I'd give her that much. Whatever it took, I swore to finish her off!

I took a moment to think about who we had here and the moves we had available.

Our allies here were Raphtalia, Glass, and S'yne. Then there was Itsuki and me, now without our weapons. We also couldn't use any magic or skills. The C'mon Raph that called Raph-chan was also a skill, so we couldn't use that either. I should have called her sooner!

Based on what Miyaji had said, it was the weapons belonging to the members of the four heroes from another world—Itsuki and me—that had been eliminated. I had been hoping to remove his weapon from him, but instead we were faced with not having our own weapons!

"Wonderful, Hidemasa! Let us hurry up and bring an end to these holy heroes and vassal weapon heroes from another world. We have our own mighty ambitions to fulfill, after all!" This came from another woman, speaking as she also came in through the door. She was sounding a lot like Witch already. I felt like putting my head into my hands. *No more bitchy women!*

The newcomer had striking cream-colored hair. She was relatively tall and quite beautiful. A mature woman, but different from Sadeena and Rat . . . and if what she had just said was anything to go by, she was completely ugly and stupid on the inside.

She looked like a variant on Witch, basically.

She was wearing highly revealing clothing that had large buttons placed on it in random places. For some reason, she also reminded me of S'yne. Perhaps it was because her clothing was so similar. The weather here wasn't hot or cold, but while the design was like S'yne's clothing, she was using some kind of fur material as well. The cool, collected look in her eyes—at odds with her actions and appearance—was also the same as S'yne.

"You—" As this woman appeared, S'yne's own gaze became even more intense. It filled her with murderous intent as she rushed forward and attacked the woman with her scissors.

"Well, well, well! If it isn't S'yne," the woman said. The woman stepped forward and took a chain out from . . . somewhere, catching the scissors on it.

I had a real nasty feeling about that chain. It had a gemstone on it, a characteristic of the weapons—including the four holy ones—and the gemstone looked cloudy.

"You move quickly, S'yne. It's been so long since we last met," the woman mocked.

"I won't forgive you—for your betrayal!" S'yne replied, even as the woman easily avoided the follow-up attack from S'yne's familiar. I could tell already that she was skilled in combat.

"You're still harping on that old stuff? Wandering the worlds with that broken-down vassal weapon, seeking revenge? That's why you are stupid. Having such a stupid younger sister is no joke, I can tell you," the woman replied.

"Sister?!" I exclaimed, which drew her attention to me. For some reason, she looked surprised for a moment.

"Well, well, well. I'm so shocked I can hardly speak," she said. That response only served to further enrage me. What had she seen when she looked at me? "Some things don't change, S'yne. But nothing good will come from such stubbornness. Why keep wishing for something that can never come true?" she asked.

"Shut up!" S'yne's emotions were clear even amid her skipping voice, and she swung her scissors in a wide arc at the woman again. The tip of the chain the woman was holding proceeded to strike S'yne in the stomach, sending her flying away with a grunt.

"Dammit!" I grabbed her before she crashed into the wall, wondering exactly what power the woman had used to do that. I was lacking the protections of the shield and was low on strength myself. I had almost been sent flying right along with her.

Shit. If we could use healing magic or skills, we could have defended against this!

"I love to see you on the ground. That's where you belong,"

the woman said, laughing to herself with disgust in her eyes. "Hidemasa, darling! She's my plaything, so even after you've killed these other foolish vassal weapon holders and holy weapon holders from another world, please let her go. Do you understand why I'm asking? She's so rebellious, but I'm looking forward to the day she realizes her rebellion is pointless and she finally joins me."

"I understand completely. It isn't much fun just having lackeys who obey your every word. Having someone like that among your allies brings a real spice to things," Miyaji replied. Spice? What was this, a cooking show?!

With another supremely annoying laugh, the moron woman glanced at the rest of us again.

"I'm not sure what to say. You seem too pathetic and so helpless it makes me want to spoil the method we used to do this to you," she said. So she was just like the rest of them—just like Witch, Kyo, and Takt. She wasn't going to say anything of value! I knew that already!

"You must have grasped that we have suppressed your holy weapons. But you don't understand how, do you? To put it plainly, we have captured all of the holy weapons in this world and used a technique to suppress the power of any opposing holy weapons—nullifying the holy weapons and techniques from other worlds," she patronizingly explained. She had distinctively said "our." That suggested this wasn't something

THE RISING OF THE SHIELD HERO 17   241

Miyaji had come to on his own, but something he had been provided with in order to contain us.

"The medium is the dragon hourglass. It suppresses the holy weapons. This was apparently a defensive mechanism for this world, created by the spirits of the holy weapons. It was to be activated if holy weapons were ever used in an invasion. Of course, it only works on holy weapons, magic, and techniques. It wouldn't be worth using if it stopped us as well," she continued.

I had pegged her as a Witch-type to start with, but now she seemed to be telling us pretty much everything. From everything she was telling us, it seemed fair to also call this approach pretty stupid. There was a chance she was a liar, but the explanation made too much sense to be a lie.

"The holders of the holy and vassal weapons are basically slaves to the weapons, correct? The weapons won't lend their strength to anyone who won't follow their orders. So we have confined those weapons and are forcibly drawing out their power. Don't make the foolish mistake of comparing those other vassal weapon holders to us, thank you," she said. So they were suppressing the holy weapons, allowing them to also suppress any vassal weapons resisting them, and then forcibly drawing out their power? Damn, my analysis had been this: even if they knew some power-up methods, they probably weren't drawing their full power! Holy crap, I had completely underestimated these guys. We could have easily got ourselves killed, walking into this the wrong way.

"Hey!" Miyaji said.

"What are you telling them all of that for?" Witch said.

"Right! What value is there in conversing with evil?" Armor added. The three of them seemed quite displeased with the direction this stupid newcomer had chosen to take.

When I read it another way, however, their displeasure also suggested she was telling the truth. The idiot woman faced her allies with her arms crossed.

"Well, well, well. It seems the musical instrument hero from this world and our newcomers are feeling the pressure already," she said, tauntingly, while spreading one hand to the side.

"What was that?" Miyaji replied.

"Are you looking for a fight?" Witch responded, glaring at the trash-woman with hate in her eyes. They were having a falling out already, were they? *Go ahead, morons, kill each other for me!*

"You agree with my stance here, correct? Rather than killing them without them knowing anything, we should give them the slightest opportunity to win and then rip it away, allowing us to enjoy the despair on their faces even more," the idiot said, taunting Witch. It was a textbook line from a villain. But I had to presume she didn't know how many such villains we had defeated already. "Defeating such scum, with all their pathetic efforts and cowardly schemes, like the insignificant insects they are, is the law of the truly powerful, no? If you use your own stingy, cowardly means to defeat your prey, then you are no better than the scum you defeat!" she went on.

"What?!" Witch flared up. "You have a problem with how we do things?" It looked like Witch and the moron woman were not on the best of terms. They were probably too similar to get along. I couldn't even work out why they were fighting in the first place.

Not that I was about to stop them. This suited me.

"You have to bring your enemies low with a correct and just strategy. Otherwise, how are you any different from the cowardly scum who will sink to any means necessary?" the moron woman said.

"Hah!" Witch didn't seem to like that either. It was a weird branch of logic, one that seemed to interchangeably weave together "correct" and "cowardly." The main thrust seemed to be that she considered using a strategy as cowardly as this one and defeating enemies who didn't know what was happening to make some kind of bad impression. She desired showing some level of respect for the enemy, and yet still defeating them with some kind of display of strength and justice.

Even if the greatest sage formed a mighty strategy, for the one beaten it was still just a cowardly attack. She was saying that no matter how good it might feel to perpetrate, she was dissatisfied with how cowardly this strategy had been.

I had trouble understanding it though. If that was her issue, then just come at us head-on—or realize your ambitions through discussion, even.

"Or what? We've set everything up for you, and you're still going to let them defeat you? Pathetic. You seemed so strong and beautiful, so I came to you with this, but I'm quite disillusioned now," S'yne's sister said.

"Gah, very well! It's not like we're letting them leave alive, anyway. Telling them how to stop this would make things fair and square, right? So go ahead," Witch spat and turned to look at us. "You'd better be thankful for this!"

We'd been weakened to this degree and then sat through a condescending lecture that didn't reveal how to undo it all, and they called that "fair and square?" The only thing I could think of was that we had to get back the holy weapons from this world. I certainly wasn't going to be thanking anyone for any of this either!

"If you want to return all weapons back to where they belong, you first need to recover and release the captured holy weapons," the moron woman said. If what she had just said was true, getting back the captured holy weapons was our only choice.

It was time to make use of this opening they had presented. I just hoped it would work.

"What appallingly selfish logic," I said.

"Indeed," Glass chimed in. "I hardly have a response, having suffered all of this and yet also having it called 'fair and square.'"

"Don't be so naive!" Witch fired back. "This is combat. There's no such thing as cowardice in combat! But we're telling you this because we aren't cowards! If you have an issue with that, you can share it—after you turn this situation back to your own advantage!" Crazy people of this type really did love this kind of argument—that the winner got to decide everything. Was there a book somewhere that they learned all these lines from?

"Well, well, well. You have the technology we've provided you with, so you can still use your own magic even under these circumstances," the moron woman said to Witch, pointing to an armband she was wearing. "Good luck!" Hold on. Did that mean Witch and Armor could use magic from our world?

"Why do I have to do all the fighting?" Witch whined. "I'm only here to support Hidemasa from the rear!" Even under these conditions, Witch just wanted to have an easy time of it in the back. Her position hadn't changed at all from when she'd been allied with Motoyasu.

However, our enemies were still only arguing amongst themselves verbally. It hadn't created any kind of advantage for us yet. I took a breath, calming myself, and tried to think of an effective move.

The biggest threats were Miyaji, Armor and his axe, and then the moron woman and her chain vassal weapon from S'yne's world. The other women were, when compared to what I'd seen Raphtalia and Glass do, not much of a threat.

We could still win this.

Not to mention, based on the information that they were suppressing the holy weapons to draw out their power, the capabilities of Armor's axe had to be reduced. The axe seven star weapon was under our jurisdiction, rather than the four holy weapons of this world.

That said, with Itsuki and my own weapon now out of action, there was no way to test that assumption. It was better to keep our guard up. It would have been great if we could have used sakura stone of destiny weapons or protections, but they weren't compatible. If I could have used them, I'd have sent Raphtalia in with a preemptive strike.

"Let's get this fight started, shall we?" the moron woman said. Weakening an opponent into the ground, splitting them up, and then coming at them full force—this was no different from the approach Takt had taken. It might only be a little better this time because of the hints the moron woman had unleashed so imperiously. "Now, in the name of all that is just and fair, we shall end you!" I didn't even have the energy for a caustic reply.

"Our justice shall destroy the ambitions of the shield

demon king and his minions!" Armor added.

"This is where you die! Go! Crush them!" Witch crowed. I was sick of that pair already. I was sick of all of these losers.

"Mr. Naofumi, please fall back!" Raphtalia said, probably including Itsuki in that.

"We will deal with this," Glass said. The two of them raised their weapons and stood in front of Miyaji and his allies.

I was still holding S'yne, and in that moment, she came around with a moan.

"S'yne, are you okay?" I asked.

"I'm—" She staggered to her feet but was clearly still intending to fight. In fact, scissors quivering, she looked ready to leap at the moron woman at any moment.

Then S'yne unleashed threads toward Itsuki and me.

"Marionette Assist—" she said.

"It is a support skill. We will aid you as best as we can!" her familiar explained. I checked to see my stats had been boosted a little. So she had these kinds of skills too. As I'd been using Aura up to this point, it hadn't really been needed until now.

"Master Hidemasa! We will aid you!" Miyaji's women were still eager to fight. The situation was bad. I wanted to retreat, but I couldn't use Portal Shield. If L'Arc's party could remove the lock on the dragon hourglass and give us access to Scroll of Return, that might turn this situation around . . . But in light of everything that had happened so far, the end of the fighting over there might just allow even more annoying enemies to show up here.

"Die! This is where our justice seizes victory!" Armor said. Mixed with the shouts of other enemies in the room, he swung his axe into action.

"I don't have anything personal against you, but I must fight too," Miyaji quipped, sending out notes from his musical instrument once more. The moron woman sent her heavy-tipped chain flying like a snake for S'yne, and Miyaji's women all attacked with each of their own weapons.

"Stardust Blade!" Raphtalia unleashed sparkling slashes laced with stars.

"Circle Dance Combination Formation: Formation One, Formation Two, Formation Three, Formation Four!" A quick combination from Glass made short work of the notes from Miyaji and also blocked the attack from Armor.

"Well, well, well, if you don't stop me soon, I'll send you flying again," the moron woman said with a laugh.

"I won't lose to—" S'yne replied, scattering sparks as she deflected the incoming chain. I could tell that her sister's attacks were too strong for S'yne to resist for long.

"Now!" S'yne's familiar appeared behind the moron woman and charged in, but she crossed the chain over her back and stopped the attack.

"You are naive as ever, little S'yne," the moron mocked.

Dammit. Was there no way to turn this around? Even as I thought that, a familiar-sounding spell rang out.

"As the source of your power, the next queen commands you. Let the way of all things be revealed once more! Blazing flames of hell! Drifa Hellfire!" Witch was still fixated on being the next queen, clearly! Melty was the queen of our world now! There was no place for Witch!

I thought for a moment about what I could do . . . and then realized I had heard the incantation, in which case, it had to be worth a go!

"As the source of your power, the shield hero commands you. Let the way of all things be revealed once more! Scatter that wretch's blazing flames of hell! Anti Drifa Hellfire!" The magic I unleashed quickly cancelled out the massive ball of flame Witch had summoned up.

"Magic nullification? And how are you casting it so fast?!" Watch raged. She hadn't been there in the second battle with Takt, so she didn't know about that particular trick yet.

My incantation interference had worked anyway, so it looked like the Way of the Dragon Vein could still be used too. In either case, I couldn't use attack magic, and there wasn't much support magic I could offer in this situation. It might be better to have Itsuki cast it.

I was basically without my shield though, meaning I probably could attack a little.

"For Master Hidemasa, death to the hero from another world!" Miyaji's women came at me, swinging a selection of blades.

"Mr. Naofumi!" Raphtalia shouted.

"Don't worry about me!" I shouted back. Considering the kinds of enemies I had fought in the past, it was easy to read the attacks of these women. I pushed life force through my body using Hengen Muso Style and danced through the attacks.

"He dodged them?!" one woman exclaimed. Now that I knew I could use life force, I had at least some hope for fighting back. Even as that thought came to me, Armor charged in.

"Great Quake III!" he shouted, swinging down his axe and causing an earthquake!

"You moron! Stop it!" I shouted. This was an underground maze! Was he looking to bury us all alive?

"I'm not listening to anything you have to say, Demon King!" Armor cackled. Maybe this place was earthquake-proof. The ground still split open, however, making it hard to dodge around. He was definitely stealing my power-up methods! He wasn't able to use X class, from the look of it, but if he was applying all the power-up methods he was aware of, his attacks would likely hurt me even if I had my shield!

"Eat this!" shouted one of Miyaji's women, even as Armor roared again. I grunted as the attack landed, unable to avoid it due to terrible footing.

"What?!" one of the women reacted.

"I put all my strength behind that, but it didn't cause any damage!" the attacker said. A combination of Muso Activation, the capabilities of the armor I was wearing, and the life force technique called Wall that S'yne had taught me, had just about managed to prevent any damage. My level was pretty high too, which was a help.

"Hiyah!" I used Muso Activation, focusing my life force and punching the woman. It felt strange, like hitting a wall of air, almost. Perhaps it was some kind of protection Miyaji had on his allies.

"You were never taught not to punch women? This is the problem with trash like you," Miyaji said, giving me a disgusted look and launching more notes in my direction. Raphtalia and Glass intercepted those.

"Like I care! This is combat! Gender doesn't matter here!" I retorted. Just more feminist claptrap! Enough! He was happily attacking Raphtalia and Glass himself!

"Everyone! I'm going to get serious! I need you to pin down the vassal weapon holders. I'll target the other world holy weapon holders!" Miyaji said.

"Okay!" his women replied. It sounded like he hadn't been serious up to this point. That might be a problem.

"Now! Face the hammer of justice!" Armor was also narrowing his attacks on us . . . more like Itsuki. In that moment, for some reason, Itsuki took out a medicinal herb. I wondered what he was planning on doing.

Itsuki put the medicinal herb to his mouth and started to play it, like a grass reed. The light of magic immediately sprang up in the vicinity.

"Magic?! Impossible!" Miyaji looked disproportionately surprised, even though the weapon he was holding in his very own hands was similar.

"Bow Imposter! What trickery is this?!" Armor gave a roar as he swung his axe again.

"I won't allow that!" Glass stepped in and blocked the attack. "Hardly what I would call powerful."

"You're weaker than I was expecting. No justice wants someone so pathetic as an ally!" Miyaji mocked, looking down on Armor.

"Hah! This is how you use real strength!" The axe gave a suspicious glow and then changed shape . . . into a curse series weapon!

Armor grunted again and was rewarded with a cry from Glass. A large wound appeared in her shoulder. She had been unable to stop his second attack.

"A penetration attack?" Glass asked. She swept her fan to the side and forced Armor to drop back. She hadn't taken especially severe damage, but she had a pained expression on her face from the cursed attack.

"That could be nasty," Glass said and applied some soul-healing water to the wound, but the curse was slowing the healing. These stolen weapons continued to have some bothersome abilities, from the look of it. It was like a vassal weapon for our holy weapons, so he couldn't be maximizing its stats, but it was fair to assume that it was still loaded with all the power-up methods from when Takt had owned it. Armor and Witch had probably heard about other power-up methods too. They were probably using them all, including the ones from the holy weapons. That definitely made them a threat.

Enough molehills could become a mountain. The danger was real.

"Now, eat this!" Armor shouted.

"Allow me to get in on this performance!" Miyaji's weapon also changed into what looked like a twisted electric guitar. These guys seemed to have a thing for cursed weapons. They probably weren't paying the price for them either.

"Chain Bind III! Chain Needle III!" Chains covered with spikes appeared from the ground and closed in with Itsuki and me.

"Well, well, well, allow me as well," The moron woman cackled and unleashed her own chain.

"No!" S'yne tried to stop the chain, but it wrapped around her own weapon. It looked like she could probably shake it off, but then she wouldn't be able to stop the chain coming for us.

"Go!" she commanded.

"I've got it!" her familiar said and flew to our rescue.

"Mr. Naofumi!" Raphtalia turned her focus toward us too.

"Don't worry about us! Continue the attack!" I told her.

"But . . ." Even as she replied, Miyaji's women attacked her.

"Raphtalia! Look out!" I shouted. Multiple spears suddenly erupted from the ground at Raphtalia's feet, trying to skewer her. With a shout, Raphtalia jumped away and chopped the spears down before they could extend too far. But as she was busy with that, the attacks on the rest of us increased in intensity.

"You won't hit me!" I shouted as Itsuki and I moved to dodge through the incoming chains. But the playing of Miyaji and his musical instrument seemed to have turned the air around us into water, making it much harder to move around. It felt like a debuff skill or magic. That could be super dangerous too!

With a clinking sound, both Itsuki and I were wrapped up in the chains.

"The name of the punishment I have decided for these foolish sinners is execution via beheading. Now face the despair of your head parting your body without even the time to scream!" Armor was incanting something, and I'd heard it before. "Guillotine!" Massive guillotine blades suddenly plunged toward my and Itsuki's necks.

"Not today!" I stacked Walls all the way above me. But I didn't have the defense to stop curse skills at the moment, and my walls of life force shattered one after the other. As each one broke apart . . . time seemed to slow down. Dammit, I raged to myself. There was no way Itsuki's justice-spouting ex-lackey was going to kill me with a curse skill like this!

S'yne's familiar was still running to save us.

"Hold it, little guy! You're not getting through here!" Miyaji's women grabbed the familiar and stopped her in her tracks. She didn't have the strength to fend them off.

"Naofumi!" Glass shouted.

"Hey, little lady! You should worry about keeping yourself alive! Take this!" Miyaji swung his electric guitar, attacking Glass head-on. He was fast too! Maybe as fast as Glass . . . maybe a little faster! Glass barely managed to avoid the attack, leaving a few strands of her hair dancing in the air. Hidemasa plucked those strands out of the air and smiled.

"Master Hidemasa! For you!" One of the women pressing the attack on Raphtalia proceeded to pass Miyaji some hair wrapped in paper.

"Ah! Thank you!" Miyaji said.

"Anything for you, Master Hidemasa!" the woman replied. I barely had time to wonder what they were planning before Miyaji used a skill.

"Cursed Song: Woodo-Voodoo!" A clashing sound rang

out, and a straw doll appeared in Miyaji's hand. "Let's see what we can do with . . . this!" He placed Raphtalia's and Glass's hair on the doll, stabbed a nail that had appeared in his other hand into its breast, and then hammered it home with the electric guitar.

Raphtalia and Glass immediately started to moan and suffer, clutching at their chests . . . in the exact spot the nail had been hammered into the doll—right around their hearts. It looked very much like some kind of unavoidable curse skill! It likely had pretty specific conditions for use . . . The hair looked like the medium for activating it. If it was affecting them both, it had to be pretty powerful too.

"Mr. . . . Naofumi!" Raphtalia gasped, desperately trying to reach me as she staggered on her feet. Right now, Itsuki and I were pretty tied up, however. My own stack of Walls, created with all the life force I could muster, were being smashed down one after the other. The guillotine blade was only gaining in strength as time passed. I needed to shatter it somehow, but that was hard when I was also wrapped in binding chains.

It was starting to look like my only choice was to circulate as much life force as I could, then let it hit me . . . and pray it wasn't enough to kill me.

I wasn't sure my neck was up to that task, quite honestly.

With a rage-filled shout, I brought all the life force I had to bear.

"What an impertinent demon king you are!" Armor chided me, gritting his teeth and letting out another roar. "Take the judgment of justice!"

"What is this justice?! You've got to be kidding me!" My own retort was lost amid my own screams of rage. I finally broke free of the chains, reached out to stop the guillotine blade with my hands . . . and in that moment, two brilliant shining balls of light appeared in front of my eyes.

Chapter Eleven: The Mirror Vassal Weapon

"What's this? What's happening?!" Surprised by this unexpected turn of events, Miyaji looked over at the moron woman. She was still wrestling with S'yne but stopped and shook her head to show she didn't know what was going on either. The two balls of light whirled around in the space between Itsuki and me, slowing down the progress of the guillotine blades. For a moment, I thought it was support magic from someone . . . but that wasn't it. There were faint shapes within the light—a mirror and a book.

The mirror was the one who had sent us on this lovely vacation in the first place. The book though . . . What was it playing at?

The balls of light containing the mirror and book rammed into me, as though they were competing with each other, and then one of them flew away. Light dazzled my eyes, but when I blinked, the light was gone.

However, there was also a strange feeling in my shield hand. Very similar to how it had been acting until now, but also slightly different. Text appeared in my field of vision.

Confirming connection of mirror vassal weapon to the shield holy weapon—performing conversion.

Then a familiar-looking but also slightly different status item popped up.

Unlocked compatible weapon!

Weapon book items slid in at high speed and formed into a single shape.

I entrust my intent to protect this world to you.
You liberated me, and I have come to repay that debt.
Please save the trapped holy weapons, brave Shield Hero.

The item locked in place along with this message.

Amid exclamations from those around me, I looked at my hand. There was a mirror-like shield there. I immediately stopped the guillotine blade and then blew it away. In my field of vision, I saw a mirror that was shaped like a shield, called the Spirit Tortoise Carapace Mirror. This looked like an exception weapon that might work much like the staff had. I opened the weapon book to check. Countless mirrors—which looked basically like shields—all hovered in my field of vision. I could only use them in this world, from the look of it. I'd only been able to use the Fenrir Rod when I had the staff equipped, so this didn't look like an exception weapon after all. It was more like the vassal weapon had chosen me.

I looked over at Itsuki to see the ball of light with the book swirling around him. Then the book within the light snapped shut and backed off. It looked like the vassal weapon wasn't able to choose its owner. Then the ball of light with the book vassal weapon seemed to just give up. It then proceeded to pass through the wall and vanish.

"Well, well, well!" said the moron woman.

"Wait! Catch it!" Witch shouted orders, trying to get after the book vassal weapon.

"We're not finished here yet!" I flourished my new mirror and stood in front of Witch and the other foes. I also quickly checked my status. It was a mirror, after all, not a shield. I prayed I would be able to attack.

All I saw were numbers that looked like a weakened shield state. "Dammit," I cursed, even as I placed myself in the line of fire. I still couldn't attack! The previous owner . . . Albert, wasn't it? That guy had been able to attack all he liked . . . when Kyo controlled him, admittedly. So was this a different situation?

"Naofumi, the mirror vassal weapon chose you?" Glass said.

"Mr. Naofumi!" Raphtalia and the others suddenly looked a lot more cheerful.

"You've obtained a vassal weapon?! There's no way this kind of last-minute save happens to someone so evil! Enough with your theatrics!" Armor swung his axe again, and he was now firmly fixated upon me as his target.

"Air Strike Shield!" I shouted, almost on instinct, but nothing happened. It looked like the skill system was different too. Then the skill item popped up. I didn't normally spend much time looking in there . . . but I spotted a skill I could use. Perhaps the two weapons were still sorting out the sharing of information between them, as many skills were grayed out. But there was one that I could definitely use.

"Formation One: Glass Shield!" I willed it into existence, and a semitransparent glass shield appeared in the air.

"Hah! This won't stop me!" Armor swung his axe at the glass shield I had created. With a high-pitched shattering sound, the glass shield shattered into fragments. Armor laughed.

"See, Shield Demon King? This is all the strength an imposter can manage!" he crowed. It certainly looked weaker than Air Strike Shield. Armor was using the axe seven star weapon, after all, not to mention a curse series. When I gave consideration to its potential attack power, smashing that shield seemed expected. I tried mixing in some life force, just in case, but it hadn't seemed to do any good.

Even as I considered this apparent failure, the fragments of glass swirled through the air . . . and flew toward Armor. One after the other, glass shards stabbed him. Blood started to gush from all over his body.

"What! What the hell! Damn you!" he roared. Bleeding profusely pushed him to further heights of rage.

"You cowardly otherworldly scum! Relying on the power of the legendary weapons like this! Don't think this is over yet!" Miyaji shouted.

"Cowardly . . . is not a word you have any right to use! And you're from another world here yourself!" I shot back. Getting himself summoned here and then acting like this, seriously. Almost everything he said was a contradiction of something he said earlier. I didn't think we were going to be able to reach him with words anymore.

Not that I'd ever really thought that.

"Die!" The still-raging Armor swung his axe at me again. I mixed my power with life force and concentrated on a skill name that I often used. Okay, that felt like I was getting the hang of it.

"Stardust Mirror!" An enhanced Shooting Star Shield was instantly deployed, stopping Armor and his axe in their tracks.

"Impossible! This can't be allowed! We are justice! This means the vassal weapons of this world are evil, if they are willing to side with a demon king!" Armor raged. I was pretty impressed myself—even without any enhancement, the mirror had decent capabilities. Recalling the mirror that had shattered, however, I realized it was true that it offered lower defense overall compared to the shield.

In either case, we now had a new means to fight back.

I was also pretty amazed by Armor and his incredible logic

that everything that opposed him had to be evil.

"Ha! No need to get all excited just because you picked up a vassal weapon," Miyaji said, still so full of himself. And he then started to play again. In the next instant, however, magic spheres hit both Miyaji and Armor. Both of them gasped and shouted at the attack.

"You should not get distracted," Itsuki told him. At some point, he had started his own performance again. The magic spheres created by Itsuki proceeded to turn into the shape of rocks and fly toward Miyaji's allies and Witch.

"Element Harmony? You can activate such high-level magic using a blade of grass?!" Glass was suitably shocked as she saw the magic swirling in the vicinity. I didn't really understand it myself, but from Glass's reaction, this was quite something.

"Is that difficult to do?" I asked.

"It's attack performance magic that requires a solid performance before it will activate. I think even Filo would have trouble activating it by just singing," Glass explained. Filo, who loved singing, had even become something of an idol singer.

"Well, well, well, that's pretty smart of you. If you can't use magic from your world, use magic from this one," the moron woman said. She sounded pretty impressed, even as she continued her engagement with S'yne.

"Hah! I'm the specialist at musical instrument magic! Now you'll see the true terror of the Musical Instrument Hero!"

Miyaji clicked his fingers and the room filled up with more of his allies, including more soldiers. So he planned to just overwhelm us with numbers now?

"Listen to me, you're trash! This is the ultimate support magic! Tremble before the might of my enhanced allies!" Miyaji crowed. He placed his bow on the strings of his violin-like musical instrument and started to play. Itsuki immediately started to resist him.

". . . I've captured the flow of the piece. Now I'll put into action something Filo and the others taught me," he said. He blew on the leaf again. All of a sudden, the music Miyaji was playing turned into a horrible cacophony. The barrier of thickened air that had been surrounding his allies scattered, and the magic spheres that had been hovering around Miyaji were also all dispelled.

"Hey, scumbag! Stop interrupting my playing!" he shouted at Itsuki.

"This is the art of dissonance. Can you perform your magic under these conditions?" Itsuki asked. So it wasn't incantation interference, but more performance interference? I didn't know much about dissonance, just that it involved making a sound at odds with the others being produced.

Just like in cooking, the right additions could be used to bring out a pleasant flavor, but persistently adding the opposite could ruin the taste. The same was true here, which clearly prevented magic from being used in this world. Miyaji was glaring in anger and disgust at Itsuki.

"I'll keep trying to block his performance magic. Naofumi, please try to turn this situation around," he told me.

"I'm on it!" I quickly responded. Even without his weapon, Itsuki was still more than pulling his weight, and without making use of his Accuracy ability.

"Raphtalia, Glass, are you both okay?" I shouted.

"This is . . . not going too well," Raphtalia managed, clutching her chest with one hand. She was still on the receiving end of an enemy curse skill. The same was true for Glass, but she was up and fighting Miyaji's women; she was also clearly at a disadvantage.

"Oh, baby S'yne! Aren't you a clever little baby!" the moron woman taunted. S'yne broke free of her hold and fought back, but she didn't have the time to worry about us.

"We'll aid you!" someone cackled. Miyaji's women rushed to help the moron woman. This was bad! The rest of us had our hands full dealing with Armor and Miyaji already!

"I do so appreciate the offer, but you deal with Hidemasa's enemies. I am enjoying myself too much to let anyone else interfere," the moron said. Then she plunged her chain into the ground, creating a cage of chains and shutting out those trying to help her.

She really was enjoying messing with S'yne. That was one twisted sister.

That also meant we didn't have to worry about the enemies ganging up on S'yne though, so that was something.

"S'yne, you just focus on your own battle! Make sure you don't lose to her!" I shouted. S'yne glanced in my direction, gave a nod, and then attacked the moron woman again using her scissors.

Meanwhile, I had to focus on defending Raphtalia, Itsuki, and Glass. I had to fight Witch and Armor too.

"Hah. You have to know that the true value of this musical instrument doesn't lie simply in performing. Even if you interfere with my playing, I can win if I use cursed songs against you vassal weapon holders," Miyaji gloated. He made a good point . . . but just going on the defense seemed unlikely to stop that mysterious curse skill. The attack wasn't coming right at them—right at their faces—so it wasn't something that could be stopped by interrupting it. It was a gradual thing, but both Raphtalia and Glass were progressively taking damage. Those straw dolls looked like the medium of the attack . . . There wasn't much we could do without taking them back. Even as the curse skill continued, Miyaji was still attacking with his notes, preventing us from aiding our allies.

Even as I mulled the situation over, I felt the skill conversion bringing other skills online. One in particular stood out. It didn't have "shield" in the name, and so the name hadn't changed. Maybe because it was only activated using SP. Still, we needed all the help we could get. I decided to give it a try.

"C'mon Raph!" I said. Weaving in some life force, I activated the skill to summon Raph-chan. In response to my call . . . a light appeared.

"Raph!" said Raph-chan.

"Pen!" Chris had come along too! They both landed, looked around, then looked at me.

"Thanks for coming, Raph-chan and Chris," I told them. They both gave cheerful responses, but then their fur raised in response to the threat from these enemies. Then Raph-chan and Chris rushed over to Raphtalia and Glass, respectively.

"Shikigami!" one of Miyaji's women shouted.

"Adding two more small fries to the mix won't make a difference!" said another. They moved to attack the cute twosome, but with a puff of smoke, Raph-chan activated her illusion magic. There suddenly seemed to be a countless number of her and Chris in the room.

"What's this?!" one of the women cried.

"Isn't their magic sealed away?" said another.

"Bad luck for you. These are shikigami, meaning they don't use the same magic we do," I told them. The way in which Raph-chan's illusion magic worked had actually not really been determined. She could also use the same magic that we did, but considering how she had just used it here, she could clearly also use a similar but different type of magic too. She was a monster after all, and the circumstances of her birth placed her close to a resident of this world. All of which meant it was hard for them to block her.

Then, as the women tried to batter an illusory Chris, a massive Chris—at least two meters—appeared behind her, unleashing a mighty smack with his powerful flipper. The woman screamed as she went flying away.

"Pen!" Chris said triumphantly.

"Is that Chris?!" Glass exclaimed.

"Pen!" Chris affirmed, striking a body-building pose at Glass, as though to show off how strong he had become. Glass was stunned and then glared over at me. Hey, I wanted to say that had nothing to do with me.

Chris immediately returned to his small size and then the two other small ones dashed over to their respective owners and climbed onto their shoulders. That was all it took for Raphtalia and Glass to look like they were in considerably less pain.

"Has the pain in your chest improved?" I asked.

"That's right," Glass remembered. "These shikigami have the power to resist curses."

"What?!" Miyaji was hammering the straw doll over and over again. Each time he did, there was the sound of something hitting Raph-chan and Chris.

"Raph!" Raph-chan batted it away with her tail.

"Pen!" Chris pecked something with his beak. In the same moment, the doll Miyaji was holding split apart.

"They repelled the curse attack?!" Miyaji shouted. With a pained grunt, Miyaji placed his hand on his own chest, glaring intently at Raph-chan while he did so. As the saying went, of course, if you curse someone, you'd better dig two graves. It was a standard trope in manga and anime for a curse like this "voodoo" to bounce back on the user if it failed. Maybe that was also an element of the attack he had used—or maybe Raph-chan and Chris had just bounced it back at him.

Now we could disrupt Miyaji's curse attack and use support magic against it. That should stabilize the battle a little more.

"Stardust Blade!" Raphtalia unleashed a wide-range skill that consisted of sparkling stars and sent them flying at Miyaji's women and Witch.

"That's not going to hit us!" one of them yelled. They all dodged the incoming stars, then moved to strike back. I could completely nullify Witch's magic though, so that didn't get her anywhere.

"Zero Formation: Reverse Snow Moon Flower!" Glass shouted. Next Glass unleashed one of the skills she was most proficient with, sweeping away the women who were closing in to counterattack. Then she and Raphtalia dropped back to my position.

"Thank you for calling in Chris. I might have some comments about what has happened to him later, but for now, you have my gratitude," she told me.

"Mr. Naofumi! The mirror vassal weapon is lending you its power! How great is that?" Raphtalia said.

"Pretty great," I replied. "Can you tell me the power-up method to draw out the power of this weapon?" I asked her. There was a power-up method she had learned from Kizuna, but I hadn't asked for the details. I vaguely remembered it being something like getting stronger if you were using the same weapons. Glass's method was for her weapon to absorb the magic leaking out from opponents during battle. In any case, if we didn't have a quick way to power up right now, we would lose purely on the basis of raw stats.

"Do you think I have time for that now?!" Raphtalia exclaimed in response. Miyaji was firing notes at me again. He really knew how to pick his moments!

"Formation Two: Glass Shield!" I shouted. Just before the notes appeared, I made my own glass shield appear right in front of Miyaji's eyes. It could be used exactly like Air Strike Shield, so I was proficient with it already. It also didn't require Change Shield, so that made it one beat faster.

"Shit!" Miyaji shouted, even as the glass shattered and flew at him. Even Miyaji didn't have time to avoid that one, and the glass stabbed into him—but maybe due to the difference in our levels, it didn't look like he took any damage.

"Why must evil always thrive?! Taste the hammer of justice!" Armor raged.

"Raph!" said Raph-chan, activating magic of some kind.

"I don't plan on letting you do that again," Glass followed up, parrying the attack using her fan. His strikes were too powerful to take head-on, so she had adjusted by sweeping them to the side.

"Curse you, Shield Demon King! Only a coward would resort to illusions!" Miyaji bellowed. He had also been hit by Raph-chan's illusions and looked completely disoriented. This looked like our chance to take him down.

"What the hell are you letting them do to you?!" Witch raged at him. She hadn't done enough to warrant complaining about anyone else, surely. Her magic spells had just been nullified one after the other.

"What was that?! If you have a problem with how I'm handling things, put some pressure on the shield demon king yourself!" Armor shouted back.

"Hah! You've got a seven star weapon and you still can't handle your business! Why would I help you out?! If that weapon had come to me, I'd be able to make much better use of it than you! But who was the one shooting off his mouth?! I won't get my own weapon unless we win this battle either!" Witch screamed back—seemingly revealing more of what she was really thinking than perhaps seemed like a good idea. It also sounded like they still had a trump card up their sleeve.

I could probably guess what it was. The chain S'yne's sister used was one thing, but seeing the axe Armor used . . . it seemed safe to assume that they had possession of the missing seven star weapons.

Which just meant we had to take them back.

"Stop playing around and finish them off!" Witch barked. Armor gave a wordless shout of rage. If this had been a cartoon, there would have been smoke coming out of his ears. As someone accustomed to a bit of rage myself, I decided to offer him some advice.

"You need to review your reality. Getting all enraged like that isn't going to change the facts in front of you. Push down your murderous rage and think calmly about the most horrible, graphic way to kill your enemy," I told him.

"Only a demon king would say such a thing!" Raphtalia commented from the sidelines. This all took me back a bit, honestly. It had been a while since things were quite like this. I was finally finding my groove again. Time to ramp things up.

"Can you keep your taunts down to a minimum?" Glass said. I would have told her this was what we were always like, but that wouldn't have made her think any better of us.

"Everyone. Focus," Itsuki called out while still playing his support magic on his leaf. He was right, of course. I was feeling lighter on my feet too. My wounds were gradually healing. This performance magic was pretty convenient to have around.

"Raphtalia, the power-up method!" I reminded her.

"Ah, of course!" Raphtalia proceeded to tell me in a whisper. We didn't need our enemies overhearing it. "Still, the method for the katakana is refinement, correct? You said it added a plus." So there were overlapping methods? Even if that was the case, when I took the examples from the past into account, there was no way you could just guess your way into using them. You needed an awareness of skills, levels, and weapon power-up methods.

I decided to use materials I had on hand to enhance the mirror. I wasn't sure if the failure rate was the same or not, but I raised it to +6. I made it in one go, so I guess I was lucky.

"You know the one for the fan, Glass?" I asked her.

"Yes," she confirmed. It involved absorbing the magic, or whatever leaked out from opponents during battle, and using that to make enhancements. That wasn't the kind of thing I could do right now. "L'Arc can imbue the souls of monsters he has defeated."

"Spirit Enchant?" I asked. That was the power-up method from the spear, as Motoyasu had taught us.

"It sounds pretty similar," Glass said. I didn't like the sound of that—so it might be compatible, and it might not.

Then I noticed that the Spirit Tortoise Carapace Mirror had a fixed Spirit Tortoise soul attached to it. Was that thanks to Ost? It looked like it boosted all status and centered around defense. It could also deflect and nullify a single powerful attack, although that one had a long cooldown—and if the attack was too powerful, it couldn't handle it all.

That must have been what I used to stop Armor's attack. That made sense.

Of course, in my case, my attack wasn't increased. But it also had bonuses to health, magic, and even auto SP regeneration. The Spirit Tortoise was something else! As it was fixed, I could also apply another for myself . . . In light of the effects of the shield, I decided to use the White Tiger Clone materials I had inside my shield on it. It looked like they increased agility. Maybe I could expect some effects from Atla as a result of that.

We were still connected, even if we couldn't talk. Maybe it was a bit much on my part, but I wanted to believe that Atla and Ost were lending me their strength.

"What about ofuda, like Kizuna said?" I asked.

"I think this would be good for you," Raphtalia replied, taking one out and giving it to me. I put it inside the mirror and took a look. It appeared to increase defense. Yes, that was perfectly suited to me.

"Ethnobalt's ship had provided bonuses based on the type of items placed inside it, right?" I confirmed. It was a power-up method that any hardcore item collector would love.

"That seems to cover it. What is the mirror's power-up method, anyway?" Raphtalia asked. I checked the help . . . and quickly realized it wasn't something we could do right away.

"Not something we can do in a hurry!" I replied.

"Okay. Understood," Raphtalia responded.

"Can you please start concentrating on the battle again?!" Glass interjected even as she protected us from Armor's raging attacks. I was periodically putting out Glass Shield and Stardust Shield so she could hold on a little longer.

"I'm ready. Let's do this," I finally said.

"Okay!" Raphtalia agreed.

"Hey, Glass. Do you think I could use that magic that Trash #2 . . . Tsugumi's guy used?" I asked.

"It will probably be hard to just start using it," she replied. "Hold on, what did you just call him?" Oh crap. She'd realized that I never learned his name.

"Hardly something we should be discussing right now," I said. We didn't have the strength to take out Miyaji, his women, Armor, and Witch too. Ah. Then I remembered a certain skill.

I raised one hand, saw a skill in my mind, and then activated it.

"Formation One: Float Mirror. Formation Two: Float Mirror." Two mirrors appeared, just like with Float Shield.

"Hah! There's no way you can fight back!" Miyaji yelled. He appeared to only have one trick up his sleeve, as he proceeded to launch off more notes once again. They had different shapes and colors this time, so they were probably a different type of skill.

"Mr. Naofumi!" Raphtalia shouted.

"I'm fine. Defense is my job. Also, Raphtalia . . ." I started.

"Yes?" she replied. Then the floating mirrors adjusted their angle in the air to catch each note. The notes slipped inside the mirrors before being shot back directly at Miyaji.

"Uwah! Reflection?! You are joking! I'm not allowing such a cowardly attack!" Miyaji raged. So reflection was cowardly now, was it? Still, these mirrors could not only reflect magic—a property of Float Shield—but could also reflect skills. That was pretty convenient.

Time to put the boot in.

"Your magic is nullified and your skills reflected. Looks like we've got you on complete lockdown, Miyaji!" I crowed with a mocking look on my face as I taunted him. We were establishing a nice situation for countering Miyaji—a real textbook example of strategy.

"What did you just say?! Are you insinuating that I'm weak?!" he raged back.

"Yes. Itsuki and I could take you alone," I told him. We would actually prefer to have an attacker help us as well, but if we could nullify everything he was doing, then we could probably subdue and capture him. If we defeated each of the attacks he unleashed, one at a time . . . Then I remembered why we were here. Our purpose was not to defeat the musical instrument vassal weapon holder—it was to rescue Kizuna.

If we could just save her, we wouldn't need to be here fighting in enemy territory. And there would be so much more we could do.

Chapter Twelve: A Falling Out

"Glass! Take Chris and go on ahead!" I said.

"But . . ." she started.

"Don't forget what we are here to do! Get moving!" I repeated. The most frightening thing right now was having Kizuna be held hostage. That fact alone could turn the entire situation against us.

"Very well. Naofumi, I'll leave the rest of this to you," Glass said.

"Go get Kizuna back!" I told her.

"We will!" Glass said.

"Pen!" Chris chimed in. Following my instructions, Glass put the shikigami on her shoulder and charged toward Miyaji and Armor.

"You think we'll let you through?!" Miyaji said.

"No escape!" Armor yelled.

"I'm going to let them through. Like this!" I said. I proceeded to use the Way of the Dragon Vein to activate the magic in the gemstone on the scabbard of Raphtalia's katana. She had a scabbard that could activate Filo's Haikuikku. I wasn't sure if it would activate or not, but I just had to hope that Dragon Vein could activate it. I could feel something like intent from the gemstone on the scabbard, but unlike Therese, I couldn't hear what it wanted to say. I could just tell it wanted to help me. It was hard for me to reach for the magic, but the scabbard gemstone was reaching out for me.

The puzzle that appeared was the same as for the Way of the Dragon Vein. I knew how to handle it, so I activated it at once. The magic was assembled.

Now! Just for a moment! Please, lend me your power!

"Jewel High Speed!" I shouted. The support magic flew toward Glass and accelerated her just for a moment. She was already pretty quick, and that instantly sent her around and behind Miyaji. I confirmed that she had scattered his women and made it through the door at the back of the chamber.

"No! Wait!" a woman shouted. Three of Miyaji's women chased off after her.

"Guwaaah!" Armor bellowed. Hah, Glass had left Armor with a parting gift too—a quick attack. He was roaring and writhing in pain.

"Well, well, well, this is most disappointing. Allowing someone to escape, are we?" the moron woman spat at Miyaji.

"Not at all! Dear Hidemasa, you just need to bring more power to bear! You've got this, I'm sure of it!" Witch told him. She was looking to earn some points of her own perhaps, because she was only saying nice stuff. Her eyes looked cold and dead, however.

"Boosted Mirror Fragments," I said. Sharp pieces of what looked like glass flew at Miyaji.

"Don't forget about me!" Armor was up again, finally seeming to have overcome Raph-chan's illusions. He smashed the fragments out of the air. He had more dexterity than I'd given him credit for.

"Don't underestimate me! Without all this interference, I am clearly the strongest here!" Miyaji shouted. He proceeded to turn his musical instrument into a piano and then started to play like some crazy virtuoso. Itsuki continued to impede the magic with his own grass playing—but it activated anyway. *I guess there's a limit to how much you can do with a blade of grass.*

"Hero's Melody!" Some kind of magic went out to Miyaji's allies. "Now go!" he shouted.

"Okay!" his women responded. Miyaji, flanked by his women, attacked at twice the speed they had been moving at before.

"Stardust Mirror!" I shouted.

"I'll destroy your flimsy mirror in an instant!" he shouted back. My protective walls were quickly shattered, and the women came pouring in. Relying on strength in numbers . . . I didn't hate it as a tactic, but I also didn't really want to be on the receiving end of it.

"This is just another way to use my weapon! Reflect this, if you can!" Miyaji yelled and turned his musical instrument into the gaudy-looking guitar and swung it at me. I already knew this was a cursed weapon.

"Die! Shield Demon King!" Armor was still harping on that. Talk about a paper-thin character!

"Please don't think we were just standing around doing nothing for all that time!" Raphtalia said.

"Raph!" Raph-chan was with her, leaping forward and casting some magic. Her tail was all fluffed up.

"Dream Illusion: Shadow Single Strike!" It was a combination attack, bringing together Raph-chan's and Raphtalia's magic. The chamber was suddenly filled with countless copies of Raphtalia, making it impossible to tell which was the real one.

"I won't allow that!" Armor shouted. "What?!" When he actually attacked one though, the fake vanished in a puff of smoke. Armor and Miyaji's women had no idea which one was the real Raphtalia, allowing her to successfully perform her attack. Two slices appeared in the side of the room from her sword stroke.

"You mock me! Taste the hammer of justice!" Armor raged on. He swung his axe. The armor from which I had given him his clever name was now covered with blood. I caught his axe on a mirror and turned it aside, eliciting an annoyed grunt.

With a boing sound, Miyaji and his women were protected by that same mysterious barrier from before. Itsuki's magic must have landed between castings. While Miyaji was actively performing, we couldn't hope to get that lucky again.

"You're tough . . . but there's more I can do!" Raphtalia responded.

This "Hero's Melody" had an innocuous name for all the trouble it was causing. Repelling such a powerful attack from Raphtalia was another—in this case unwanted—example of the power of support magic. In this case, it appeared to boost stats and provide the defensive covering.

"What . . . what's this?" someone spluttered. "My insides!" Wow, wonderful! So Raphtalia had woven in a Point of Focus to perform a defense rating attack! The defensive covering had seemed to stop her attack at first, but it had been unable to prevent the follow-up effect.

Maybe it was magic that reduced the damage by a certain amount, rather than simply a wall like Shooting Star Shield that stopped it.

I had to wonder why these kinds of opponents always seemed so ill-prepared. That said, immediately after being summoned, heroes were generally pretty ill-prepared—me included. Mistakenly thinking that everything would go their way was how situations like this one came about.

"Dammit!" Miyaji wasn't giving up yet. He fired off another skill. "Demon's Melody!" Countless notes were ripped forth and came flying toward us.

"Futile!" Raphtalia really needed to work on her putdowns. "Stardust Blade!" She unleashed the skill Stardust Blade, which launched a scattering of stars, repelling the incoming horde of notes. It was starting to look like the musical instrument vassal weapon was mainly based in performance magic, and vassal weapons like the katana had the edge when it came to skill attacks.

Any notes that Raphtalia missed just hit the Stardust Mirror and vanished. I would have still liked to enhance it a little more, but with some added life force, I was achieving sufficient output to get by.

"Everyone! Stand fast! Listen to my performance!" Now he was riffing on the lines of a pilot who saved the world through song! Miyaji summoned giant speakers and started to perform even harder.

Meanwhile, Raphtalia and Armor were clashing, weapons locked. His attacks had been powerful enough even to damage Glass—and in that moment, Armor gave an unsettling grin. He was about to launch the exact same attack.

"Formation One: Glass Shield!" I had been waiting for that very moment and made a mirror appear to protect Raphtalia. With a shattering sound, the mirror broke and its pieces embedded themselves into Armor.

"Gah!" Armor grunted. "All you can do is fall back on petty tricks!"

"I've got tricks even pettier than this. Formation Two! Formation Three: Glass Shield!" I put out additional mirrors in front of and behind him. If he tried anything, they would shatter and stick him—in fact, he could barely move at all. The shards weren't all that powerful, but it would help keep him in place.

"As the source of your power, the next queen commands you! Let the way of all things be revealed once more! Blazing flames of hell! Drifa Hellfire!" Witch incanted, trying her magic again.

"Get off my back, Witch! If you think piling on will let your magic work, you are mistaken! Anti Drifa Hellfire!" I shouted. I had a reading now on all of Witch's quirks when she unleashed magic. Stopping her would be easy under all but the most stressful circumstances. Even if it hit us, I knew it wasn't going to hurt. That was how low Witch's and Armor's levels were. I didn't know how long they had been here and what their levels were, but they should have been able to overwhelm us under these conditions. It was the vassal weapon holder Miyaji who had the most powerful attacks in this group.

"Gah! Stop making those cowardly shields!" Armor raged.

"Everything is cowardly if it stops you, right? How old are you, ten?" I retorted. He had no right to complain if all it took to hem him in was two shields. I'd fought a woman once who had been surrounded by no less than three shields, and she had still avoided them and turned them against me.

"Hah! Great Tornado III!" Armor proceeded to launch a skill that created a tornado centered on him, smashing the mirrors using a power attack. The shattered glass fragments proceeded to whirl up in the wind and rip into Armor. He gave a pleasing roar of pain. There seemed to be more fragments than just breaking them would have created.

Still, the countereffect wasn't all that strong, and Armor didn't seem too badly hurt—more was the pity. He also seemed to have just the positive effects of the curse weapon active, meaning his wounds were gradually healing.

A number of Miyaji's women were sent flying by the still-swirling tornado. They screamed as they were blasted across the chamber and then passed out. Protecting himself by attacking his own allies! What a dumbass.

"What are you doing to my women?!" Miyaji shouted.

"It's their fault for getting too close!" Armor responded. What impeccable logic! Did he have any understanding of working as a team? "Anyway . . ." The black aura around Armor became thicker and more enhanced. He started to cackle. "I'm getting a handle on this now. Things aren't going to go your way again! Jason Murder IV!" Armor put on a hockey mask that suddenly appeared in the air and started to swing his axe wildly.

"Raphtalia! Itsuki! Get down!" I shouted, grabbing their shoulders and dragging them down. It was a spur-of-the-moment decision, but it quickly turned out to be the right one. A moment later, a massive attack smashed through the barriers. It happened right in the position where our heads had been. It had come right through the Stardust Mirror! If it had landed, it would likely have caused serious damage.

"See, you can do it if you try!" Miyaji managed, regaining his footing. "Right. I'll cast Hero's Melody on you too." Now he seemed pretty sure of his victory, praising Armor—however, he was still coming from a position of arrogance. It was quite a departure from his rage at his women getting blown away.

"Hah! Play the theme of our justice, then! You worthless fiddler!" Armor growled.

"What! Don't get too full of yourself just yet. A 'please' or two would be nice!" Miyaji fired back. These guys really didn't get along.

In any case, Armor was starting to master his seven star weapon. After I sent Glass on ahead, that left us with Raphtalia and Raph-chan handling attacks. That could make things difficult. Miyaji and his women still posed a threat, and Armor's attacks were gradually increasing, even as he unleashed them without thinking of his allies. Witch wasn't part of the equation. If she closed in, then I was planning to order Raphtalia to take her head. But at a distance, all she could do was keep trying to cast the same magic, and it would keep getting nullified.

S'yne maybe presented the greatest risk.

If she was defeated, that one development alone would turn the dangerous moron woman on us. Perhaps the only saving grace in the situation was Miyaji's attacks not really being that potent. Itsuki's contribution from the rear was definitely having an impact.

I hoped Glass would save Kizuna soon . . . but not much time had passed since she left. As I was thinking about all of this, Miyaji turned a murderous gaze on Armor.

"If you don't stop this, I'm going to have to kill you," he rasped.

"Give it a try, if you think you are capable. That will be the moment in which our justice judges you," Armor replied.

"Hurry up and defeat the shield! You can bicker once the demon king is dead!" Witch cut in.

"Of course," Armor responded. I cursed to myself. Even with the mirror, I didn't think I could stop Armor's attacks at my current level of defense. Even if I could draw out more of its potential, it wouldn't be enough.

This situation had been more than a possibility once Aura X was sealed. Not to mention, Miyaji could use performance support. If they kept working together like this, they would overwhelm us before too long.

"I'm focusing on killing these losers now, but once this is done, you too will pay the price for your deeds here!" Miyaji shouted. And with that, Miyaji started to play Hero's Melody again. Itsuki was playing interference from the rear again.

"Now learn that your tricks mean nothing to our justice!" Armor shouted, launching a relentless series of attacks toward us.

"Formation One. Formation Two: Glass Shield. Chain Binding Mirror!" I shouted.

"Not this time!" Armor retorted. I had launched Chain Binding Mirror, the modified version of Chain Shield, but it was unable to stop Armor's raging attack! We needed something decisive!

Itsuki was still desperately playing interference, but he couldn't stop the magic completely.

"Hero's Melody! Come on! Finish them off!" Miyaji shouted. The completed skill was finally cast on Armor and Witch, further increasing the power of Armor's attacks.

"Moon Katana: Crescent!" Raphtalia launched a skill at Armor's arm from a Draw Slice stance, but it couldn't penetrate the aura from the cursed axe and the protection from Hero's Melody.

"Raph!" Raph-chan tried some illusion magic, but it was scattered by a tornado skill from Armor. Miyaji's women sensed the threat and fell back, so they didn't take any further damage. They sought to interfere from the back, with performances, magic, arrows, and ofuda.

"This is the end! Jason Murder IV!" In the moment he was about to unleash that skill at us—

"Air Strike Throw X! Second Throw X! Torrid Throw X! Tornado Throw X!" Three projectiles suddenly hit Armor, and a tornado formed around him. He gave a roar of pain. I recognized the skills at once and turned in the direction of the voice that shouted them to see Rishia smashing in through the wall.

"I've finally found you!" she said.

"Rishia!" I exclaimed. I should have expected this from her. Her "main character" quality was still in full effect. She appeared at just the right moment to save her allies. She hadn't waited and picked this moment, had she? That seemed unlikely, based on her personality.

"The book vassal weapon just appeared and led me here. It seems I made it in time," she explained. So the book had guided Rishia in! That was something to be grateful for.

Good! It looked like the moron woman had been right and seven star weapons could still be used. The holy weapons had been sealed. So the seven star weapons could still be used.

"Rishia," said Itsuki.

"Itsuki! Are you okay?" she asked.

"Yes, I am fine. Thanks to you, Rishia," he responded. After Rishia had confirmed Itsuki's safety, she looked around the room and then glared at Armor.

"Well, well. If it isn't Rishia, the woman who ran off to join the shield demon king," Armor snarled. He was completely dismissive of Rishia. *Does a piece of trash like you really think you can defeat our own shining main character, Rishia?* But no, giving it a little more thought, this guy had no idea about the new, awakened Rishia. He probably thought of her as little more than that girl who'd pulled off that move with the barrel of rucolu fruit at the Cal Mira islands.

"Mald?! What are you doing here?" she said. Then Rishia looked over at Witch, and her expression hardened.

"What do you think? We are fighting the good fight. We shall defeat the shield demon king here in this other world, bring peace to our own world, and display the light of justice to the people," Armor replied to Rishia.

"Naofumi hasn't done anything wrong. Even Itsuki acknowledges that," Rishia replied. Itsuki said nothing. He just stared at Rishia. That was super suspicious. One interpretation was that he was only going along with me because of the curse.

"Hah. What does the approval of a false hero mean? If you don't get a clue, Rishia, then I will have to turn my hammer of justice on your weakling face as well. I suggest you surrender at once and hand over that weapon." Armor really was just a pathetic bully.

"He's right, he's right! Then that weapon will come to me!" Witch chimed in.

"What's with all these annoying reinforcements you keep receiving? I've had enough!" Miyaji exclaimed. He was one to talk! How many women had he brought into the chamber? The trap had split us up, but these were just our friends coming

to try and help their allies in peril. What was so strange about them coming to save us?!

"Mald, I've got lots of things I want to ask about how you manipulated Itsuki in Zeltoble. Like where you ran off to afterward," Rishia said and looked around the chamber, glared at Armor with contempt, and then prepared to fight. "This situation, and that weapon . . . I clearly can't underestimate this. Even the weapons in this world are telling us that you are mistaken," Rishia said. She was drawing in life force from the vicinity and starting to weave it. "I use my power for the justice that I believe in." Rishia gripped her projectile weapon and stood to defend Itsuki. Good, she was awakened. This all turned the tide back a little in our favor. After all, once Rishia knew what evil was, she got very emotional about dealing with it. Armor had clearly done something cowardly, deceiving Itsuki and then running away. Witch being here was just the cherry on top when determining who was in the wrong. Even better, Rishia was completely awakened due to completing her training. She could make complete use of her weapon!

"So many people thinking they are justified! I'll show you who holds the real justice here." Miyaji was as arrogant as ever. Rishia crept forward a little, and a little more, closing in with Armor . . . and then she dashed forward.

"You dare turn your weapon on me, Rishia? Weakling! Pathetic! Now you will die in the name of justice! Jason Murder IV!" Armor unleashed his previously interrupted skill at Rishia.

Rishia turned her projectile weapon into a short dagger, applied some life force, and then deflected the attack—deflected that powerful strike from Armor!

"Bolas Blast X!" Immediately afterward, Rishia turned the projectile weapon into a bolas—a thrown weapon with heavy weights attached to multiple ropes—and threw it. The bolas wrapped around Armor's body, then immediately exploded and started to burn. It was a skill she had obtained from the bolas that had been created by modifying Filo's morning star.

"Curse you!" Armor managed amid his roars of pain. "You dare oppose me, Rishia! You weakling!" He was blown backward by the explosion but managed to land safely and then roared again while charging at Rishia.

"Haah! Knife Rain V!" Rishia immediately leapt backward, turning the vassal weapon into a short dagger and throwing it forward. The knife proceeded to divide up into many more knives, creating a rain of blades much like the Hundred Sword skill that Ren had used in the past. Armor roared in response.

"Power Break III!" Armor smashed through the rain of daggers, like some boar charging forward, and struck at Rishia; Rishia placed a hand on Armor's wrist and flipped backward, then used his back as another stepping stone to leap through the air.

"Shadow Bind IV!" Rishia proceeded to throw a short dagger at Armor's shadow.

"Gah . . . I can't move! I see what you did there! Shine Axe Burst III!" Armor immediately realized that his shadow had been pinned and used a skill that made his axe light up, freeing himself.

I was just impressed by how incredible Rishia was in action.

"Look at you, flipping around! So these are the cowardly human modifications you've been put through by the shield demon king?" Armor snarled. He hadn't learned a thing. He was still using a cursed weapon himself.

"There's nothing cowardly about this. This is how I use the power that Naofumi, my master, and so many others have taught me!" she replied. I recalled everything that Rishia had done since we discovered she had a talent for Hengen Muso Style.

"Can you afford to get distracted?" Miyaji taunted Itsuki.

"I'm not." Itsuki was indeed continuing to interfere with Miyaji's attempts to enhance his women and Armor.

"You are such a pain in the neck!" Miyaji whined.

"That's my line. I won't overlook you trying to interfere with Rishia's duel," Itsuki replied. He was involved in his own full-on performance duel with Miyaji. Raphtalia and I were taking out the skills that came flying in from Miyaji, while Raphtalia's skills and techniques and Raph-chan's support were dealing with his women and their attacks.

If we had just one or two more people on our side, we

could turn the tide. If someone else would show up, like Rishia did, we could start to push them back. Either that or if Glass finally saved Kizuna. That would work too.

Then I noticed that the dull, dead-looking gemstone on the musical instrument vassal weapon Miyaji was holding had started to glow with a faint light. Itsuki appeared to have noticed it too, because he was looking back and forth between Rishia and Miyaji.

What was Miyaji doing? Storing up the energy to attack? I was also concerned by the presence of that accessory that looked like the one Takt had. Was that the reason why Armor even had the axe? It seemed worth a try.

"Raphtalia, can you destroy that accessory?" I asked.

"I'll try," she replied. At that, the moron woman looked over with surprise on her face.

"Well, well, well. Hidemasa, you had better be careful. If you don't protect the accessory I gave you, the vassal weapon will be released and leave your control. The vassal weapon is being energized by the presence of someone more suited to be its owner than you," she explained.

"What?!" Miyaji exclaimed.

"Hey! Why are you telling them that?!" Witch accused. As soon as I heard her mention his accessory, I looked at the suspicious purple thing on Miyaji's musical instrument. That was the same as the one that had been on Rishia's seven star weapon that we'd taken from Takt. I'd used the power of the four holies to forcibly strip it off, which had likely sent the seven star weapons flying into their hands.

"Well, well, well, even if I didn't tell them, a random attack might hit it and knock it off. They were about to target it anyway," she said, covering herself. But she couldn't cover the fact that she'd made it totally clear what we were meant to do. Moron.

"So it was already pretty suspicious as to whether you were worthy, and now there's someone here who's definitely more worthy," I said. I looked over at Itsuki, who was still resisting Miyaji with his leaf playing. In terms of strength, technique, and pretty much everything, Itsuki definitely seemed better suited. I was already using the mirror vassal weapon myself, so it wouldn't come as a surprise if Itsuki ended up using the musical instrument vassal weapon. "So that accessory is what completes their hold over the weapon," I announced. An excellent piece of information. "Rishia! You target Armor's accessory!"

"Bah! Targeting my weak spot? Shield Demon King! Another cowardly strategy!" Armor exclaimed. I'd had more than enough of them lecturing me about being a coward!

"I'm not allowing that! This weapon is mine! I'm the one most suited to it! Everyone! Bathe in my incredible music!" Miyaji jabbered. Regardless of Itsuki sealing it or not, he was still planning on playing some more. What he should really be doing was closing in or using some skills, but I didn't feel like telling him that. If the rules of magic were similar to those I knew, Itsuki wouldn't be able to interfere with cooperative magic. But if they tried to pull off anything time-consuming, Raphtalia would surely finish off the women. They had to be aware that they didn't have time for that.

"How much longer are you going to be playing with your sister? Get over here and join in the real battle!" Witch rasped, realizing the tide was turning and seeking aid from the moron woman.

"I'm having too much fun playing with S'yne. I can't be worrying about you too. Do you want me to unleash S'yne on you?" the moron answered, pointing at Miyaji and Armor. "S'yne is skilled at capturing her foes. With your half-assed weapons, forget performances! You'll just be sitting ducks."

"That's when you show us how strong you are!" Witch countered.

"Right! Time to prove you're strong enough to give us orders!" Armor added. They were such a whiney bunch! As soon as they started losing, this was what happened? Likely feeling much the same as me, the moron woman gave a sigh.

"You poor fools. What is there for you if you can't overcome this? Might is right, correct? Can relying on someone else when you get into trouble truly be called strength?" the moron continued. I wasn't really down with that way of saying things—but this was coming from one who had to rely on others all the time!

"You worthless woman! I'll make you pay for this later!" Miyaji spat, all theatricality gone from his voice. So this was the real Miyaji. It wasn't like he'd done a good job of hiding it. "Time to play my true trump card! Hero's Melody has nothing on this! Come on!"

"Of course! All for Master Hidemasa!" one of his women said, then turned into a semitransparent spirit and covered Miyaji.

"I really didn't want to have to do this," Miyaji commented. A strange pressure filled the chamber. They were about to unleash something. "You rabble surely don't know the correct way to use a spirit, so now I'm going to tell you. This is the correct way to use the power of a spirit and a human!" Miyaji said triumphantly . . . and then lightning rained down around him.

Chapter Thirteen: Forced Possession

All of a sudden, I heard one of Miyaji's women screaming. Miyaji shouted out her name, but I couldn't hear it.

Then the door behind Miyaji opened, the one Glass had gone through, and Shildina came into the room.

"Master Hidemasa! I'm sorry!" a spirit woman overlapping Shildina, just like Miyaji, whined. This one had a pained expression on her face.

"Quit resisting," Shildina said. The woman moaned again. "Are you okay, sweet Naofumi." Shildina ignored the enraged Miyaji and instead directed her attention at us.

"We're not badly hurt. What's that though?" I asked her.

"When this spirit attacked me, I used my oracle powers on it and caused a sort of forced possession. It's a single-use thing, but it's made me super powerful," Shildina explained. That sounded wrong on all sorts of levels!

"How dare you!" Miyaji raged—even though he seemed to be using the exact same technique. I also didn't think her oracle powers had been behind the attack she used when she appeared.

"So you can use magic now?" I asked.

"No. I imbued this with power and used that," Shildina

explained, holding up an ofuda. It looked like she had access to some pretty different attacks from Rishia.

"So she was too much for them to handle . . ." Miyaji muttered. It sounded as though Miyaji had taken steps against Shildina, but they clearly hadn't worked out. "But to make use of her yourself! This is the height of cowardice! Release her!" he yelled. I guess it made sense that he would have placed a trap for everyone after splitting us up.

"Sweet Naofumi, watch this!" Shildina said and turned to Miyaji. "You get defeated by this!"

"Ah! My power . . . she's draining it! Master Hidemasa!" The transparent spirit split off from Shildina and collapsed. Shildina threw out a bunch of ofuda and then incanted by passing magic through them.

"I call upon your power. Ofuda! Respond to my word! Become a torrent and wash these enemies away! Watatsumi!" Shildina's cards unleashed a flood of water created from magic, which rolled like a tidal wave toward everyone she considered an enemy! She was pulling off what looked like cooperative magic on her own. Just like Itsuki, she seemed to have a pretty solid understanding of magic in this world already. She had also taken the spirit and was using her as a magic tank . . . What was she, a monster?

"What is this?!" Miyaji raged as his allies screamed and flailed. "More cowardice, interfering in our battle!" The magic hit Miyaji, Armor, and Witch too. The moron woman spun her chain around herself. She was a moron, but she was also the strongest one here. S'yne was struggling, that was for sure. If we didn't save her soon, she'd be in trouble.

"I heard everything you were just talking about," Shildina said, her voice warped by the fact that she was still casting magic. A number of mysterious ofuda swam smoothly through the air like they were water, targeting Miyaji's musical instrument, sticking onto it.

"Paper Splits Rock: Explode!" The ofuda flashed and then exploded, blowing Miyaji away. He managed to recover—but he was gripping his stomach, a pained look on his face and groans coming from his mouth.

"I'm not finished yet! What . . . what's this feeling . . . like my insides are being stirred around?!" I saw something moving through Miyaji's body, a flicker of light that I recognized. It looked like a Hengen Muso Style Point of Focus.

After the tidal wave Shildina launched had passed, Ethnobalt appeared behind her. He was surrounded by layers of paper, even using it to stand on in the air. In his hand, there was a book. From the shape, it looked like the vassal weapon Kyo had used.

"Ethnobalt," I said.

"I am here!" he replied.

"Me too!" said Filo, popping her head out from behind Ethnobalt.

"It seems the book vassal weapon wanted to guide us here after we were all scattered," Ethnobalt explained.

"That book?" I said.

"Once it finished guiding us, it settled in my hand and seems to have accepted me as its owner," Ethnobalt continued. That made sense. Ethnobalt was a type of monster called a library rabbit, so this might suit him better than a ship.

"With my acquisition of Hengen Muso Style, all of my training, and now a vassal weapon . . . you can't count me out in battle any longer," Ethnobalt said.

"Glad to hear it," I told him. "So defeat these guys." There was no time for heartfelt reunions.

"Of course. If they are binding the vassal weapons with illegitimate power, I will free them from that binding!" Pages from the book flew up, obeying Ethnobalt's will, and wound themselves around Miyaji. "A skill mixed with Hengen Muso Style . . . you might call it: Life Force Style Magic Explosion." The name was similar to a skill Kyo had unleashed. Ethnobalt must have added some life force to it. Miyaji was certainly moaning enough about it.

"What have you done to me?!" he shouted accusingly.

"I'm simply circulating some life force through your body. It's just that each of those pages is also holding it inside, causing further damage," Ethnobalt explained. That was a pretty nasty trick too. It was the kind of attack that would have shredded me to pieces before I learned how to let life force flow out of me.

"It only has one exit," Ethnobalt said. "That accessory."

"You can't be serious!" Miyaji raged. The life force from Ethnobalt passed through Miyaji's body and then erupted out from the accessory, which was itself about to break anyway. With a high-pitched sound, the accessory shattered.

"No! Stop! You're mine! Don't leave me! You're mine!" Miyaji shouted, trying to cling to the musical instrument. Like shedding its skin, the musical instrument popped into a ball of light, moved away from Miyaji's hands, and then flew into Itsuki.

Then, as I had expected, the musical instrument was in his hands. It was shaped like a violin. The small accessory representing the bow became large enough to be used as a violin bow.

"I heard the voice of the vassal weapon. It wants us to protect from this invasion from evil powers. I don't know if I'm suited to this task, but I want to respond to that desire, if I can," Itsuki told us and checked the violin over with sleepy-looking eyes. He then ran the bow over the strings. Clear and beautiful music, incomparable with the dirge Miyaji had performed, echoed out in the vicinity.

"Amazing, amazing! I'll sing too!" Filo said. She turned into the humming cockatrice and circled around behind Itsuki and then started to sing in accordance with the music. The music seemed to be the one Miyaji had called "Hero's Melody"—but the breadth of the sound was so different it was hard to believe it was the same piece. Numerous magical lights immediately floated up in the vicinity.

"Hero's Melody . . . wasn't it?" Itsuki said. The support magic was cast on everyone, greatly boosting our stats— although not to the extent of Liberation Aura X. Still, this was great timing.

I flicked my hair up like Miyaji had and gave the same kind of exaggerated laugh. Eventually I managed to speak.

"What a dumb look you have on your face, dumbass! I simply can't hold my laughter in!" Then I returned to normal. "That was the line, right? So now the shoe is on the other foot." He'd pissed me off enough, so I was happy to rub things in a bit.

That did feel better.

"You bastard!" Just my laughter had already set Miyaji off, and now his face was so red with anger it looked like it might start giving off smoke.

"What are you screeching for, you chimpanzee! You did all of this to us first! If you don't want it to happen to you, don't do it in the first place!" I told him. A little childish perhaps, and maybe I felt like I'd fallen to his level, but I also wasn't going to just sit there and take this.

"Can you please stop taunting our enemies?" Raphtalia said

and looked at me with exasperation on her face. But I didn't care about that.

"You dare steal my weapon?! You bunch of thieves! Do you have any idea how wonderful I am?! How much I've done for this nation, as its hero?!" he raged.

"The musical instrument vassal weapon is under new ownership. How do you hope to explain how you treated it now?" I asked him, just out of interest. Not to mention, he had kidnapped Kizuna and killed the other holy heroes! There was no talking his way out of this one.

"Master Hidemasa . . ." one of Miyaji's women began and put a hand on his shoulder in worry.

"Death! I will bring death to every single one of you who have made me feel this way! Come on, everyone!" Miyaji shouted, as if he hadn't been planning on killing us all along. Even as I had that thought though, Miyaji continued. "But first . . ." He suddenly attacked Armor from behind.

"What are you doing?!" Armor shouted.

"Give me that weapon!" Miyaji shouted back. He grabbed the axe in Armor's hand and tried to wrestle it away from him. It was such an insane thing to do we were all suitably shocked— even Rishia, who was still fighting. "I didn't want a dumb musical instrument in the first place! But that was the only vassal weapon in this country, so I was told I didn't have a choice. Now I do, so give that weapon to me! I have the power to control vassal weapons even without that accessory! I'll make better use of it than you!" It sounded like he had a similar ability to Takt. But he was caught up in someone else's summoning, right? Tracing that backward . . . this guy had to be a vanguard of the waves, no doubt about it!

In the moment after I came to that realization—

"Mountain Break IV!" Armor slashed his axe down hard at Miyaji! Miyaji howled in pain. With the loss of his vassal weapon, he couldn't hope to withstand the attack, and he was promptly sliced in two with a single stroke. Blood vividly erupted from the pieces just after Miyaji gave a final scream.

"Master Hidemasa!" one of his women screamed his name as all of his allies involved in the battle were thrown into confusion.

"All your arrogant talk just reminded me of that fake over there! I hated it, and I hated you! Without a weapon, that means you are basically evil yourself! Your death is just the natural order!" Armor said. He swung the axe again, just to be sure—I mean, Miyaji was clearly dead.

"Raph . . ." said Raph-chan.

"Wow. He's real mad," Shildina said. It seemed they were both seeing the soul of Miyaji. Armor swung his axe around, slung it up onto his shoulder, and turned a taunting expression on us. "Ah! He destroyed it," Shildina revealed. I almost felt sorry for Miyaji, for a moment. He had been caught up in all this, trying to look cool, and ended up dead, his soul destroyed.

I had to wonder if this was all some kind of psychological attack. It was all so pathetic—beyond pathetic—a farce I no longer wanted to take part in.

"Next, I'm going to do the same thing to you," Armor gloated, turning the axe that had just killed one of his allies onto me.

"You just cut down your number of allies. Literally. Do you think you stand a chance?" I asked. Miyaji's women weren't going to cooperate any longer either.

"I won't allow that anyway!" Rishia raised her projectile weapon and leapt at Armor. "I just need to destroy that accessory, correct?"

"That's right," I confirmed before turning to Armor. "Now it's your turn. We're stealing that axe off your corpse if we have to!"

"Isn't there a better way of saying that?" Raphtalia commented. She made a good point, on reflection. I was sounding like the bad guy again.

"Hah!" Armor launched a bold swing at the incoming Rishia. But he couldn't hope to hit her as she darted around, using the walls and even the ceiling to launch herself freely through the air.

"Air Strike Throw Z Second—" Rishia started.

"Great Tornado IV!" Armor interrupted, intercepting her

projectile skill with a tornado just before it landed. That trick again!

"Well, well, well. I hardly know what to say. I'm so disappointed. Right, S'yne?" the moron woman said. I looked over in that direction to see S'yne wrapped up in the chain. She'd been holding her own until a moment ago! The situation was that bad?

Then I noticed a number of Miyaji's women bowing their heads to the moron woman. Were they going to try and get some revenge?

"Please, let us join those who follow you!" one of them said. I almost fell over in surprise.

Chapter Fourteen: Quick Adaptation

"I've hated his stuck-up attitude ever since I met him," one of the other women said.

"Please! Let us join you!" another said. Man. There were witches in every world—displaying whiplash-like quick adaptation to a situation mere moments after their man had been killed. It was almost worthy of respect. It was all so sordid, but almost exhilarating too. Scary stuff.

"Not a bad idea, maybe," moron woman pondered. "There's been interest in you too. An opportunity to make myself look good." I had already understood that they were in an alliance with Miyaji, but this seemed like needless exposition at this point in time. "Anyway. It looks like it's finally time for me to clean up this mess," the moron said. After trussing up S'yne, she proceeded to ignore her and turned to face the rest of us. S'yne was struggling to get away but couldn't move at all.

"Raphtalia, Shildina, Ethnobalt, target that woman now," I told them.

"Okay!" The others also nodded at Raphtalia's shout. But then—

"Huh?" The moron woman shifted her attention from us and put her hand to her ear. "Well, well, well, so they've taken back the hunting tool. That ends our fun! Oh, and the hourglass has been captured too? So much for the former musical instrument hero and his pathetic country," the woman said. Who was she communicating with? It sounded like she was talking about the activities of Glass and L'Arc—and it sounded like things had worked out with them. "This feels like a good time to get out of here. The musical instrument has been stolen, and the mirror and book have shown up too. Things are no longer in our favor. I thought this might all work out, but look where we're at now. I'm leaving!"

"You think we'll allow that?" I said. But before she even heard my reply, the moron woman had already turned to face Itsuki, Rishia, and Armor.

"All false heroes will face the hammer of justice!" Armor roared. "Any who flee are evil!" He was busy attacking Itsuki and Rishia and hadn't heard anything anyone else had said.

"Mald. I'll give you what little respect you deserve," Itsuki said. "I'll fight you myself."

"You arrogant fake!" Armor shouted but then gasped as he noticed notes that Itsuki launched all around him. I'd thought Itsuki and Filo had just continued to play Hero's Melody, but at some point, they had switched to this instead. "The attacks of one as evil as you cannot harm me!" Armor used his axe to smash the notes out of the air, but Itsuki didn't miss that opening.

"Music Strike!" Itsuki muttered. Something—basically an arrow—was fired from his violin and struck the accessory with deadly aim. His Accuracy ability was at work again.

Armor grunted at the notes, then started to strike him, sending him staggering. He'd woven in some life force, meaning Armor's high stats were now working against him. He spat up some blood.

"I'm not finished yet!" Armor raged. "The attacks of evil cannot defeat true justice!" He was doing better than I expected—but Itsuki continued to play.

"Imposter! I know your weakness! You can't handle close combat!" Armor dashed in close to Itsuki and swung his axe, but in that same moment, Itsuki turned the musical instrument into a large bell and swung it to the side. It made a pleasant ringing sound. Itsuki proceeded to fall back, the bell ringing out each time he did so, and he played more music simply by moving around. Armor shouted in rage and frustration.

"Unfortunately for you, having trained with Rishia, I'm no longer vulnerable to close-distance attacks," Itsuki informed him.

"Owww! Curse you!" Armor exclaimed. I was pretty impressed. Itsuki was developing too, being able to cover close range as well now. "Stop moving around!" What did Armor expect, honestly? For Itsuki to just stand still?

"I'm ending this," Itsuki said and jumped quickly backward.

He placed a foot on the wall and hopped to the side and then unleashed a skill that fired a lot of those same arrows at the accessory on Armor's axe. They flew so swiftly that all of the arrows hit him.

"Music Stream," he intoned. I was impressed again. He was moving pretty much exactly like Rishia did.

"Gah! More of your cowardly long-range tricks! Fight me fair and square!" Armor raged. Of course he wanted to fight at close range; he had a massive axe!

"Impossible," said one of the women who had betrayed Miyaji. They were all looking at Itsuki with shock on their faces. "The arrows should all just fly out randomly from that attack. There's no way to focus them all like that!"

With a splitting sound, a crack appeared in the accessory.

"Never! Hah!" Armor swung his axe and started to chop down the arrows Itsuki launched.

"It's not easy to pin you down when you move around like that. Please stay still. Stun Beat!" Itsuki turned the weapon into a guitar and started playing it. Multiple notes flew out and surrounded Armor.

"What?! That attack means nothing before my justice! Great Quake III!" It sounded like he was planning to use that earthquake skill to wipe all the notes away!

"Very naive of you, Mald," Itsuki chided in his monotone voice. The very notes Armor had been trying to wipe away now exploded in his face. I narrowed my eyes and saw light and what looked like lightning flickering around Armor. He moaned, holding his face. It looked like maybe he was under a status effect.

"Hey!" Witch yelled and dodged through Itsuki's attacks, dashing directly at the stunned Armor. "You give me that weapon!" She snatched the axe and then turned an unpleasant smile toward me. I was at a loss for words. These guys had no idea of the concept of allies, or working together, or anything.

"Eat this! Drifa Hellfire IV!" she yelled. Interesting. She'd finished the incantation ahead of time, stolen the weapon with it charged, and then unleashed upgraded magic. That was pretty smart—for Witch, anyway.

Shildina and Itsuki looked ready to prepare anti-magic, but I raised one hand and cut them off. The main event here was the moron woman—Witch was just an annoyance. I was will-ing to give her a few points for choosing to stick around, even though she had to see how the situation turned against her. It would have been easy to stop the activation of her magic too. There was a reason why I had decided not to. I'd had more than enough of this bitch and finally wanted to make her hurt by my own hand!

"Die!" she screeched, balls of fire flying directly toward me at high speed. I proceeded to catch them on my mirrors. "Are you simple? My magic is boosted by the protection of a seven star weapon! You won't stop it like that—what?!" she whined. Her tirade was cut off by my roar as I reflected the magic right back at her like a baseball pitcher throwing a burning curveball. Even if this hadn't worked out as planned, I still could have applied some life force and bent the magic's trajectory to return it.

It went exactly as planned, however. I was really getting a feel for handling the mirror. If the shield was based in physical defense, the mirror was more magic related. The way reflection worked actually seemed easier to use than the shield. I applied some life force to the mirror . . . and also added some magic to the reflected magic as well, just for good measure. The flames proceeded to increase in size, become wreathed in life force, and then crash right into Witch. Adding some magic when reflecting gave the attack a nice power boost.

"Back, stay back!" Witch shouted, her cries quickly degenerating into a scream. She rolled around on the floor, burning from the magic she herself had unleashed.

"She burns like dry twigs!" I laughed. It felt great. Witch, burning in her own hellfire. This was one of the first times I had ever been able to really strike a blow against her. That only sweetened the experience. Finally, I had brought down some punishment on her myself.

Then I heard Armor screaming as well. It seemed some of the sparks had leapt over to him.

"Now! Let's finish this! Take back the axe! And get that armband off Witch too. Then I'll finally be able to use Liberation Aura again!" I directed, instructing Raphtalia and the others to destroy the annoying accessories. Time to get everything back!

The moron woman gave a sigh. "Chain Defense!" She swung her chain and bound Witch and Armor. "Please stop causing trouble for me," she told them. The pair could only gurgle in pain. "I told you that we're leaving." The moron woman wrapped the two of them up more tightly, and Witch and Armor's voices could not be heard any longer. The axe had been wrapped up with them too, I realized. We still needed to destroy that accessory!

In any case, taking care of the moron woman had just become our top priority.

"Well then, you rabble," she said and looked us over. "You fought a good fight, I'll give you that. Worthy of some praise." She really was looking down on us. "The tides of this battle have turned against us, so it really is time for me to leave."

"Like I already said," I reminded her. "You think we're just letting you walk out of here?" The moron was surrounded and yet still looked at ease.

"I'm pretty sure I can. From what I've seen so far, anyway," she replied, still smiling.

"You really think you can get away from this many people?" I retorted.

"You are making the mistake of underestimating me," she replied. Her chain started to give off a suspicious light, which proceeded to envelop her entirely. A mysterious aura proceeded to fill the chamber. S'yne grabbed the chain, her eyes intent, and glared at the moron woman. We still needed to save S'yne, but I wasn't sure how.

Then the moron woman threw her at us.

I reacted on instinct, grabbing her, and then a horizontal shock wave hit and sent us all flying. Even as I hurtled away, I looked around the room to see chains erupting out of everywhere and knocking away my entire party. Everyone reacted in their own way, including cries of pain and one "fehhh." Then we were all smashed into the wall and stunned.

It was such a powerful, such a fast attack, I almost wanted to ask why she hadn't done that to start with.

"Your defenses are insufficient for any real purpose. Look how easily I made a mockery of you. Now do you understand that I've been playing with you the entire time?" the moron woman said. I'd just been selected by the vassal weapon, so the lack of enhancements really hurt. Her attitude didn't really impress me either, considering this had all started with a carefully laid trap.

I laid the unconscious S'yne down on the floor, stood up, and readied my mirrors, directing them toward the moron woman. I couldn't attack on my own, but I also couldn't just stand by and watch more of this unfold. This was the moment to use skills like the Glass Shield or weapons with a countereffect to fight back.

Perhaps sensing what I was thinking, the moron woman smiled unsettlingly. As soon as things appeared to have turned in her favor, Miyaji's gaggle of women started clamoring again too.

"Amazing! Now, quickly! Finish these infidels off!" one of them said.

"Master Hidemasa died because you showed up!" said another.

"Avenge him!" shouted a third. The moron woman raised her hands, seemingly having no time for these women herself.

"No. This is all such a pain. I already told you, I'm leaving," she said. The women were stunned, faces in shock at being rejected so plainly. "They didn't kill former musical instrument hero, either. It was one of our own. You are assigning blame in the wrong place." That was true. Armor had done the killing, not us.

She might be a moron, but sometimes she did make sense.

"If we provide any further stimulation, who knows what kind of miracle they will pull out next? I don't need the additional hassle right now," the moron went on.

"But . . ." started the women.

"The hunting tool has been lost, which means that fan

woman will be coming back, and their allies on the surface will bring in reinforcements too. If we don't run away now, we will be overwhelmed and killed," she reasoned, looking over Miyaji's women with nothing but contempt in her eyes. "We might win the battle, but I want to win the war. I'm leaving." The moron woman waved at me, blew me a kiss, and then turned away. "Oh, one thing. You seem to be getting pretty full of yourself, having learned some powerful new support magic, but there's plenty of ways to deal with that other than what you've seen here today. For example, magic that removes it, or our own buffing magic or skills," she revealed. I gritted my teeth at the pinpoint accuracy of her assessment. The mention of removal magic reminded me of the enemy we had faced when S'yne saved us.

If All Liberation Aura X was removed, I could just apply it again. But I could imagine a tug-of-war with the enemy removing it ensuing. If they started using the same kind of buffs . . . then we'd be on the back foot, having to remove them.

All stuff to be very careful of.

"I've heard you fought some of our low-level thugs. Maybe that's given you the impression that we are easy to handle, but I promise you one thing: think too little of us and you'll get burned," the moron warned. So they had been "low-level thugs"?

It did sound like Motoyasu had fought them off pretty capably. "Honestly, there are so many races concerned about their souls. There was already a whole bunch of them who didn't want to go and get attacked and die before they could come back. What a pain! The way you wiped out those who've been sent to your world has caused quite a scare," the moron woman explained. That made sense—they were attacking so aggressively due to the presumption that they couldn't die. But with the techniques we possessed, we could kill them completely without any chance for revival, which made it far more difficult for them to invade.

I did understand how they were feeling. I'd want to attack them right down to the last one—even as a zombie myself, if it came to it. Still, this woman loved to run her mouth.

"Ah, what a pain this all is. I have to take back the holy weapons, as well as the hunting weapon too. Anyway, S'yne, the next time we meet, I won't take it so easy on you," she said. The moron woman looked at S'yne with taunting contempt in her eyes, and then she pointed at me and spoke.

"Well then! Time to finally leave. See you again, Iwatani!" Throwing out these final words, the moron woman suddenly vanished into thin air, taking the still trussed-up Witch and Armor with her. Just when I thought we had a chance to turn the tide . . .

She'd known my surname too. She probably heard it from Witch or something. But still, it didn't line up with what S'yne had said when we first met. She hardly talked about herself, after all. This seemed like a good time to have a serious discussion about that.

Raphtalia staggered shakily to her feet. I offered her some support.

"We lost," she said.

"Not really. We achieved what we came here to do. But it's true they let us go," I conceded. Immediately after that, Glass and Sadeena appeared.

"Are you all okay?!" Glass asked.

"Oh my! What's going on here? Did I miss all the fun?" Sadeena exclaimed and tilted her head to the side. The next moment L'Arc and Therese also arrived—and from the look of it, it was by getting caught in the teleportation trap.

"Kiddo! Are you okay?!" L'Arc asked. That moron woman really had picked her moment to escape. Had she just been lucky, or had she sensed the best moment to retreat? The second one, clearly.

So she'd had a full understanding of the entire situation . . . and yet chose to just play with S'yne instead of really using it. She'd had a lot to say, but she had analytical abilities that clearly outstripped the likes of Witch. She surely could have easily taken care of S'yne too . . . but maybe she had wanted to cause trouble for Miyaji and the others. Something she said had also suggested that Witch and Armor were newcomers to the organization. If she was one of those types who enjoyed reporting the failure of rookies to her superiors, that might explain it. So we had been saved by internal backbiting, at least in part.

"Glass, did you recover Kizuna?" I asked.

"Yes. I encountered Sadeena fighting along the way, so we joined up and managed to save Kizuna soon after that," Glass reported.

"I don't see her though," I said, looking around.

"This situation came as quite a surprise to me as well," Sadeena said.

"Chris is currently protecting Kizuna. I'll explain about all that in a moment. Having recovered her, I rushed back to support you," Glass said. Then I looked over at L'Arc. His use of "kiddo" had not gone unnoticed.

"We captured the dragon hourglass. The reinforcements we called in are still fighting up top," he said.

"I was able to make excellent use of the strength you provided, Master Craftsman," Therese added.

"Okay, glad to hear it . . ." I said. They'd proceeded down here because they had enough people helping out up there. *Dammit!* A few moments more and we could have had her.

Then S'yne staggered back to her feet. Her stuffed familiar was battered as well, with stuffing bleeding out of her tummy.

"Are you okay?" I asked. "I still can't use magic, but Therese should be able to do it. Do you need healing?" I asked.

"I'm fine," S'yne responded.

"Good to hear. Your sister sure had a mouth on her though, doesn't she!" I said.

"Yeah. She's always been a talker," S'yne replied. For some reason, she wasn't skipping as much. "A chatty traitor who'll just prattle on about anything. Heroes mean nothing to her, nothing—" S'yne was quite literally shaking with anger. I rapped her on the shoulder and gave her a thumbs-up.

"If you're after revenge, I'll lend a hand. I hate liars and traitors," I told her. An eye for an eye, a tooth for a tooth, and death to all traitors! Just being allied with Witch meant she was worthy of death!

"I'm not sure I'd really recommend that, considering who we are talking about, but thank you . . . I never expected to meet her here in this world," S'yne said.

"I'm sure. Finding out they are connected behind the scenes is a useful piece of information though," I said.

"I'm going to kill her! The villain who joined with those who destroyed the place I loved . . . my sister!" S'yne's intent was firm. We were starting to learn some of S'yne's backstory as well, which had been clouded to us until now. We'd known she was the holder of a vassal weapon from a destroyed world, but if someone else had survived and was now working with these enemies, that was information we couldn't overlook.

She had enjoyed beating on S'yne too. She seemed to have a sadistic taste for combat.

"Sounds like a lot has happened here, but tell me, Naofumi, Ethnobalt, and bow dude . . . what's that you are holding?" L'Arc asked. Of course, we needed to explain that too. I proceeded to give L'Arc and the others a breakdown of everything that had happened with Miyaji and the interference from S'yne's enemies.

"Um . . . I'm Naofumi Iwatani, the Mirror Hero, at your service," I announced.

"And I'm Itsuki Kawasumi. I just obtained the musical instrument vassal weapon," Itsuki added.

"Fehhh . . ." Rishia gave one of her usual pathetic sounds, switching out of combat mode. Maybe she wasn't able to keep up with what was happening.

"This has apparently been traditionally handed down by a library rabbit," Ethnobalt said, a wry smile on his face and the book in one hand. "I didn't expect to get it back in my generation though. I was originally the holder of the ship vassal weapon, of course." With his intellect, this suited him more than a ship.

"Fine," L'Arc said. "Itsuki having the musical instrument vassal weapon suits our purposes, anyway. If we announce the death of the hero of this nation, the others still fighting should settle down. We've got a little more work to do, so let's get moving."

"Okay," Itsuki said, nodding at L'Arc's request.

As a result, the battle with Miyaji, Witch, and the enemies of S'yne resulted in just the defeat of Miyaji.

Chapter Fifteen: Mirror

"The hero you believed in was an imposter! This is the proof!" L'Arc announced. With this announcement, and with Itsuki playing performance magic on the vassal musical instrument as we marched to the surface, unrest swelled among the soldiers of this hostile nation, and their desire to fight melted away.

Some of them still resisted for a while, but eventually the king realized their defeat was evident and ordered an end to all hostile action. L'Arc and Itsuki acted as representatives for the negotiations and managed to achieve an alliance with this nation. It was closer to an occupation, perhaps, but the negotiations had gone very well.

Thanks to L'Arc and Therese's rampage, the entire area around the dragon hourglass was in a bit of a mess. In regard to the women who had been following Miyaji, some of them had gone missing, joining up with the moron woman. The rest of them had mostly been stripped of their privileges and then let go. It sounded about right for the handling of the losers. Miyaji had done some pretty heinous stuff though—a few were likely facing execution. The authority of the four holies and their role in this world was very much like our own, after all.

Killing them was serious stuff.

Not to mention kidnapping Kizuna from another nation. They didn't have a leg left to stand on. It seemed their queen was missing though. Perhaps she had also joined up with the moron woman's faction.

As Itsuki and L'Arc dealt with these issues, we went to get Kizuna at long last.

"It's this way," Glass said, leading us toward Kizuna's location. "She was first being held in a room with some kind of machinery, but Chris, Sadeena, and me worked together and freed her."

"Pen!" We came in through a doorway to find Chris standing guard in big mode. After he confirmed it was Glass and the rest of us, he shrunk and came over.

"Why didn't you just bring Kizuna with you?" I asked. If they were able to free her, they should have brought her along. But instead, Glass and Sadeena had come back to me alone. It did sound like something had happened. I just hadn't confirmed it.

"Look over there." Glass pointed. I looked . . . and there was something that looked like Kizuna.

Not someone. Something.

A statue of Kizuna, standing like some temple effigy, with a fishing rod out in front of her. Was this really Kizuna? Not just some carving? The fishing rod looked accurate, but I didn't really like the design overall.

But think. This world had status and status effects, just like a video game. I combined my video game experience with the fact that Glass said this was Kizuna.

"Has she been petrified?" I asked.

"That's right . . ." Glass confirmed. Wow, so there was a petrification status effect! Now that it came up, I remembered seeing resistance to it among the effects when a shield was unlocked. I'd never been attacked by it myself, but the proof of it was right in front of me.

"She isn't dead, right? She can be turned back, right?" I asked.

"It should be possible. It will take a little time, but she can be restored," Glass said.

"Fair enough. So we've recovered Kizuna, at least. I guess this counts," I replied. She was in one piece—even if that was one big piece of stone—so we should just be happy at having been reunited with her.

"I can't use much magic at the moment, so I can't provide much healing magic. We'll just have to hope we can resolve the petrification as quickly as possible," I concluded. After defeating Miyaji and the others and driving the moron woman away, I'd thought I would be able to use the shield and my magic again, but they still weren't working. Whatever trap they had set, it seemed to still be covering the whole world and was continuing to seal away our weapons and magic.

"Let's carry her out then," I said.

"Good idea. Thank you for your help," Glass replied. We proceeded to carry out the petrified Kizuna. She was pretty heavy . . . but I had a high enough level to manage it.

"Let me help too." Ethnobalt also lent a hand carrying the statue. There wasn't much room for anyone else to help.

In any case, we'd successfully taken Kizuna back.

After that, thanks to having captured the dragon hourglass pretty easily, we used Return Dragon Vein and returned to L'Arc's country.

"Looks like we got you back on your feet pretty quickly," I said.

"You sure did. You've been a big help, kiddo," L'Arc replied. We were talking in one of the facilities in his nation, watching Kizuna's statue as she was gradually healed.

"You've still got that bad habit," Ethnobalt noted.

"Hah! Stop bringing that up. It feels strange to call him 'Naofumi,' so you'll all just have to put up with it," L'Arc said. I gave a sigh. There was no putting him right. I was getting sick of constantly pointing it out too. I guess he could call me whatever he wanted.

"Stay on topic, please. How long will it take to return Kizuna to normal?" I asked.

"Good question. This is a dense, heavy case of petrification. We have Therese, others from my nation, and Ethnobalt doing all they can to heal her, so she should be back to normal in maybe two days," L'Arc replied.

"Good to hear," I said. Glass was looking at Kizuna and her treatment with sadness in her eyes. Just that was enough to reveal the powerful bond of trust between the two of them. I continued. "Onto other things, then. After these events, L'Arc, we've become more than just the visiting help. We need to increase our activities in this world in order to defeat the enemies at work here." Once Kizuna was back with us, the situation would swing back in our favor. The main problem was that Itsuki and I still couldn't use our original weapons and magic—oh, and Witch and Armor were also here and up to no good. This had started out as just having to defeat the presumed vanguard of the waves in this world, but now Witch, Armor, and S'yne's enemies had been added to the equation.

If this had all been happening back in our world, we would have had more leeway to deal with it all. All sorts of stuff had happened over there, but cooperation between the nations was running pretty smoothly now, and most of the hostile countries had been dealt with. We'd at least eliminated those nations trying to pull some shady stuff.

But here in Kizuna's world, they didn't have that cohesion. And apart from Kizuna, all the holy heroes were dead. The moron woman had said their holy weapons had been rounded up too. It would be nice to do something about all of that, if we could. I also didn't want Raphtalia to keep getting teleported over here each time this world was in trouble. Unless we gave up the katana vassal weapon completely, our fates were intertwined.

I had no intention of abandoning them. No plans to lose any more allies.

"S'yne's enemies and Witch have a nasty habit of just popping up. I would guess they are likely working with someone in authority," I said.

"Looking at the enemies we have left . . . the Harpoon Hero has the biggest force," L'Arc said.

"Hmmm . . . and we're going to have to fight them at some point, right? We should consider the harpoon vassal weapon holder as our next enemy," I said. If our enemies were at work in this world, that should help draw them out. The one with the harpoon was likely the one who killed the holy heroes too. We'd need to try talking to them, but we should also probably presume that they are a vanguard of the waves—until proven otherwise.

"Still . . ." L'Arc muttered with one hand on his chin, looking me up and down.

"What?" I asked.

"Just never thought you'd get picked by the mirror vassal weapon, kiddo," L'Arc responded.

"Hey, same here. It's probably just a temporary thing, seeing as I can't use the shield," I said.

"The bow kiddo has the musical instrument too, so who knows what might happen next? There's still so much stuff going on that we don't know about," L'Arc replied.

"Itsuki can play better than Miyaji could, so I think he's well suited to the musical instrument. The book seems to suit Ethnobalt too," I said.

"It even looked like the vassal weapons were fighting over you, Mr. Naofumi," Raphtalia commented. I nodded. I wouldn't say they had been waiting for the right moment, but both vassal weapons had come pushing into me.

"I guess the book weapon felt indebted to you after the whole Kyo incident, kiddo. We had no idea where it was though," L'Arc said. I remembered the two spirits circling around in the shield spirit world. Maybe it had been hiding close to me in order to avoid more people like Kyo, Miyaji, and the other vanguards of the waves. The mirror holder had been pretty suspicious too, so maybe being liberated from that situation also created some goodwill toward me.

"Still, now I've got a mirror," I said. It looked like I could handle it much like a shield. Easy enough to use, but I would have liked some attack capabilities. It didn't look like I could use Iron Maiden.

"If the choice was between the book and the mirror, I think the mirror suits you the best," Raphtalia said, nodding to herself.

"Why do you say that? You think I'm some kind of narcissist?" I said.

"No. What I mean is, if someone does something to you, you like to turn around and do it right back," Raphtalia explained. I made a puzzled sound, so she continued. "When your name was raked through the mud after being framed for rape, you changed the name of the woman responsible and raked her name through the mud. When someone is unreasonable to you, you reply by being unreasonable yourself. You give as good as you get." Hearing all that and thinking back on what had happened to me so far, I could only nod in agreement. I always repaid kindness with kindness, that much was for sure. In the case of Takt, I only did back to him what he did to me. "Don't you think that sounds like a mirror, reflecting back your opponent?" she asked.

"I see. A real reflection of the life of the kiddo here," L'Arc said with a cheeky grin. I wasn't happy with them accepting this so easily . . . but if that was how they saw me, it couldn't be helped. It was definitely true that if someone did something to me, I wasn't satisfied until I got some payback.

In any case, Witch had to pay. She had to pay dearly.

She'd betrayed the trust of the queen, betrayed Trash's feelings, and then sided with the scum who killed Atla—all with no sign of regret. Leaving her alive was simply not an option.

"Okay, okay. I get it. Good, bad, whatever. If someone

does something, then I do it back, so the mirror suits me. Fair enough," I said, finally accepting it. While one way of looking at this was that the shield was manifesting itself through the medium of the mirror, in terms of power-up methods, we had to work with the vassal weapons of this world. Once I got back to the world I was responsible for, the shield was likely to return to normal, but I couldn't use it here.

We also didn't know what weapons the moron woman and S'yne's other enemies were holding. And we had to get the seven star weapons back. It was worth giving some thought to what the moron woman had said about our lack of enhancement. Various holes had also quickly been poked in the seemingly almighty Liberation Aura X, although I considered that a good thing in the long term.

Whatever happened, our fight here was going to be a complex one.

As I worried about what was coming, Filo and Raph-chan arrived.

"Master!" said Filo.

"Raph," said Raph-chan.

"Hey. What's up?" I asked.

"I'm hungry!" Filo chirped.

"Raph," Raph-chan agreed.

"Not this again," Raphtalia said, starting to caution Filo. "I understand how you feel, but Mr. Naofumi is exhausted." I gently pressed her shoulder and waved my hand.

"No need to worry about it, Raphtalia," I said.

"Really? I think . . ." Raphtalia started, looking at me with a concerned face. It's fine, I told her with my eyes. This was going to be something we needed going forward.

"Filo, no need to worry. I'll cook for you every day going forward," I said.

"Really?! Yay!" Filo replied, starting to get all excited. In the corner of my eye, I saw Raphtalia tilting her head. She was likely surprised by this sudden generosity, considering she knew how aggravated I generally got when it came to cooking. Without any other reason, I normally just told them to let the state chefs feed them.

"I mean, a lot happened, but everyone did their best. That's worth a reward," I said.

"It feels like you have another reason," Raphtalia said.

"You noticed," I replied.

"I've been around you for quite some time now, Mr. Naofumi," she responded. That was true. A fair amount of time had passed since I was summoned as the shield hero. It really felt like I'd been fighting for years, but in actual time, it hadn't been that long. It did feel good to have allies who understood how I felt.

"It's related to the mirror vassal weapon's power-up method. Let's eat and I'll explain everything. This will be worth it, so you come too, L'Arc," I said. I heard from Albert's women—the previous mirror vassal weapon holder—that Albert hadn't shared the mirror power-up method or any other details with anyone else. I thought this power-up method was a pretty easy one to spot . . . Maybe he had just thought it was simply the hero's protection. I'd experienced something like that in the past myself.

"Your handmade cooking, kiddo? That's the best! I definitely want some of that," L'Arc said.

"Yeah, make sure you come and get some," I replied.

I proceeded to the castle kitchen and started to cook using the castle's ingredients.

"Here you go, Glass. Have another helping. Eat up!" I said. Glass was also joining in with the meal, taking a break from treating Kizuna. I'd made a big pile of rice, and I heaped some onto Glass's plate now.

"Whoa . . . Naofumi, I've had enough. Let someone else get in on this," she said.

"What are you talking about? You need to eat to get stronger. Look at Filo!" I said. We both turned to see her gobbling her way through even more than I'd just given Glass.

"This is great! Can I have some more?!" she said, mouth full.

"Fehhh . . . I'm stuffed. I'm so full but I can't stop eating! Itsuki! Help me!" Rishia had tears rolling down her face as she ate, begging Itsuki for help. I'd not seen anyone eat like that before. Itsuki himself was caught up in his playing, eating a little between practicing. The musical instrument . . . was shaped like a grilled fish. I couldn't overlook that detail.

"This is the Glutton God Tango, a skill that enhances digestion, it seems, so please relax and enjoy your meal," he said.

"I can't relax at all!" Rishia replied.

The musical instrument vassal weapon power-up method was very similar to the projectile power-up method in that they both used money. The projectile one mainly offered things like erasing failed enhancements or increasing the effects of other power-up methods, but in the case of the musical instrument, you could buy status for cash—like spending 100 yen to get +1 to magic. However, it was a bit more complicated than that, and after making one purchase, you had to buy a different item the second time. There were various prices for each item, such as magic +3 for 500 yen, and in some cases, you could even purchase increased maturation rates or magic recovery speed.

It was pretty convenient but also looked to be quite an outlay of cash. Maybe it was derived from the fact that musical instruments were normally so expensive.

I had to smile at the thought that even Itsuki's power-up method was now like Rishia's. He was certainly bound to her.

"Raph!" Raph-chan said, stuffed full and rolling on her side.

"Pen!" Chris agreed, right there with her. Raph-chan's big tummy looked so fluffy. I just wanted to stroke it. Probably not the best idea right now though.

"I want more to drink!" Sadeena shouted.

"Me too!" Shildina agreed. The two of them were packing it away and drinking like fish. I guessed that being giant killer whale therianthropes meant they could eat quite a lot if they put their minds to it.

"Come on, Raphtalia. Tuck in, just like you used to!" I told her. Raphtalia's face paled a little, and she started to eat the food in front of her.

"Do I really have to try and fit all this in?" she asked.

"I want you to eat as much as you can. Are you checking the status icon?" I asked her.

"I am, but still . . ." she said.

"Ah, another dish is ready. This is the fastest way to boost our combat power at the moment. I need you to eat and get strong!" I told her. I used the status icon to check the new dish. Hmmm, so adding some life force had improved the numbers considerably. It was definitely more effective than just cooking normally.

This was all coming from the mirror's power-up method. I still didn't really understand why, but eating food now increased a new level that was separate from regular levels—it might be called the "food level." It felt a bit like the system that Itsuki had described once. Eating food I had prepared caused experience to be earned and a separate level and status to increase. It looked like the type of food that was eaten changed the status that increased, but I still wasn't sure how that all worked either.

Basically, I wanted to stuff them with high-quality, high-capability, highly efficient food and raise that food level as quickly as possible.

Even better, feeding vassal weapon holders with a careful eye to their enhancement would let me enhance them even without them being a hero. This was pretty convenient. I was up for anything that involved enhancing my allies. The mirror knew what I liked!

"I know this is enhancement . . . but it isn't easy," Ethnobalt said, finally finishing the plate in front of him.

"We should have some medicine on hand to aid with digestion," I said.

"The people in your village would make short work of all this, I think," Ethnobalt commented.

"Yeah, I bet they would." If everyone at home could get a boost from eating like this, that would have been a great reason to cook for them. There would be some long faces at home when I told them about this feast.

"Hmmm. I'm going to have to experiment on everyone here in Kizuna's world in order to feed them once I get back. Otherwise, they may defeat me," I said.

"Defeat you at what, exactly?" Ethnobalt asked.

I took some of the food over to L'Arc too.

L'Arc and his table had been stuffing themselves to start with, but they were reaching their limit now. Therese was already tapped out. She liked jelly, so I'd made some for her that looked like gemstones—she'd like them so much she forgot about pacing herself and filled up too quickly.

"I'm stuffed and yet this flavor makes me want to keep on eating. That's cheating, kiddo!" L'Arc complained.

"I'm really starting to have a good time," Sadeena said. "My skin feels so lustrous." She was being literal too—there was a strange glow coming off her. S'yne, meanwhile, was also stuffing her face! It probably wasn't my place to comment, being the one stuffing her, but I had to wonder where she was fitting it all in that slender body of hers. Filo and Sadeena were big girls—in their original forms, at least—so that went some way to explaining it, but S'yne was positively petite. I had difficulty imagining her tucking quite so much away.

"Another helping," she said. I recalled the first time I'd encountered S'yne in my village—she'd tried to eat my food then. She always showed up for breakfast, lunch, and dinner in the village too. Maybe she was actually something of a glutton.

Anyway, it was Filo, Sadeena, Shildina, and S'yne who were eating the most.

"Naofumi, kiddo, can I stop now?" L'Arc asked.

"Hmmm . . . I guess I can just feed you again in a bit. I'd better start making preparations," I said. The quality of the food seemed to influence how much levels increased, so getting the ingredients ready now would help out a lot later. I didn't want everyone getting sick of eating the same food either.

"Gah . . . that mirror of yours is starting to look more like a tray to me . . . You're the Food Hero," L'Arc said. I wasn't going to let a comment like that slip by.

"Right! It sounds like you still need some more! I've got a deluxe-size riz a l'imperatrice here that I was going to feed to Filo and the others as dessert." I slapped the dish—basically a cake made using rice—down in front of L'Arc.

"Hey! Hey?!" L'Arc protested.

"I want to see that dish clean, L'Arc. Eat all of it. This is so you become stronger and ultimately to protect this world. You've been watching your power-up methods closely, I'm sure, so you can see the experience and bonuses my food is giving you, correct?"

"Okay! I'll eat it! That's what you want, right?" L'Arc raged and then tucked in with a roar, stuffing his face with my food. Before long though, he collapsed like a puppet with its strings cut. *Take that! Calling me "Food Hero"!* It had reminded me of that soldier who once said my shield looked like a pot lid. Seriously!

"Filo, you take care of the rest of this!" I shouted.

"I'm on it!" Filo replied, heartily tucking in. Filo had already changed out of her humanoid form, and her bird tummy was looking pretty extended from all this eating. "Master, I'm actually starting to feel full! I've never felt this way before in my life!" Filo marveled. She had to be nearing her limits, as even her eating speed had fallen.

I continued the terrible-for-your-health food doping for a while longer.

Epilogue: A Responsibility to Justice

It was around the time that almost everyone had gone off to bed, nursing their distended bellies and moaning about being force-fed. I sent Raphtalia off to bed as well, finished cleaning up the kitchen, and was just heading back to my room when I encountered Itsuki taking in the night air and the wonderful view on a terrace.

Rishia . . . was, what, sleeping in her room? She was supposed to be keeping an eye on him . . . but from everything he had done so far, it seemed safe to trust him at least a little now.

"Ah, Naofumi," Itsuki said and turned his gaze from the night sky and directed it to me. There was something about how he'd been acting recently . . . He was almost too quiet. It was a bit unsettling. "Passive" sounded nice in theory, but it was also hard to tell what he was actually thinking. "The moon looks so beautiful. I was just taking it in," he told me.

"It is nice," I said. These other worlds still had a moon. There was also one in the world I had been summoned to. I mean, it was a world with werewolves and demi-humans liked Fohl and Keel who could transform.

The silence drew out between Itsuki and me. I wondered if I should just leave. As though answering my thought, Itsuki broke the silence.

"You know about me, don't you?" he said.

"Know what?" I asked.

"That . . . my curse has broken and my awareness is back to normal," he said.

"Yeah, I know." I wasn't a moron. Itsuki's ongoing increase in self-assertion had definitely started to become suspicious.

"I expected as much," he said.

"I mean, the curse should have definitely lifted by now, so I thought something was going on," I said. There had also been the possibility that he was just permanently broken, like Motoyasu. If I had to classify it, I'd basically been treating him the same as Motoyasu. But he'd responded to questions normally and talked when required. So long as he didn't display any hostile intent toward us, and in considering Rishia had been watching him, I had just not been worrying too much about it.

"With my curse broken and having recovered, aren't you wondering why I remain with you?" Itsuki asked.

"Not really. Having Rishia close to you has settled you down, I thought. That's about all the thought I gave it," I said. Of course, I had wondered whether he was broken like Motoyasu.

"That's just an indication of how broad-minded you are, Naofumi," Itsuki told me. That didn't sound right to me—I considered myself to be pretty narrow-minded. I was fine with him having the wrong idea about that, but I knew the truth in my own head.

"To be honest . . . I didn't have the bravery to say that I was wrong and you were right, Naofumi," he finally told me. His pride wouldn't let him accept me, even though inside he knew the truth. A particularly thorny feeling. I had my own times when I didn't want to acknowledge someone else being right—even when, inside, I knew that they were.

And so, without the bravery to say anything, he had just carried on.

"I can say it now. You weren't in the wrong, Naofumi. If all you collect is bad information on someone, even a saint could look like a demon," he said.

"But I am a bad person," I told him. It was my fault that the people from the village happily went to their deaths—happily went into battle. I still thought making people happy with products and getting them to pony up their cash was the best way to get rich. But I didn't consider someone who made people happy to place themselves in combat to be a good person. "I haven't been able to save anyone from the ravages of war," I admitted.

"But you always try to. Everything you do is to protect them," Itsuki said.

"And yet I failed," I continued. It was true. I had repeatedly failed my villagers. We had lost people in the Phoenix battle—not just Atla, but many others. Losses against Faubrey might have been smaller, but ours hadn't been zero.

"They know all about the ravages of war, right from the start. They were born into it," Itsuki said. I took a moment to think about them. However you framed it, they had a hard life. And yet I could only see their smiles. I wasn't exactly getting homesick, but I did feel like a trip back.

"Being able to protect everyone from violence . . . that only happens in stories. But I deeply respect your desire to do so," Itsuki told me. I had no reply. "I understand now that a village where everyone can fight for themselves and want to help you shines far more brightly than one that doesn't."

"Sophistry," I said.

"I don't disagree. But I finally understand everything that Rishia and Ren tried so hard to tell me about you," he continued.

"You mean how I was like the slave of everyone in the village?" I said. I'd sworn that wasn't the case, but the two of them had been quite passionate in their defense of the idea. I'd never felt quite so strange about a concept before.

"That's not the case though, is it?" Itsuki said.

"What do you mean?" I asked.

"When saving and leading people, you need to think about the kind of people they need to be in the future," he replied. That was a roundabout way of saying things. "The world is full of corruption, starting with but not limited to the Church of the Three Heroes. It all comes from the idea that if anything goes wrong, they can just rely on a hero to save them. If they are trusting their very lives to someone else, it doesn't do them any good if that person saves them."

"I won't deny that," I said. It was just common sense. You only ever noticed the power that had been quietly protecting you when it was finally gone. Even worse, if people relied upon something completely, once it was gone you were left with people who could do nothing for themselves.

"We heroes . . . have to be more than just self-satisfied. We really needed to be more like you, Naofumi—working to make people happy and to prevent them from slipping into that same corruption." As Itsuki talked, I was having flashbacks to my time as a merchant in Melromarc. Itsuki had joined a revolution and defeated an evil king, but the people saw nothing but a change in their leadership, and their daily lives had only gotten worse.

That wasn't what it meant to save people.

"That's why you say you're creating a place for these people to live after you've gone home, right?" Itsuki said.

"I started out just wanting to thank Raphtalia," I said.

"Even so. By learning the importance of protecting other people, everyone also feels what it is like to be protected themselves. That's why your village is such a nice place. I want to protect it myself—the justice that you protect, Naofumi," Itsuki told me.

"Justice, huh?" I said. I had no intention of saying things

that I thought to be true were justice. I'd made a whole bunch of mistakes myself. But Itsuki saw justice in what I had done. "If you think you see justice in me, then stick with Rishia. You don't have to worry about me." I had some mental leeway myself, and thanks to Raphtalia and Atla, I was now capable of accepting the feelings of the others as well. I knew I had better things to do than pick over everything Itsuki had done in his past.

"I did something really horrible to Rishia. She was struggling with her low status and wanted to become a hero . . . but I looked down on her, just like so many had looked down on me. I thought it was only natural that I be praised and respected. I saw my past weaknesses in Rishia and so I discarded her," he muttered, his voice full of regret, eyes downcast. "I have to spend my life to make amends to Rishia and stop Mald and the others. That's the punishment for my sin."

"Yeah, I feel you," I replied. Armor had been rambling on about his own warped sense of justice. He wasn't the kind of person we could come to an understanding with. L'Arc had said Armor was trouble the first time he saw him too. I didn't know whether he had been warped into that under Itsuki, though, or whether he had started out that way.

"In the past, I would have thought anyone opposing me was evil to be defeated. I don't know how many times I've judged people simply based on one-sided opinions," he said.

I recalled when Witch had framed me. I wondered what might have happened if Itsuki and Ren had read the situation better back then. When I thought what Trash and that stinking Witch would have done to Ren and Itsuki if they had known the truth though, I couldn't imagine a good outcome.

"I don't think you can generalize," I said. Things could have turned out a whole lot worse—like being down a holy hero or two. Considered in that light, the seemingly rash decision that Itsuki had made didn't look too bad in hindsight. It was hard to accept, but that's just how bad that situation had been. "There are lots of people who wouldn't have been saved without your justice—Rishia among them," I said. Itsuki was definitely the only one who could have saved her from that particular situation. I had basically been on the run, and Ren had only been interested in getting stronger. Motoyasu might have been able to save her, but with Witch around, there was no guessing what was going to happen next.

"Thank you. Just hearing that makes me feel so much better," Itsuki said. I turned to look at the same scenery as Itsuki. The lights of the castle town . . . everything so different from Melromarc and from Siltvelt, was really driving home how far we had come. I was meant to be the Shield Hero, but now I was the Mirror Hero too. "I've learned not to make judgments based solely on what I personally feel. Without that, I may have ended up like Miyaji. You always need to have a discussion, even with people who appear completely evil," he told me.

"Decide whether to fight or not after talking first," I agreed. Indeed, Itsuki had talked at length with our foes this time. Talking to determine someone's nature was never a bad thing.

"Rishia always says that it takes a fine hero to call someone out when they are wrong, but pushing your justice onto someone is—probably—a different matter entirely." Rishia really had come a long way to be able to say such things to Itsuki now. The "probably" was also just like her.

This all reminded me of when Yomogi had confronted Kyo, demanding to know if he had done something wrong. That was bravery—it felt like. Kyo's reply had been half-assed, and he hadn't shown any repentance for his actions. But Yomogi had worked out what the right to do was and proceeded to aid us.

"I know Rishia will teach you all about justice, but you should also talk to a woman called Yomogi here in this world. She's a good person and a straight shooter," I said.

"Okay," Itsuki said, his voice faltering a little. "Justice really is a difficult concept, isn't it?" he pondered. I could tell he was trying to change, and that prompted me to ask him something.

"Once the waves are finished, what do you want to do?" I asked. We were still locked in a fight with no end in sight. Once I'd achieved a satisfactory result, I planned on returning home, but I wondered what Itsuki was planning.

"I'm thinking of staying in that world and doing some traveling," he told me.

"Traveling? Where to? Why?" I asked.

"I want to help people in trouble. I've decided to try and bring satisfaction to other people rather than myself. To choose to continue to think about things. Even if people end up throwing stones at me, I won't make excuses," he said. He had it worse than I'd expected—the "justice" sickness. But as for the arrogance, the self-justification he'd been full of before, there seemed to be less of it now. I really wanted to believe he was making progress. Itsuki had caused all sorts of problems, but he had saved people too. Rishia was a prime example—even if he had messed up after that.

In any case, Itsuki was changing.

"Let's both continue to do our best, Naofumi. We can start by using the time waiting for Kizuna to recover as productively as possible," Itsuki said.

"Of course. You can start by getting some rest," I said.

"I will," he replied. I decided to do the same.

More conflict awaited us tomorrow.

The Rising of the Shield Hero Vol. 17
© Aneko Yusagi 2017
First published by KADOKAWA in 2017 in Japan.
English translation rights arranged by One Peace Books
under the license from KADOKAWA CORPORATION, Japan.

ISBN: 978-1-64273-053-1

Written by Aneko Yusagi
Character Design Minami Seira
English Edition Published by One Peace Books 2020

Printed in Canada
1 2 3 4 5 6 7 8 9 10

One Peace Books
43-32 22nd Street STE 204 Long Island City New York 11101
www.onepeacebooks.com